THE GIRLFLESH CAPTIVES

'Angela, you are the perfect secretary,' Vanessa said.

'I try to give satisfaction, Miss.'

'Then clear the desk, strip off and bend over next to your daughter . . .'

'With pleasure, Miss . . .'

Vanessa bound them side by side with their inner ankles strapped together and outer bound to the desk legs. She strapped their wrists together in front of them and pulled their arms over the desk, making them bend across its top, and secured their wrists with longer straps to the front legs of the desk. Two fine sets of buttocks and vulvas now presented themselves to her.

For a moment Vanessa's head swum with a dizzy sense of power. Mother and daughter were utterly at her mercy. Their most intimate orifices were open for her to use as she wished. It was a loving surrender of total trust and the greatest compliment they could pay. Yet why should it surprise her? She had assumed a position of responsibility and control in the company. Angel and Sandra were loyal company slaves. It was natural that she should enjoy them.

THE GIRLFLESH CAPTIVES

Adriana Arden

This book is a work of fiction.
Always make sure you practise safe, sane and consensual sex.

Published by Nexus 2009

2 4 6 8 10 9 7 5 3 1

Copyright © Adriana Arden 2009

First published in Great Britain in 2009 by
Nexus
Virgin Books
Random House
20 Vauxhall Bridge Road
London SW1V 2SA

www.virginbooks.com
www.nexus-books.co.uk
www.rbooks.co.uk

Addresses for companies within The Random House Group Limited can be found
at: www.randomhouse.co.uk/offices.htm

The Random House Group Limited Reg. No. 954009

Distributed in the USA by Macmillan, 175 Fifth Avenue, New York, NY 10010,
USA

A CIP catalogue record for this book is available from the British Library

ISBN 9780352345417

The Random House Group Limited supports The Forest Stewardship Council
[FSC], the leading international forest certification organisation. All our titles that
are printed on Greenpeace-approved FSC-certified paper carry the FSC logo.
Our paper procurement policy can be found at www.rbooks.co.uk/environment

Typeset by TW Typesetting, Plymouth, Devon
Printed and bound in Great Britain by CPI Bookmarque, Croydon CR0 4TD

Symbols key

 Corporal Punishment

 Female Domination

 Institution

 Medical

 Period Setting

 Restraint/Bondage

 Rubber/Leather

 Spanking

 Transvestism

 Underwear

 Uniforms

One

'First I'm going to strip you naked, then I'm going to screw your head off!' the machine promised as it rolled towards Vanessa Buckingham with a whine of electric motors. She retreated into a corner, feeling a thrill of fear as it loomed over her.

It stood over two metres tall and ran on a tank-like twin-tracked base unit. Out of this rose a column supporting a transverse chest and shoulder unit, from the ends of which extended a pair of jointed arms with clamps for hands. Its voice issued from a speaker grille in the middle of the chest. Atop the shoulders was an extendible neck supporting a head fitted with auditory receivers and a pair of large glowing red binocular eyes.

Just above the junction between its tracked base and main body was a large ball socket. Extending forward from this on a hydraulic ram was a shining phallus as long as Vanessa's forearm with a screw thread spiralling about it. As the machine moved, this shaft whirred and pulsed in and out while LEDs set into its tip and sides flashed. Stencilled onto the machine's base panel was the name: ROBOSCREW.

A mechanical hand reached out and caught the arm of the old jacket Vanessa wore. Desperately she tore at its metal arm but could not break its hold. With a twist and a wrench and a popping of buttons she shrugged off the jacket, leaving the remains in its grasp. With her skirts and ponytail of fluffy dark hair flying she dashed away round the zigzag walls of cardboard cartons and packing cases that turned the warehouse floor into a virtual maze.

A robot hell-bent on ravishment and equipped with a huge screw-shaped cock was chasing her. It was the stuff of fantasy and nightmare . . . except that it was very real.

A sound system was pumping out a medley of background music to accompany her desperate flight. Eerie tinkling breathless pauses were followed by sudden bursts of gunshot percussion and racing strings. Vanessa thought she recognised some of the film scores from which they had been lifted. The lighting scheme complemented the music. Dim washes of red and blue picked out the shadows of the high roof and distant walls, contrasting with dramatic pools of stark white light cast by banks of focused spotlights.

It was an appropriate setting for a helpless heroine to be pursued by a malevolent inhuman enemy. The thought of the fate that awaited her if she was caught made her stomach knot, even as the crotch of her panties began to dampen. Her chest was heaving and her loose blouse was already sticking to her back with sweat. As she ran she wiped a hand across her bright hazel eyes to clear the stinging perspiration.

She rounded a corner and almost collided with another of her robotic stalkers.

It was a squat glossy red machine with a shell-like body no higher than her waist, carried by six legs with two large pincer arms facing forward. Smaller crablike feeding mandibles flanked a mouth from which another corkscrew phallus protruded. Across its rounded back was written: CUNNY CRAB.

'Those tits could do with a little nip!' it hissed, its stalked eyes flashing, its mandibles writhing lasciviously and its claws snapping as it lunged at her.

Vanessa sprang aside but she was a fraction too slow. One of its rubber-lined pincers locked about a fold of her faded skirt while the other made a grab for her leg. Vanessa tried to pull away and there was a ripping of cloth as her skirt was torn from her, leaving her with only her flimsy white panties between waist and sock tops. Gasping for breath she staggered back and ducked behind the nearest stack of crates. With a whir and click of many feet Cunny Crab waddled after her. She was faster in a sprint but it would not get tired until its batteries ran down.

She ran on through the maze, her trainers slapping over the hard floor, straining her ears for the whine of electric motors above the rise and fall of the background music. Then a metal door set in the warehouse wall loomed ahead of her out of a wash of cool blue gloom. Vanessa rattled the door handle and banged on it with her fist, but it was locked. Of course, it would not be as simple as that. Her fear cranked up another notch. She was trapped.

She looked about her. Could she climb up the crates and evade her pursuers that way? Most of the spotlights were focused on the floor. Maybe she could hide out of sight of their camera eyes. She saw a tall stack of cartons with a stepped end. If she could get on top of that she would be safe as she was sure none of her pursuers could climb. But would the boxes be strong enough to support her weight?

She clambered gingerly up onto the first carton. The top sagged but there still seemed to be some packing material inside it to give it additional strength and it held. Emboldened she reached out for the next one.

Vanessa heard the hum of motors and squeal of rubber wheels above the thud of drumbeats a second too late.

There was a phut of compressed air and something struck her back. With a crackle, a numbing jolt of electricity coursed through her, scrambling her thoughts and sending her muscles into spasm. She fell over backwards, twitching helplessly, to sprawl limply across the top of the lowest carton. As she lay there she felt a shameful hot wetness flowing though her panties across her thighs and along her bum crack. She'd wet herself.

Pussy Dog rolled up, reeling back into its mouth as it did so the small electrode-studded globe that formed the tip of its long electric tongue lash. 'No you don't, bitch,' it growled triumphantly. 'This dog's going to have you!'

It had an angular dog-like head with red eyes and large sharply pointed ears. This was mounted on a cylindrical body supported by four short slightly bowed legs with independently powered rubber wheels for feet. From under its belly pulsed and whirred another huge screw phallus. Its name stencilled across its side was accompanied by an image of a girl's upturned and bare backside with dripping pudenda.

But though Pussy Dog had her temporarily at its mercy, it could only just reach her as she lay on the top of the packing case. Its screw cock whirred in frustration.

Snapping its jaws, it tried to get a grip to drag her down to the floor. Its hard rubber teeth closed on her out-flung arm and with a whine of wheel motors it began to tug backwards.

But life was returning to Vanessa's limbs as the numbing effects of the shock faded. With a wrench, a popping of buttons and rip of fabric she rolled off the other side of the carton minus her blouse, revealing the white metal collar that enclosed her neck. She tumbled to the floor, leaving the shredded remains in Pussy Dog's frustrated jaws, and staggered away rubber-legged, clad only in her trainers, socks, bra and sodden panties with the shadow of her pubic delta showing through them.

But she could hear the other machines closing in on her now. There was no escape. To one side of her Roboscrew swung into view round a pile of boxes, baleful red eyes blazing. Click, click, click, Cunny Crab's claws sounded ever closer, while a mechanical

4

howl from behind told her that Pussy Dog was still on her trail.

Vanessa stumbled on, aware that they were driving her before them like a wild animal, backing her into a corner of the warehouse.

Then there was nowhere else to run. The corner was devoid of cover. Her robotic pursuers emerged from the shadows. She tried to make a dash to one side along a wall to get round them but Roboscrew twisted at the last moment and caught her right wrist in its left clamp-like hand. She kicked its metal sides and tore at the clamp, but the rubber lining made it impossible to slide her hand free and she could not force the halves apart. It caught her other wrist and pulled her arms wide, lifting her off her feet.

She hung with her back to the robot, her smooth stomach palpitating and breasts heaving. Its screw cock flashed and whirred and extended in a mechanical parody of tumescence until the tip touched her bottom, probing the tight wet fabric of her panties. Vanessa gave a shriek of alarm and kicked and squirmed in mid-air. The phallus swung about, trying to find its target, grazing off her buttocks. But while her legs were free and she could twist about it could not penetrate her.

'Keep still, slut!' it commanded.

'No way, bolthead!' Vanessa retorted with desperate bravado.

She heard a snarl of frustration from Roboscrew's speaker. Holding her aloft like a trophy, it carried her back to the others.

Pussy Dog and Cunny Crab both made a lunge for her, their metal sides grinding against each other with a screech and whine of motors.

'Hey, I want a piece of that bitch's ass!' Pussy Dog barked.

'Wait your turn, Fido,' hissed Cunny Crab. 'We've got to peel her first and you haven't the tools for it.' It

5

focused its eyestalks on Roboscrew. 'If I help strip and hold her, tin man, we share her, agreed?'

'Agreed, just get on with it,' Roboscrew snapped impatiently, his phallus twitching and bobbing.

Cunny Crab reared up on its front feet and reached out a pincer towards Vanessa as she fluttered and squirmed in Roboscrew's implacable grip. The claw closed about her cleavage, scraping her skin as it pinched the tiny strap between her bra cups, and then tugged. Vanessa was jerked forward as the elastic fabric stretched, cutting her shoulders and squeezing her breasts, and then snapped. The two halves of her bra fluttered aside to hang about her shoulders while her pale softly rounded breasts bounced free, their sharply defined red-brown nipples standing up stiffly.

The robot crustacean lowered its claw to Vanessa's panties. The tips pinched the swell of her pubes through the wet fabric, making her squeal in pain. She stopped kicking her legs and held still except for a shiver of fear she could not quell. In a macabre chorus the three robots laughed at her distress. They were metal and rampantly male and she was just feeble female flesh. They had all the power. She was their toy now.

The Crab ripped the side bands of her panties in half and the sodden scrap of fabric fell to the floor, exposing a close-cropped delta of dark hair trimmed back from her well-rounded pubic lips that were gaping hungrily. A pair of small golden rings were threaded though the sides of her impudently pouting inner labia. Cunny Crab's eyestalks moved in for a closer look at Vanessa's sex.

'That is a nice hot slot,' it hissed, probing it with the tip of one claw and making Vanessa whimper. 'And her clit's standing up nicely. Is that pee or your juices? Are you a hot metal slut girl?'

'Please . . . don't hurt me,' Vanessa whimpered.

'Her arse is pretty good as well,' Roboscrew commented from behind Vanessa's trembling body. She felt the tip of its cock probing her bare bottom cheeks.

'Get on with it, you two,' Pussy Dog growled.

Cunny Crab raised a pincer and clamped it about Vanessa's right breast, squeezing until her tender flesh ballooned between the halves of its claw and began to go purple. Vanessa yelped and snivelled in pain.

'Are you going to be a good girl?'

'Yes!' she sobbed, her stomach churning.

'Do you beg for a big crabby screw?' it asked, its mandibles snapping.

'Yes . . . yes!'

The Crab freed her breast, now indented with the serrations of its claws, and clasped Vanessa's dangling ankles. It pulled them wide and then lifted its body. Its mandibles spread as its screw cock extended. Pulsating madly, the screw tip slid between her wet labia. At the same time she felt the tip of Roboscrew's cock sliding between her bottom cheeks, probing for the mouth of her greased anus. Her eyes bulged and she gave a choking gasp as they both penetrated her.

The soft spiral flanges of the twirling vibrating rubber cocks tickled and flexed sensuously within her, curving upwards even as the shafts plunged deeper until half their lengths were sheathed inside her and they plugged both her passages to the limit, driven by the force of hydraulic rams that her poor orifices were too weak to resist. Her belly swelled and bottom bulged as they filled her front and rear, drilling and pulsing and churning. It felt as though they were going to meet inside her, separated by such a thin membrane. She shrieked in pain, shame and delight as she rode the flashing sex screws.

Grunts and gasps were coming from the robots' speakers as they screwed her, almost as though they were living things. They were grinding her between their metal bodies as they ravished her mercilessly, impaled upon their mechanical parodies of manhood. Then hot oil was pumping and spurting up inside her as they came, filling every nook and spraying back out of her front and rear, running down her thighs and dripping to the floor. With a wail her own orgasm ripped though her and her juices joined the flow.

Roboscrew and Cunny Crab sagged. Their clamps and claws relaxed, dropping Vanessa's limp sweat-streaked body to the floor. She fell onto her face, her arms stiff, twitching and trembling. Oil shone on her pubes and bottom and began to form a puddle as it continued to leak from her. Her anus still gaped wide. Her groin was so stretched and pummelled that she could not close her legs. But her ordeal was not over yet.

With a desperate growl Pussy Dog drove up between her splayed legs. Its front wheels rode over the backs of her thighs until they were level with her chest, then the front legs closed together, pressing the rubber tyres against her sides and clamping her firmly. At the same time the Dog's back legs spread, holding her thighs wide. It lowered and twisted its head and clamped its jaws on her hair, holding her in place. Then its body settled down on top of her, pressing her flat, its pulsating screw cock probing for her dribbling anus.

Her ability to resist had been shattered and it went in easily. Grunting and growling the robot began to sodomise her, rocking back and forth on its legs, grinding her breasts into the concrete as its cock twirled and drilled her insides out. Under its weight she snivelled and sobbed, knowing she was spent and bruised and utterly unable to respond to this third invasion of her body. And then something very perverse gathered inside her and the aches and bruises became a pleasure bomb that went off in her brain and she came again, mingling her discharge with the hot oil pumping into her. Then she slumped to the ground utterly exhausted.

The background music cut out. Fluorescent tubes flickered on, banishing the artful shadows and bathing the test area in cold white light. From the observation gallery spontaneous applause broke out.

'Well, um, what did you think of our robotic trio, Vanessa?'

It was an hour later. Vanessa was drinking tea in the office of Derek Shepherd, the manager of Robotikine, a subsidiary of the Shiller group of companies.

Shepherd was a thin, prematurely greying and slightly hunch-backed man of indeterminate age who blinked out at life through large glasses. He was awkwardly polite and clearly uncomfortable in her presence. This might have been due in part to the fact that as a Shiller company slave Vanessa was naked and lapping her tea up from a bowl on the floor in front of him.

Even after a shower and a thorough douching both front and rear, Vanessa still felt a happy ache within from her robotic screwing. She was also sore and unnaturally slippery and was aware of lingering traces of the sunflower oil the robots had pumped into her as simulated ejaculate. Not that any of this worried her. A Shiller girl should always be well lubricated.

VANESSA 19 WHITE was inscribed on her collar. A leash running from it was hooked over the arm of Shepherd's chair. Her borrowed trainers had been replaced with white open-toed sandals and her hat had been restored to her. It was a white fedora with a black silk band, into which was tucked a card on which was printed the word: PRESS. In the last few months it had become her trademark in the strange secret world of corporate slavery. It was the hat worn by Vanessa Buckingham, the only slave reporter working on the *Girlflesh News*: the unique house magazine for Shiller slavegirls.

Vanessa looked up from her bowl in response to Shepherd's question. 'I thought it was amazing, Master.

9

The chase and stripping was a great build-up. I really enjoyed it.'

'Did the limiting circuits work properly?' he asked with sudden concern. 'The claw pressure was never too high when they took hold of you? We don't want our machines to inflict any injury.'

'I feel sore and there may be a few bruises, but it's nothing, Master. I expect to feel firmly secured and helpless when I'm screwed and I was. That's what chain girls like.'

'Yes, you really do, don't you,' Shepherd said in mild wonder.

At that moment Vanessa was aware of the gulf between them. Not simply between man and woman but free man and natural masochistic slave. Even people familiar with slavegirls sometimes had trouble accepting the fact of their needs and desires. Not so long ago she would have found it impossible to believe as well.

'I assume from what I heard, Master, that the operators enjoyed themselves as well. Is the virtual penile feedback system that good? Did they really feel as though they had their cocks up inside me?'

'Oh yes, it was all very successful,' Shepherd said proudly. 'That and the ease of control mean that almost anyone can use an avatar robot with five minutes' practice. Of course the test area is just a mock-up. If it was offered as an experience to paying clients the set dressing would be refined.'

'Well, I'll be able to write a great article on it for *GN*, Master. I think plenty of girls, private slaves as well, would love to try it. And I'm sure their owners will enjoy giving them a good robo-screwing.'

Shepherd grinned uncertainly. 'I suppose ultimately that's what it's all about. But I hope you'll mention our other work as well. We've got some special projects under development and we're testing a lot of them this week, as we've got Peach Chain at our disposal.'

'I'm sure they're excited to be your guinea pigs, Master.'

'Oh yes. Of course some of our female staff volunteered to try out the devices first, but we can't use them at full strength or, um, go all the way . . . if you know what I mean.'

How ironic that this slightly shy and modest man should end up designing machines to capture and screw slavegirls, Vanessa thought. How he got here would be a story in itself. Aloud she said helpfully: 'Which is why you need proper slavish, bondage-loving masochists to experiment with, Master.'

Shepherd blushed slightly. 'Uh . . . exactly.'

'Please don't be embarrassed on my part, Master. I know what I am and love being it. Now I'm here for the day so please show me more . . .'

A little self-consciously, Shepherd led her round the facility. Vanessa trailed after him on the end of her leash with her camera slung round her neck and notepad in hand.

'Have a look at this,' Shepherd said, opening a door onto a small viewing room. 'It's still in the prototype stage and it's not interactive but it is, well, amusing. Probably for private use or small gatherings, perhaps on a stage. I think they're about ready to run another test . . .'

Through a large pane of one-way glass they could see a plain white room with rubber matting floor. A second one-way window, looking from this side like a mirror, was set in an adjacent wall. A pretty naked blonde girl in an orange collar was standing in one corner. Her wrists were cuffed behind her and she had a ball gag in her mouth. Above this her bright eyes were darting round expectantly. The lips of her sex were smooth and looked recently shaven. Through a speaker beside the window Vanessa could hear the slight sound of her shuffling feet and rapid excited breathing. In the corner opposite her was a large metal box.

The operating light on a video camera set high up in the corner of the room blinked on and it turned and zoomed in on the girl. A man's voice came through a speaker mounted beside it. 'Screwsnake prototype "C" test 31 commencing. Natalie 7 Peach as test subject. Activating units now . . .'

The lid of the box flipped open. Natalie's eyes widened and she pressed herself back against the wall. Multicoloured snakes were squirming out of the box.

They were over half a metre long with thick bodies sheathed in a shimmering metallised plastic skin. Each had a code number marked on its back.

A dozen multicoloured screwsnakes had poured out of the box by now. They spread out and raised their heads, moving them from side to side as though scanning their surroundings. Their snouts were blunt and bullet-like, with a ring of metal studs about their necks, and quite plain except for two tiny black eyes and a small central hole out of which a tongue flickered.

'They're guided by simple movement sensors and smell,' Shepherd explained. 'They have olfactory sensor chips that can be programmed to recognise human body scent from some metres away. Closer to, this can be refined to distinguish the difference between the scent of a vagina and an anus.'

The snakes had stopped weaving about and flicking their tongues. They put their heads down and began moving towards Natalie, who by now was looking quite nervous with her nipples trembling distinctly as she edged along the wall. The snakes undulated along in a slightly stiff, jerky manner, enough to show they were not living things, but they were still surprisingly fast.

'They're programmed to enter either orifice,' Shepherd continued. 'These are simple shapes that they can recognise by contrast and orientation. That's why she's shaven to ease identification. She's gagged so they don't enter her mouth by mistake.'

And it also makes it much more exciting, Vanessa thought, watching the girl's teeth clenching on the ball that filled her mouth.

'When they've penetrated the right target they will deliver a series of small electric shocks and then disengage.'

Natalie was shuffling along the wall but the snakes were turning to follow her and fanning out. She reached a corner and found she was hemmed in. As they got closer they raised their heads and flicked out their tongues, focusing on Natalie's naked groin. In a panic Natalie began to kick out at them. Her foot connected with the head of an emerald green specimen, only for her to jerk it back with a muffled yelp and hop about in pain. Her face screwed up and tears sparkled in the corners of her eyes.

'They also activate their shock system to protect themselves,' Shepherd added dryly.

Vanessa was surreptitiously squeezing her thighs together as her stomach fluttered and slippery warmth seeped through her labia. She was watching a pretty young woman being subjected to a freakish sexual torment and loving every moment. In any other circumstance it would have been a horrifying and cruel spectacle. But no girl wore a Shiller collar who was not ready to enjoy humiliation, pain and pleasure as one.

As Natalie had been distracted a red snake had coiled about her left ankle. She stood on one leg to try to shake it off, but it was coiled too tightly. Now a blue one attached itself to her right ankle.

'As you can see, they are programmed to coil round any suitable object and climb to reach their goal,' Shepherd said.

Natalie tried to rub her calves together to scrape the screwsnakes off, but they must have shocked her again in response to the pressure for she shrieked and shuffled her legs wide. Now she was trapped leaning back against the wall, her eyes bulging as she looked down in horror to see the snakes climbing up over her slim knees and about the smooth swell of her thighs towards the fleshy pouting slot of her sex.

Vanessa felt her loins churning in delight.

Now the red snake was nuzzling at the mouth of Natalie's vulva, pulsating and surging forward. The blue was probing deeper between her thighs and curving upward into her bottom cleft. The red parted the fleshy curtains of Natalie's labia. The blue jabbed upward.

Natalie threw back her head and wailed as they entered her, their bodies whipping from side to side as they forced their way into her front and rear passages. In seconds half their lengths seemed to have vanished up inside her, with their wriggling tails protruding grotesquely from between her legs.

Then her hips jerked, her bottom slapped against the wall, her teeth clenched and her eyes rolled up.

Half a dozen times Natalie convulsed in this manner as the robot snakes writhed and wriggled inside her. Her face was a picture of sensuous distress with her eyelids fluttering masochistic delight and tears dripping down onto her heaving breasts to mingle with the saliva drooling from about her gag. Then her head dropped and she slid down the wall as her legs folded under her, splaying her thighs wide, helplessly opening up her body to the robotic invaders.

The red and blue snakes slithered out of her, their bodies now shiny with her juices. The others surged forward in a twining mass, fighting to get inside her.

Natalie's anus could only take one at a time but her vagina was elastic enough for two. They wriggled and writhed, mindlessly obedient to their instructions, fighting to screw, pumping their sensuous bodies into her until her stomach bulged, making Vanessa wonder how

14

far they had penetrated. They churned about so much they beat Natalie's juices to a froth that bubbled from her pouting, abused and swollen red-lipped lovemouth. Below her sex her well-stretched and jolting anus hung open like a tunnel, quivering with helpless spasms. She flinched and twitched and heaved making her breasts bob and jiggle. Then she groaned and jerked her hips, adding her own orgasmic convulsions to the shocks that wracked her body.

Only when the last snake pulled out did she slowly topple over onto her side, dribbling from both ends, half-sensible and utterly drained.

'Test 31 satisfactory,' said the voice. 'Deactivating all units. Uh . . . maybe somebody should get Natalie a glass of water . . . or something?'

I've just seen a girl gang-banged by robot snakes, Vanessa thought. It had been one of the freakiest things she had ever witnessed. Was this the sort of thing men in white coats inevitably got up to when you gave them a gaggle of slavegirls to play with? Yet the slickness down her thighs could not be denied. It had turned her on, and that was all that mattered.

She realised Shepherd was looking at her expectantly.

'I think they'd be a great icebreaker at parties,' she said.

'Now, where next?' Shepherd wondered as they left the viewing room. He checked his watch. 'Ah, yes, you must see the robot jockeys we've been trying out. They should have cleared the test area for a race by now.'

Ready for anything, Vanessa trotted obediently after him as he led her back to the control room that opened onto the old converted warehouse adjacent to the research centre that was used for larger-scale trials. Her recent robot sex partners had been put aside and covered by sheets and new equipment was being set up.

The curtains that had closed off the operator booths were now drawn back and the devices inside them had been changed. The 3D imaging goggles were on their hooks ready for use, but instead of sensor boots and gloves for robot limbs there were now what looked like saddles hung with stirrups mounted on an array of small hydraulic pistons.

Where the saddle pommels would have been were the soft rubber folds and wires of simulators that would link their users' cocks with the passages of their selected mounts via radio links. Why men would want to couple with rubber vaginas, however realistic, when they had a baker's dozen of real and very willing pussies to hand seemed ludicrous but, as Vanessa had learned over recent months, there was so much more to sex than reproduction and the direct exchange of bodily fluids. This was all part of the wonderful game of domination and submission and often nature took a back seat.

Looking out into the warehouse she saw that the maze of old cartons she had been chased around earlier had been rearranged to form the perimeter of an oval running track, with the spotlights adjusted to illuminate it.

'The jockey system we've developed is more compact than the larger robots,' Shepherd was explaining, 'so they could be used individually in a secluded garden or paddock, for instance, but I think competitive races would be more entertaining. Of course if it was run in a dedicated facility there'd be stands and proper rails and that sort of thing.'

The course was ready and four Peach girls were being turned into ponies. They were harnessed up with standard ponygirl bridles and bits, but with short reins that ran though their cheek rings and down to clips clamped about their nipples as a convenient means of control. At the sight, Vanessa's own nipples pricked up in sympathy.

On their feet they wore calf-length boots with ankle and instep braces that forced them to point their toes.

These then tapered and curved around under the foot to form horseshoes.

'Ah, yes, their running boots,' Shepherd said, following her gaze. 'Carbon fibre blades to give a bit more bounce to their step.'

The technicians brought out what looked like half-sized mannequins. These were dressed in riding silks, complete with caps and whips, and mounted on oddly shaped saddles that the technicians strapped to the girls' backs.

The girls carried the dummies as though they were giving piggy-back rides to children. The saddles were fat crescents sitting just above their hips, held in place by a broad waist belt, with the scallop following the curve of their backs. The side 'horns' of each saddle curved upwards and then over and out again, forming curving padded handles that hooked into the crooks of the girls' arms, pulling them backwards and causing them to push out their breasts. There was enough of a gap between their arms and their sides for the jockeys' legs to slide through. Cuffs on the sides of the waist belts held their wrists secure.

The girls were made to bend over and Vanessa realised in one respect the dummies were not true scaled-down versions of the real thing. Dangling from between the jockeys' legs under the saddle were pink rubber penises as long as those on the rapist robots. But where they had rigid cores, these were as flexible as hosepipes, except for the last fifteen centimetres of the head end which were plugged into the Peach girls' anuses and locked in place by flared flanges.

Shepherd chuckled. 'Yes, we had to employ a bit of lateral thinking to adjust reality to suit practical requirements. We wanted to simulate the sensation of riding and coupling with a ponygirl simultaneously. Unless she goes about on all fours, which will limit her speed, the rear passage is the obvious choice. The jockey is the controller's avatar but he must sit high up on the girl's back to see over her shoulders and yet not be too large for her to carry. But then the only way to couple with her would be to extend the torso and have the jockey clasping his legs round her hips, which would be absurd and interfere with her stride. So we have extended only that portion of the jockey needed to penetrate her. It will feed back the sensations of hip roll and internal muscular contraction while she runs and stimulate her in return with her controller's, ah, responses.'

'So the simulators in the control booths are set to recreate the girls' rectums, Master,' Vanessa said. 'Which the riders feel as though they're plugged into, even though it would be impossible actually to ride the girls piggy-back and sodomise at the same time.'

'It seems to work. The human mind is remarkably adaptable.'

She could not disagree with that. She was living proof.

The harnessed Peach girls beamed as Vanessa looked them over and she smiled back, still thrilled at the knowledge that she had become something of a celebrity amongst Shiller slavegirls. She did not write about slavery from an outsider's viewpoint, she did everything they did. Which meant . . .

'I'd like to be a runner as well, please, Master,' she asked, interrupting Shepherd. 'So I can write about the system from the ponygirls' viewpoint.'

'Are you sure you're not too . . . uh . . . tired?'

'Perfectly, Master.'

'Well . . . then we'll find you a jockey. I think we have a spare set.'

'Will you ride me, Master?'

Shepherd blinked owlishly and for a moment Vanessa felt that strange sense of power only a confident submissive without inhibitions could know. Today he could have her any time he wanted, but this suggestion disconcerted him. How had he ended up here inhabiting what must be a nerdish fantasy?

'Well . . . if you would like me to.'

'Then afterwards we could compare notes from both sides, as it were,' she said warmly. 'I'd know exactly what we were talking about. It would make my article much more accurate.'

'Er . . . well, of course. I'd be delighted.'

They brought out another set of harness, robot jockey, boots and saddle. As the bridle and harness were strapped onto her, Vanessa felt the familiar thrill inside her growing. It was the dark joy of being a slavegirl; it was the confinement of her movements, the loss of self-control, the anticipation of pain and humiliation and the absolute surrender to a higher power.

The boots felt strange but they were far more stable than high heels. The jockey and saddle were surprisingly light. With an expression of intense concentration set on his plastic face, her jockey hunched forward and peered over her shoulder, his booted feet hanging over her hips, her reins clasped in one small hand and his whip in the other. The end of his outrageous cock plugged snugly into her rear. A year ago she had shied away from anal intercourse. Now it felt good to have a filled rectum.

Their human virtual riders, including a self-conscious Shepherd, retreated to the control booths and drew the curtains before donning the feedback goggles and plugging themselves into the rectal simulators. When men were engaged in virtual sex they rarely wanted an audience, whereas she and the other chain girls were permitted no privacy at all. It was so unfair, she thought with a delighted shiver.

She and the other Peach girls trotted out onto the improvised course where a couple of technicians held the starting tape ready.

She felt her jockey suddenly come to life. Its eyes glowed red and it tugged on her reins, pulling on her nipples. The slug of plastic inside her rear pulsed and grew harder. Shepherd's cock was now virtually up her arse. It was a weird sensation but fun. She gave an answering squeeze of acknowledgement, hoping he would feel it. Her jockey's whip came down and flicked across the upper curve of her right buttock. She was under his control.

The five human ponies beneath their robotic riders lined up before the tape, their eyes bright and their breasts trembling in anticipation. The lights played over the smooth swells of their strong thighs and firm buttocks and telltale sparkles of excitement on their pussy clefts. Today we really are hot to trot, Vanessa thought, with a barely suppressed giggle.

The sound system cut in with bugles and some old-fashioned hunting theme, redolent of galloping hooves and flying turf. Vanessa imagined the place with a proper stand and rails and people taking bets and cheering their favourite ponygirls on. Sweating but triumphant they would be paraded in the winner's enclosure and patted and rubbed down and a rosette would be pinned to their breasts . . .

The tape sprang up and their riders' whips came down on their bottoms and they were off.

They pounded round the track in a wonderful display of straining, jiggling flesh, their shoes clattering and clopping over the concrete floor and their robot jockeys bouncing in their saddles, beating their flanks with their little whips and jerking on their nipples to steer them. With their arms bound to their sides the girls could not counterbalance the roll of their hips in the normal way, so it was accentuated, leading to a corresponding heavy sway and toss of their breasts. Our tits need halters, Vanessa thought, but it felt good.

The mirror version of Shepherd's cock inside her was getting harder, urging her on as much as the whip. In his booth she knew he was buggering her replica anus.

God, this was freaky but so much fun, Vanessa thought as she blinked the sweat from her eyes. The sheer joy of hard exercise combined with sex and bondage. What would she do if she came while she was running? Could she stay upright? She was going to find out in another lap.

A slave reporter's life was always challenging.

Vanessa was still aching happily from her exertions when she got back to her small Richmond flat that evening. The only detail making life less than perfect at that moment was that her lover and fellow slavegirl Kashika was away from London with her chain on company business and would not be back for another couple of weeks. It was a price you paid being a slave-girl and more than outweighed by the compensations.

She showered and ate, then went to bed, but not to sleep.

She took a remote control and a rabbit vibrator from the bedside drawer. Naked, she lay back on the covers and pointed the remote at the flatscreen television that hung on the wall opposite the foot of her bed.

Once, a year ago, when her life had been ordinary and by comparison terribly dull, there had been nothing on the wall there. Then a mirror had been installed with a hidden camera in its frame that her controllers employed to watch her in bed. Now there was a television with additional features.

A still image appeared of the head and shoulders of a girl with an almond-shaped face. She was a rare and striking blend of Scandinavian and Indian parentage, and her mane of mellow golden hair contrasted with her coffee-tinted skin. About her neck she wore a red metal collar inscribed: KASHIKA 5 CHERRY.

A second full-length image appeared showing Kashika standing naked and smiling. She had finely shaped neat breasts with dark nipples, a trim waist with

21

a deep navel and a vulval cleft capped with curls the same colour as her hair.

A third image flashed up. This showed Kashika chained naked and spreadeagled to the very bed Vanessa was lying on. A fourth showed her bottom with spank marks, a fifth with the very same rabbit vibrator lodged deep in her vagina . . .

While the slideshow of love and submission flicked before her eyes, Vanessa happily masturbated herself to sleep.

Two

An alarm was beeping and lights were flashing.

Vanessa jerked awake. She'd been dreaming that she and Kashika had both been racing as girl ponies. They'd just won the Grand National and the Queen had been about to pin rosettes on their breasts . . .

The bedroom screen was flashing an urgent red and sounding the alarm. She fumbled for the bedside light switch. The glowing numerals of her clock radio showed it was twenty past five.

She found the remote and pointed it at the screen. An image appeared of a slender woman, perhaps in her mid-fifties, with a strong straight nose and a narrow intelligent unlined face. Her bright blue eyes were keen and commanding.

'Sorry to wake you, Vanessa, but this is urgent,' the woman said. Her diction was precise but shaded by an unidentifiable accent.

Vanessa scrambled onto her knees facing the screen with her thighs spread submissively wide and hands folded behind her back. She bowed her head respectfully. 'Yes, Director Shiller.'

'Early this morning one of our trucks was hijacked and Canary Chain was kidnapped. We believe Harvey Rochester was responsible, so there is a possibility that you may also be a target. I have sent a security detail to your flat. Meanwhile be alert for any intrusion. You will stay with them until I contact you again. That is all for now.'

The screen blanked.

Vanessa blinked stupidly, still not fully awake. She knew Julie 5 Canary well. Oh God, she hoped she was all right. But if Rochester had her . . .

Sir Harvey Rochester was Shiller's bitterest enemy. In addition to his media empire he also ran a secret sex-slave business, but unlike Shiller he did not employ only natural willing submissives. Once, before she knew the truth about him or her own nature, Rochester had used Vanessa, then a reporter on one of his newspapers, in an attempt to expose Shiller's secrets for his own gain. He had also more recently tried to force Vanessa to work for him by threatening Kashika. Then he had employed another agent in a plot to bring down Shiller's Scottish operation in Glen Lothy, which Vanessa had managed to foil. The memories of Rochester's brutal behaviour were still fresh in her mind . . .

Vanessa threw on a robe and went round switching on lights and checking the door was securely locked. Rochester's men had broken into her flat once before and though it was much more secure now, she did not want to risk repeating the experience.

The doorbell rang, making her jump. She checked at the spyhole and breathed a sigh of relief. It was Josh Willfield and Harry Parks, security men from Shiller that she knew well. She let them in, reassured by their large solid presence.

'Everything all right, Miss Buckingham?' Josh asked with anxious formality.

'Yes, Master,' Vanessa said.

The pair secured the door and checked around the flat. Then they relaxed a little.

'Do you know any more about the hijacking, Masters?' she asked.

'The truck crew are OK, but that's all we've heard, girl,' said Josh. 'We were just told to get here as soon as possible and wait for further instructions.' He fingered the baton holstered by his side. 'I sort of hope Rochester's men do make a try for you. We'll give 'em something to think about for snatching our girls.'

'Please sit down, Masters,' Vanessa said, offering the sitting room chairs. 'Can I get you anything?'

'Some coffee would be nice,' Harry.

'And maybe some toast to go with it,' added Josh.

'And you can do it properly stripped, girl,' Harry added in turn.

'Sorry, Master,' she said, hurriedly stripping off her robe.

They were company employees while she was just company property. Well-cared-for and highly valued property, of course, but in the hierarchy of deference right at the bottom. She would not have had it any other way.

Naked but for her collar and slippers she prepared coffee and toast for her new guests. She left them watching early morning television while she went to the bathroom to shower and go through the normal slavish ritual of preparing herself to give pleasure by whatever means was required of her.

For the next few hours she kept Harry and Josh fed and breakfasted herself while worrying about the Canary girls and Julie 5 in particular. They were Shiller girls, she kept telling herself: trained submissives and natural masochists. They could take in their stride situations that would freak out normal women. But even so there were still plenty of horrors they could be subjected to. And if Rochester had snatched them what did he want them for? Ransom? Or was it to force Shiller to hand over her girlflesh business to him? Vanessa knew she would never do that.

It was while she was washing dishes at the sink, turning these thoughts over in her mind, that Harry and Josh grabbed her.

They pulled her across the small kitchen table and pushed her face down over the plastic table cloth, Harry holding her by the hair and right wrist and Josh twisting her left arm up behind her while having a firm hold of her right buttock. As this was an ambush she struggled just enough to make them hold her down firmly and satisfy their hunting urge. Then Harry's cock was being rammed into her mouth and she was gobbling it down while Josh's cock was sliding up her greased rear.

Protecting her from Rochester did not of course mean they could not use her for their own amusement. That was what chain girls like her were for.

When they were done they left her sprawled across the table to recover while they went back to the sitting room.

For a minute Vanessa lay across the table with their sperm oozing out of her. She felt better for that casual bit of rough usage. It confirmed who and what she was and the wonderful company she belonged to. Then she got up, smoothed the tablecloth, finished the dishes, went to the bathroom and cleaned herself up again.

A call came through to Harry just after eleven. He relayed the instructions to Vanessa.

'You're to pack a bag because you might have to stay at the office for a few days until we're sure it's safe. Josh will ride with you and I'll follow in our car. And don't stop for anything on the way.'

'Yes, Master.'

F.G. Shiller's London headquarters occupied a modern tower block of artfully sculpted metal and mirror glass overlooking the Thames. Outwardly it was the hub of a highly respectable general management company with worldwide interests in a score of different fields. Within it was hidden an unsuspected secret world.

Turning her beloved red Mini into the entrance of the basement car park, Vanessa could tell something had interrupted the normally smooth flow of the daily routine. There were cars and vans queuing to enter and more security staff than usual stationed at the barriers checking each arrival.

When it came her turn, even with Josh by her side and Harry right behind them, Vanessa was scrutinised carefully before being passed through, though the guards knew both her and her car well.

She drove along to the sliding mesh gate that guarded the head of the ramp leading down to the lower level of the car park that only Shiller staff used. Phil and Geoff were on gate duty. Usually they simply waved her through. If it was quiet they sometimes had a little fun such as reaching in through the side window to slip their hands down the top of her dress and squeeze her breasts or else order her to pull her skirt up to show them the colour, or the absence, of her knickers.

This time, even with Josh present, they were strictly professional, making her open the boot and checking the back of her car to be sure it was empty. 'You'll still have to go through the new security checks down below,' Geoff said before opening the gate and waving her on without a single leer or ribald comment.

This is serious, Vanessa thought.

She drove down the ramp and parked her car not far from the lift shaft. She could see the changes had been initiated since she had left the same park only yesterday. Normally the next layer of security was the camera watching the key-code protected entrance to the lift with the next human security check inside the building. Now a temporary kiosk, folding table, barrier and scanner arch had been set up in front of the lift, manned by several guards, some of whom were wearing gas masks. A handful of uneasy office staff were queuing to enter. Their bags were being checked and they were body searched before being allowed through the barrier.

Harry parked beside them as she got out of her car and they went over to the barrier.

The familiar figure of Sandra 13 White was waiting on the other side of the barrier, perfectly at ease with her nakedness amongst the clothed people about her. She was a pretty girl with a blonde bob and ponytail, small high breasts, slim hips and a neat pouting shaven pubis. She hardly looked much over eighteen, though she had a poise and self-assurance beyond her years. Like Vanessa she wore a white collar and gold rings in her inner labia, but she also had a third pierced through the hood of her clitoris.

She waved and spoke to one of the men at the barrier, who beckoned Vanessa and her escorts up to the arch.

'You'll have to strip here, Miss Buckingham,' he said. 'It'll get you through quicker anyway. We've been ordered to take no chances with anybody, not even white-collar girls. Josh and Harry can take your stuff down to B3 reception.'

'I understand, Master,' she said, pulling at her buttons.

Some of the waiting office staff watched her as she peeled, though not out of surprise or prurience. They were Shiller employees and used to the sight of naked slavegirls. Their looks suggested resentment at her preferential treatment, but they said nothing. Most would recognise her hat, but it was her white collar that gave her a strange status amongst other slavegirls and company employees. It marked her as one of Director Shiller's own personal slaves.

When she was naked but for that collar she bent and rested her hands on the table and spread her legs, shivering slightly in the concrete cold of the car park. The man checked nothing was concealed in her hair, slid stiff rubber-gloved fingers up her vagina and rectum to ensure they were empty and then ran the scanner over her. After checking her clothes and bag he gave her back her sandals, hat and the key card that hung on a short chain clipped to her collar ring, while Josh and Harry took the rest.

'Let's get you inside,' he said, passing her through the arch.

Sandra immediately took her arm and hurried her to the lift. 'The Director wants us all in the main conference room right away,' she said, a stern frown creasing her normally bright face. 'Heads of department plus white-collar girls.'

'Have you heard any more about the Canarys?'

'No.'

Inside the lift Sandra punched the button one from the top.

Vanessa did not feel that sense of welcome her arrival at the offices usually brought. This had been a place of safety, a warm caring environment where she could be her slavish self without inhibition. Now it felt threatening and suspicious.

The door opened onto a foyer along which several senior staff members were hurrying, passing between heavy double doors at the end flanked by security guards.

'Looks like they're nearly ready to start,' Sandra said, hustling Vanessa through the doors.

The conference room was nearly full, with about twenty people taking their seats around the long central table with its bowed sides. Vanessa saw Zara Fulton, her editor at *GN*, a tall attractive full-busted woman in her mid-forties with a mass of dark wavy hair and keen blue-grey eyes, sitting amongst them. She was looking uncharacteristically stern-faced. She caught Vanessa's eye and nodded. The Director's chair at the far end was at the moment empty. Behind it was a large screen displaying the company logo. A rank of white-collar girls were standing along the walls with their hands folded neatly behind them. Vanessa and Sandra joined them.

In other circumstances this juxtaposition of respectably dressed business people and a line of naked

29

collared slavegirls would be startling, but not inside the Shiller building and especially not in this room. The large boat-shaped conference table was an example of how the two were combined. Its centre was inlaid with a diamond-shaped glass panel occupying two thirds of its length. Below this panel was a long shallow padded tray lined with black felt. Lying in the tray were a pair of naked slavegirls with their heads pointing to each end of the table, their arms spread a little from their sides and their legs spread wider. Their postures were a mirror of each other so that the soles of their feet were almost touching. Metal hoops about their necks, wrists and ankles and bolted to the base of the tray held them secure. A blindfold strap holding two black rubber discs covered their eyes and a matching ball gag plugged their mouths. Lying on the black felt they seemed to be floating under the glass.

In the very centre of the table, between the spread feet of the two girls, was a shallow bowl of red roses. A spiral trail of petals extended from the display up between the legs of the girls to where a single red rose had been planted in the furrows of their smooth shaven sexes.

The pair appeared to be perfectly relaxed, perhaps even sleeping. The only movement was the slow rise and fall of their breasts that caused their red nipples to brush the underside of the glass. It was impossible not to sit at the table debating business matters without looking upon the imprisoned flesh of these sleeping beauties.

Director Shiller did not believe in denying the truth that an ethically organised trade in girlflesh formed a significant part of company turnover. Slavegirls were there to be seen and enjoyed . . . even in a time of crisis.

A door at the far end of the room opened and the Director strode in. Everybody else stood while the white-collar girls briefly went down on their knees and bowed.

Though she was physically slighter than most of those around the table her mere presence dominated the room. Not for the first time Vanessa felt weak at the knees in her presence. She was so strong and powerful. If there was any single flaw in Vanessa's life with the company it was that, although she had been a white-collar girl for many months, the Director had not yet called upon her to serve her personally, though she must know Vanessa would have been honoured. One day, perhaps, she would judge her worthy.

'Please be seated,' the Director said.

The assembly sat and the white-collar girls resumed their respectful postures.

'Some of you know the details of recent events but I shall summarise,' Shiller said. 'At approximately three-fifteen this morning one of our vehicles returning Canary Chain to London was waylaid while crossing Millthorn Heath. The crew are safe but all twelve Canary girls are missing. Their current whereabouts are unknown.'

A murmur of dismay rose up from the assembly.

'The truck crew were lured out of the vehicle by a naked woman apparently in distress who ran out into the road in front of them and then collapsed. The driver and both the cabin crew left the vehicle to assist. As they tried to move her they report that she opened her eyes, said: "Sorry," and pulled her vulva wide to expose the nozzle of what we now deduce was part of a remotely operated control device. A quick-acting stun gas, ejected from the cylinder that must have been concealed within the decoy's vaginal passage, then immobilised the crew.

'This, by the way, is the reason for the new security measures, should this be a diversion or prelude to a raid on these offices using similar means. These measures will stay in force until we are sure no such move is planned.

'The crew recovered some half hour later to find they and their truck had been driven into the shelter of a

31

copse a little way long the road. The Canary girls had been taken and this message was left in their place . . .'

The screen behind her changed to show an enlargement of a single sheet of paper bearing a printed message:

TO FG SHILLER

YOUR PROPERTY WILL BE RETURNED TO YOU IN ONE CALENDAR MONTH FROM THIS DATE IN A USED BUT STILL SERVICEABLE STATE, ON CONDITION THAT 2 (TWO) CHAINS OF SIMILAR QUALITY STOCK HAVE THE PREVIOUS DAY BEEN LEFT AT A LOCATION AND TIME TO BE SPECIFED AS REPLACEMENTS. WHILE TWO CHAINS ARE SUPPLIED IN THIS MANNER EACH MONTH FROM NOW ON UNDER THE SAME TERMS YOUR OTHER SHIPMENTS AND ASSOCIATED TRADE SHALL BE ALLOWED TO CONTINUE NORMALLY. BE WARNED THAT ANY ATTEMPT TO RECOVER THE PROPERTY OR FOLLOW A REPLACEMENT CONSIGNMENT OR TRACK ITS MOVEMENT BY ELECTRONIC OR MECHANICAL MEANS SHALL RESULT IN SEVERE DAMAGE TO THE MERCHANDISE IN HAND WHICH MAY RENDER IT UNFIT FOR FURTHER USE.

'R'

It was that last single letter that brought a chill to everybody about the table.

'Harvey . . . bloody . . . Rochester!' she heard Zara growl under her breath. Vanessa knew she would have liked to use stronger words but the Director did not approve of foul language in any circumstances.

'Apparently he has changed his tactics,' Shiller said. 'Up until now he has tried to destroy our company or take over our operation by blackmail. Fortunately he has been frustrated in those aims.' For a moment Shiller's eyes flicked across Vanessa and despite her concerns for Julie 5 she felt a brief flush of pride. 'Now it seems he has decided that what he cannot possess he will parasitise. He will use our stock of girlflesh to help maintain or perhaps even expand his operations.'

'But how did he manage to intercept Canary Chain in the first place?' a woman asked.

'This was the normal route taken by our vehicles to transport chains to and from a regular client. Rochester's men must have been monitoring our vehicle movements for some time. They chose their spot well. The Heath is quite deserted at that hour. And now he has one chain he knows we will not abandon them. In fact he is counting on that to force us to agree to his terms.'

'But we can't let him get his slimy hands on two fresh chains of our girls month after month!' Zara protested.

'No, but temporarily he has the upper hand and has had plenty of time to prepare. Canary Chain have no doubt already been concealed somewhere within his many subsidiary companies and facilities. They could by now be almost anywhere in the country. Of course we will make a search but we know how hard it has been in the past to penetrate his operation.'

'Meanwhile how will we manage with a chain down?' somebody asked. 'What will it do to our turnover?'

He must have known it was the wrong time to mention money even as the words left his lips. Vanessa felt the temperature in the room drop as the Director fixed the speaker with her gaze.

'Yes, we can manage with one or even two chains down,' she said coldly, 'if by that you mean we can continue to supply our clients with the service they have come to expect. But we cannot do so with a clear conscience while any chains are beyond our control. Those girls are our responsibility regardless of the "turnover" they generate. That is the compact we enter into when we accept their submission and they don company collars and chains. We promise we will take care of them in all circumstances . . . at whatever cost.'

33

'Sorry, Director,' the speaker muttered wretchedly.

'So then what will we do, Director?' another asked.

Shiller looked grave. 'Unless we get all of our girls back by our own means within the next few weeks, or at least have the strong prospect of recovering them, I will close our girlflesh operation and inform the police that I suspect Rochester of running a clandestine sex trade in slavegirls and hope they, with their greater resources, can find and free them, or at least frighten Rochester into releasing them to avoid being compromised.'

The people round the table were visibly shocked.

'But then Rochester will reveal what he knows about us,' somebody pointed out. 'We might be investigated as well. Even if nothing's found the suspicion could ruin our regular business.'

'That is a risk I'm prepared to take,' Shiller said flatly. 'You have all been content to live off the profits of ethical slavery. Now has come the time when we must pay the price.'

One man, perhaps braver than the others, cleared his throat reticently. 'Look, I hate Rochester and his methods as much as anybody else here, but let's not act hastily. As you say, Director, we can still do business even with two chains down. If we go along with the arrangement for a while, let him enjoy his little victory, then maybe we can make some better deal with him.'

'Pay protection, you mean?' Zara said with disgust. 'Do you really think he'll stay bought?'

'He's a businessman,' the other pointed out.

'He wants our girls,' Shiller said flatly. 'That gives him both financial reward and a sense of personal triumph. But it will not stop at two chains a month. Bit by bit he will want more and more until he has it all. That is how blackmail always ends. And I will not strike a deal with that man!'

* * *

After the department heads had left to brief their staff of the situation, Shiller motioned for the white-collar girls to climb onto the table. This they did, arraying themselves in neat ranks, kneeling respectfully with hands folded behind them and knees wide to display their charms. Vanessa could see her pubes reflected in the glass panel. Beneath her the table girls continued to add their calm erotic beauty to the setting. Enclosed as they were, Vanessa did not think they could have heard any of what had been discussed. They were simply serving, as they had been instructed, as lovely living ornaments, surrendering their freedom and dignity and putting their total trust in the company to use them as it chose. But now the limits of its ability to fulfil that trust were being tested.

'Your primary duty throughout this crisis, for however long it lasts, will be to keep the morale of the other chain girls high,' Shiller said. 'Hard as it will undoubtedly be, everything must continue as normal. Routine must be maintained. That is our strength. I will speak to the chains later this afternoon to explain the situation and assure them, as I do you now, that everything humanly possible will be done to recover Canary Chain safely. Are there any questions?'

Sandra said: 'Director, might we really have to give Rochester two more chains just to get Canary back?'

'That depends on events over the next few weeks. It will be a last resort, but I cannot pretend it will not come to that.'

Another girl spoke up. 'Whatever you decide you know you can count on our total obedience, Director.'

Shiller smiled. 'I know, and that gives me great comfort. But there are some things even I cannot order you to do, only request . . .'

After they were dismissed, Sandra went down to B3 while Vanessa stopped off at the fifth floor and the editorial office of *GN* and *Datumline*, the latter being the official house magazine of the Shiller group of companies presenting its public face to the world. The gloom in the office was palpable, with the other staff evidently distracted from their work. Zara had clearly passed on the facts of the Director's briefing.

Vanessa was the only slave reporter amongst the staff and so usually the only naked body in the room. This naturally drew more than the typical level of attention an attractive woman might expect, which she had come to enjoy. They could all have her if they wanted, and several had, as long as it did not seriously interfere with her work. But today the normal greetings, nods or cheerful leers were muted.

She went into Zara's office and knelt respectfully before her. Normally Zara opened her legs at this point and Vanessa planted a humble kiss on her knickerless crotch, but today Zara did not make the invitation.

'What do you want me to do, Mistress Editor?'

'Hang Rochester out to dry by his balls!'

Vanessa forced a smile. 'I'll do my best, Mistress. Anything more immediate?'

'Cover the Director's address to the girls down on B3. We'll put out a special *GN* supplement on it and get it distributed to all the usual outlets. We'll add it to a report on the hijacking itself. That'll help make sense of the new security measures.'

'Will it include a copy of Rochester's demands, Mistress?'

'I don't know. I'll check with the Director. What do you think?'

'I think we should publish it, Mistress. Then there'll be no doubt amongst the chains what he's asking for and why we have to be careful hunting for the Canary girls. But it's hopeful in a way because it also shows he's putting his business interests first. He can't treat the Canary girls too badly or he knows any agreement would fall apart.'

'You may be right. But for now all this is for staff and chains only, not clients. The Director will have to contact them separately.'

'Yes, Mistress. Anything else?'

'Try to keep to the regular routine as far as possible. That's what I've told the rest of the staff. We're all desperately worried about the Canary girls but the company must go on, especially the girlflesh business.'

'But for how long, Mistress? There's going to have to be a showdown between the Director and Rochester over this. Afterwards there might be nothing left of the girlflesh business to run.'

'I know,' Zara said bleakly.

Basement level B3, which appeared on no official set of plans for Shiller Tower, was one of the most wonderful places Vanessa knew. Under its overarching vaulted roof, artfully painted and lit to resemble a blue sky, and richly planted with shrubs and trees, it was in effect a tiny secret village in the heart of London dedicated to the comfort, training and discipline of slave girls. There were dormitory blocks, an exercise track, equipment stores, stables, a garden, a pool and even a tiny shopping street, known of course as 'The Mall'. Here a girl wearing nothing but a slave collar was considered properly dressed.

The largest space in level B3 was the slave-training yard, which was also used for ceremonial gatherings. By the time Vanessa and Sandra arrived girls were pouring in through its double gates. Those freed from their duties about the building joined those having a rest day. She saw the pair of girls who had been under the glass of the conference room table walk in. Breasts bobbed and bottoms rolled. Every shade of perfumed flesh, colour of hair and tint of nipple was represented. They wore a rainbow of collar colours, accessorised by coloured ribbons, beads and bangles and footwear ranging from flip-flops to sparkling high heels.

Vanessa had attended several such gatherings at happier times, such as the initiation of new chain girls, and then their graduation and awarding of diplomas. The first time she had not been able to accept that the girls were there voluntarily, or that the participants were all natural submissives eager to live a slavish life under the company's benevolent control, even when the yard had filled with the scent of uninhibited arousal.

Now she knew better. She had embraced the life herself, only to find it threatened by Rochester's rapacity.

But today the mood as the yard filled was sombre. News of the Canary Chain's absence had already spread. The girls hung their heads, exchanging anxious whispers, and normally perky nipples were flat. On a dais the senior training staff had gathered, patiently awaiting the Director's arrival. By Vanessa's side Sandra took her hand. Her face was downcast.

'It shouldn't be like this,' she said in a small voice.

'I know,' Vanessa said, 'but we'll get through it somehow. The Director won't let us down.'

At that moment Shiller appeared. The expectant murmur died away.

'Most of you will by now know something serious has happened,' Shiller said. 'A detailed account will appear in the *Girlflesh News*, but these are the basic facts. Early this morning the vehicle carrying Canary Chain was hijacked by agents of Harvey Rochester and the girls were abducted. A message was left saying the chain would be returned safely to us after one month, as long as we provided two more to take their place. Rochester clearly plans to use our girls to increase the stock of his slave houses.'

There were shocked exclamations mingled with a few stifled sobs of fear and dismay. Shiller raised her hands and it stilled.

'Needless to say, everything that can be done to find the Canary girls is being done. No expense shall be spared. But we must move with caution and the hunt will take time. Meanwhile take heart in the knowledge that Rochester has an interest in returning Canary Chain in good condition. They may not be treated as well as we would expect but I can assure you that their lives are not in danger. They will survive this ordeal because they are Shiller-trained girls, and they are strong and proud and know we will not abandon them.

'In a way, their kidnapping is a testament to the success of this company and its belief in ethical slavery. Our system of recruitment is not only more humane but also more efficient than Rochester's and we provide a better service to our clients. I had hoped this simple commercial pressure might force Rochester out of business, but sadly it seems it is not to be.

'I will keep you informed of any new developments as soon as I can. In the meantime continue to serve the company as you have always done, despite the circumstances. As you will understand when you read the full account of the hijacking, the new security measures are necessary and in no way diminish my trust in you. Also have patience. Rochester's empire is extensive and it will take time to investigate. But one way or another, when this is over, I assure you he will no longer have slavegirls in his power, whether his own or your chain sisters.

'I must warn you of one sacrifice that may be asked of you, but which I cannot order you to make. If, when the month's deadline approaches, there is the imminent prospect of resolving the situation successfully but more time is required, then I will ask for volunteers to offer themselves in exchange for Canary Chain. But that will be the only transaction I will contemplate making with Rochester and then only to buy necessary time. Before the next month is out I promise this matter will be finished for good. If there are more than two chains of volunteers, lots would be drawn to determine who is sent.'

Vanessa had not planned what she did next. She had been recording the Director's speech on the recorder hung about her neck while taking pictures of the crowd. But suddenly she stepped forward.

'I will volunteer, Director.'

And then Sandra was at her side again. 'And me, Director.'

And then another girl stepped forward. 'I'm volunteering, Director.' Then another and another . . .

Vanessa felt her heart swell and tears of pride prick her eyes.

The Director also appeared moved and had to compose herself before she said clearly: 'Let it be known that every girl of every chain present has volunteered. And that I am very proud of you all.'

Three

It was late evening by the time Vanessa finished her article on the Director's address. Zara approved it and it was incorporated in the special edition that would be distributed to all Shiller regional subsidiaries currently housing chain girls. Hard copies would also be printed off and be available for the girls down in B3 to read the next morning. Vanessa knew that Kashika would be reading the account very soon. Though she knew she would be worried about Julie 5 she hoped she would also share the pride in the united response the girls had given. She had done her best to convey the swell of emotion but it truly had been one of those 'You had to be there' moments.

Looking back on what she had started by stepping forward it did not seem extraordinary. The Canary girls were her chain sisters. If this might help bring them back how could she not have volunteered?

The rest of the magazine staff had left and she was tidying away for the night when Sandra came into the office. She perched herself on the corner of Vanessa's desk with one knee crooked, swinging her leg and innocently displaying the neat pale oyster of her pubic cleft, and looked at Vanessa with deep concerned eyes. 'How are you feeling?'

'About volunteering or the Canary girls?'

'Both. Tell me about volunteering first.'

'Queasy at the thought of actually having to go through with it, but knowing I couldn't have lived with myself if I hadn't.'

Sandra nodded. 'And the Canarys?'

'I hate the idea of them being under Rochester's control even for one second and want them back right now, but I also know they'll get through it because they're chain girls like us and I've just seen how strong we are. We mustn't think about them as though they were ordinary women facing the Full Monty BDSM. I imagine even now they'll be saying to Rochester: bring it on, we can take it. I hope they don't really, of course, because he's a real sadist, but you get the idea. And I'm not going to let worry or fear stop me from doing what I have to do. What about you?'

'About the same with both. I'm more afraid how this fight with Rochester is going to end.' She took a deep breath. 'But I can't do much about that at the moment. Anyway I've been talking to the chains in the dorms. They seem in good spirits. All full of chain-girl power . . . rah, rah!' She punched the air, making her breasts jiggle. 'I hope it lasts. But I'm still feeling sort of twitchy and ready to burst, you know.'

'I know,' Vanessa agreed.

'It's mostly anger. I want to do something right now to help get the Canary girls back but I know I can't. It's so frustrating! Anyway, I was thinking about asking Mister Winston to give me a chariot workout and I wondered if you'd like to come. He's been trying out some new pony harness that looks really exciting.'

'What's a chariot workout?' Vanessa asked.

Sandra looked incredulous. 'Haven't you had one yet?'

Vanessa felt a flush of embarrassment. 'Well, Mister Winston has screwed me . . .'

'He's lovely and big, isn't he?' Sandra said with a bubbly schoolgirl beaming smile and disconcertingly total lack of inhibition.

'He is,' Vanessa agreed, 'but you see I've never actually been a proper ponygirl. I mean this morning I had a robot jockey strapped to my back with his radio-controlled dick up my bum, but . . .'

'Tell me about it!' Sandra interjected with sudden wide-eyed fascination.

'You can read the article . . . at least you can once I've written it. My Robotikine feature was going to be front page on the next issue but it looks like Canary's kidnapping is going to bump them. But anyway I've missed out on the ponygirl thing.'

'Why?'

'Well, maybe because I saw Mister Winston whipping a team of girls in pony masks round the track the first day I sneaked down here spying on Shiller's . . .' She grinned ruefully '. . . the first day I met you, and it was a hell of a shock. It helped convince me you were all sadistic sex-traffickers. I know it's stupid but I've never quite been able to shake off that bad feeling about the stables down in B3 ever since.'

'Didn't you pull a carriage at Glen Lothy?'

'No, I did some dressage and played at being a corral pony for the guests. I enjoyed that but I never got around to actually being harnessed up and pulling anything. We had those unscheduled visitors, remember?'

'Well, it's the best exercise ever,' Sandra said simply.

Vanessa frowned. 'I'm not sure it feels right to have fun at a time like this.'

'The Director said it's our job to keep to the routine and boost morale,' Sandra reminded her. 'This'll show the other girls it's business as usual. We won't be good for anything if we just mope around. And you said you were staying over tonight. If you haven't chosen where, Mister Winston can take care of that as well.'

Vanessa took a deep breath. 'I'll give it a go . . .'

The many banks of lights that washed the pale-blue painted concrete vaults of level B3 were dimmed at

43

night, creating the illusion of a soft sky glow, and the air conditioning shifted to a cooler setting. Wall lamps came on, as did strings of coloured lights strung about the larger trees and shrubs.

Around the central core of buildings, following the perimeter of the basement level, was an oval running track of green-painted boards with banked ends. The track was thickly lined with more shrubs and small trees in pots and planters that overhung it in places. They were also up-lit by small spotlights and garlanded with string lights, forming leafy archways seemingly sprinkled with coloured stars.

Along this track Vanessa and Sandra ran, their horseshoe boots clattering on the boards. They were harnessed to the shaft of a modern-day version of a Roman chariot: a compact low bow-fronted body slung between two large wire-spoke wheels with a single shaft that rose from under the body in an 'S' curve. On the chariot rode Mister Winston, a large muscular black man wearing black leather knee boots and a matching thong pouch, with his reins in one hand and whip in the other. Its regular cracks as it kissed their flesh echoed round the walls of the track.

Their heads were encased in the latest version of ponygirl head-masks that allowed more ventilation to the wearers. They were made of a matrix of black fine wire mesh moulded into the shape of equine heads, complete with muzzles, flared nostrils and cocked ears, leaving only their eyes exposed. Integral rubber bits filled their mouths. A neck section with a flared base went over their collars as far as their sternums and curved about their shoulders, keeping the head lifted proudly. The mesh was so fine that it did not cut their skin, but it blurred their features and almost hid the true shape of their heads.

Despite the masks' comparative lightness as they pressed tight about their heads they still gave an exciting sense of enclosure and control that Vanessa loved. The girls' own hair was drawn out though slots in the backs of the masks to form flowing manes, complementing their false ponytails. These appeared to spring up from the small of their backs, rising clear of the cleft of their bottoms in a graceful arch, then to fall in bobbing, swaying plumes, clear of the globes of their buttocks. They were held in place by elongated U-shaped spring clips, with the base of the tails secured perpendicular to one prong of the 'U' and a rubber plug on the other that was buried deep in their rectums. The clips clamped tight between hot moist inner passage and outer flesh.

Their forearms and hands were encased in long rubber gloves that bent their fingers into fists and confined them within the tips that were moulded to resemble hooves. The wrists of the gloves were strapped with figure-eight loops to their upper arms just under their armpits, holding them in a begging-like posture, almost as though they were gathered up in the act of jumping a fence. A strap between their elbows crossing below their shoulder blades pulled their arms back and pushed their breasts forward. A second broad wrist-to-wrist strap across their chests passed just below their breasts. Even with their arms tucked in, this binding allowed some movement in the shoulders so they could swing their arms a little in a natural running motion, mimicking in the air the motion of a pony's front legs on the ground.

Their feet were encased in black boots with ankle braces and padded spring-steel tongues pressing down over their insteps to keep them extended. The toe mouldings were flared into mock hooves with rubber shoes to give grip.

It was as though their mutable girlflesh had undergone a chimerical transformation into hybrid creatures with women's bodies and horses' heads and extremities. But however exotic they appeared they were still working animals, controlled and harnessed, serving their master.

A yoke pole crossed the front end of the chariot's shaft like a T. Its padded ends, with double curves like a horse bow, passed through the crooks of their bent elbows, to which it was strapped, and around the curve of their backs. Reins ran though eyelets in their collars up to their cheek rings, which were linked to their bits. This gave plenty of leverage for Mister Winston to control them. Two finer chains hung from a ring under the chins of the masks. The ends of these were clipped to their nipples. As their heads turned they jerked their breasts round in the same direction.

And so they pounded round the starlit track, diving through the arches of greenery, the lights sparkling on their glistening bodies. It was amazing the speed they could get up with a whip cracking across their rears, Vanessa thought, as its end curved under their bobbing tails. The stripes burned across her buttocks stung with sweat. Her breasts tossed and bounced, swinging from their nipple chains. She was lathering at the bit and snorting for breath. The big muscles of her legs and buttocks ached with effort.

It felt wonderful.

All the cares of the day and worries for the next were purged from her mind. She was intoxicated with the high of hard exercise. Life had been reduced to the simple task of obedience without choices to fret over. Her sole purpose was pulling a chariot with a friend harnessed by her side.

When they clip-clopped back into the stable yard fifteen minutes later Vanessa and Sandra were dripping with sweat and their glossy breasts were heaving.

Like the other structures in B3 the stable buildings did not reach the roof so the false night sky glow showed over the top of their walls. There was a row of

46

wooden half-door horse stalls, polished harness hanging on the walls, a hitching rail, a horse trough, straw on the floor and a pile of hay bales in one corner. It was illuminated by wall bulbs shaded and filtered to give the soft warm friendly light of oil lamps.

Peering over the lower halves of the stall doors were more beasts with the naked breasts of women and the heads of horses. Tethers clipped to their cheek rings connected them to the side posts of the stall doors. They were girls under intensive training who might stay in their harness for a week, working and sleeping and eating as ponies. The first time Vanessa had seen such women in the yard she had thought they must have been suffering a terrible torment. Now she knew better . . .

With the other ponygirls looking on in mute interest, Mister Winston unharnessed Sandra and Vanessa from the chariot and led them to the hitching rail, fastening them to each end with ankle cuffs and chains. He pulled out their tail plugs, which came free with soft pops, and hung the flowing plumes of hair over the rail. Then he undid the straps that bound their arms to their sides, allowing them to expose their sweaty armpits, though their elbows remained crooked and hands encased in their hoof gloves.

Unreeling a hose from the tap that fed the water trough he sprayed them over. They turned about under the spray, lifting their masked heads and pulling on their nipple chains so the undersides of their breasts were also washed. The water flowed through the mesh of their masks across their faces and drained quickly away. Then with large coarse towels he rubbed them roughly down, handling them just as one would horses, rubbing the wet from their manes. And in turn they rubbed against him, grateful for his attentions.

When they were dry Mister Winston turned them round and bent them over the rail, spreading their legs

47

until their nearest ankles touched and then cuffing them together. Unclipping their nipple chains from the chins of their masks he clipped them to rings on the tops of their boots. Now they presented their red bottoms and the cleft peaches of their sexes towards him.

Standing between them Mister Winston cupped the tremulous tender bottoms of both his fillies in his big strong hands and stroked and kneaded the striped hemispheres. Vanessa shivered as he probed her sore flesh and heard Sandra making little keening noises round her bit but neither of them begrudged the pain of the whip marks. It was his right to whip them. They were ponygirls and needed to be driven hard.

Now he was fingering their vulvas, testing their heat and wetness. Vanessa groaned and snivelled, trembling with anticipation, tugging on her nipple chains despite the pain, unable to contain her need.

Suddenly the plum of a cockhead was nosing into her greased anus, and, prepared by the tail plug, the ring of muscle was gratefully opening to accept it. The head popped inside her, followed by a thick shaft. Oh God, he was big. Her rectum strained to take him. But of course it did and he rammed his full length into her.

A few quick thrusts and he pulled out. The loss, the emptiness!

Still fingering Vanessa's by now dripping vulva he rammed his shiny shaft between Sandra's soft cheeks, making her small tight anus bulge. She gave a whimper of pain and delight. Then he pulled out of her clinging passage and drove his iron-hard cock back into Vanessa's needy bottom hole once more.

Methodically he plunged into one of them and then the other, driving their hips against the railing, ravishing their bottoms. And they pushed shamelessly back against his thrusts as far as their bonds allowed, heedless of the tugging on their pendant breasts. Their inner thighs ran with their overflow.

48

Then she heard Sandra moan and knew she was climaxing even as the grunts and thrusts from Mister Winston told her that he too was peaking.

Please, please, she tried to cry round her bit.

He plunged into her anus in the act of ejaculating, splashing a hot jet of sperm across her buttocks before filling her rear with his pulsing rod. Vanessa jerked and writhed and came with a frantic jiggle of her hips and grunts of joy. Spent, she slowly sagged and hung limp over the bar, totally content and at peace.

This was the reward for being girlflesh.

Mister Winston cleaned them up and then put broad belts on them that had sets of cuffs dangling over the small of their backs. He cuffed them facing each other, locked in an embrace. Then he wrapped them in a blanket laid them out on the soft hay in an empty stall.

And that was how they slept through the night, safe and warm in each other's arms.

Four

When Vanessa checked her e-mails the next day she found a message from Kashika, sent via the branch office she and Cherry Chain were serving in. Only Shiller slave girls would be allowed to send e-mails to their lovers, Vanessa thought with delight.

We're all desperately shocked and angry about what happened to Canary Chain. I keep thinking about Julie 5. She's such a nice girl. But I know she'll be strong, like they all will, and that their training will see them through.

I suppose it shows Rochester recognises quality girlflesh. I'm sure the Director will get them all back safely soon. Meanwhile the security has already been stepped up here. Lots more body searches (though actually they're quite fun!).

Your report on the Director's speech with all the girls volunteering at the end had us in tears. But you must not go! For everybody else it would just be a hard time, but think what Rochester would do to you if he caught you. Please tell the Director that all of Cherry Chain volunteers to be swapped for the Canarys as well.

Missing you,
Love and pussy kisses,
K.

Vanessa had to wipe her eyes as she read the message. That was just like Kashika. She had such a strong sense of duty and loyalty to the company. And all the Cherry girls had backed her up. She showed the mail to Zara.

'I always knew Cherry Chain was special,' she agreed. But that was only the start.

By mid-morning the *GN* mailbox had messages relayed from chains serving all round the county who had by now read copies of the special edition. Every single one had volunteered.

Zara took copies of the mails up to the Director and came back beaming with a personal message of thanks. Another special supplement was hastily put together featuring copies of the replies and the Director's response, which was distributed all round the building and copied out to the branches. Both staff and chain girls responded well to the news.

With all this love and goodwill there was no way Rochester could beat them, Vanessa thought. Shiller girls really were the best. And Canary Chain would get through it safely. She set to work on her Robotikine feature with very nearly a light heart.

For the next three days Vanessa stayed overnight down in B3 and only returned to her flat under escort to check her mail. When it became apparent that Rochester was not targeting her specifically she returned home, though taking extra security precautions. Through the days, along with the rest of the staff, she tried to make it 'business as usual'.

And then a negative reaction began to set in. There was no specific cause of this decline because nothing had happened. That was the problem . . .

There had been no news of any progress in the search for Canary Chain. Meanwhile the clock was inexorably ticking towards the first month's deadline. Down in B3 the girls were still going about their duties, proudly marching off in chains to serve Shiller clients at exclusive functions and coming back exhausted and well used. They were concerned but they were coping well, even though it would seem they had most to lose. To

51

Vanessa's surprise it was the office staff who were beginning to gripe. She sensed a growing mood of restless dissatisfaction pervading the building. The new security measures were still in place and they were a constant reminder of the threat they were living under and the loss they had suffered. Vanessa overheard many anxious conversations. What if a confrontation could not be averted and the whole girlflesh operation had to close? What if it became public and a scandal dragged them all in? Was Rochester too powerful an opponent to hope of beating?

Vanessa talked this difference in response over with Sandra.

'It's because chain girls always have so much support,' Sandra said simply. 'They have their own chain sisters and then the other chains, like cousins. They train together, live together and work together. They understand each other's needs and get all their love in return. It may be artificial but it's equal and fair and it works and there's nothing like it. But free people have to make do with the family they've got or the friends they can make. And a lot of the staff can't tell their families outside work what the problem is. All that worry.' She shivered. 'That's why I never want to be free. I want to know exactly where I belong, what I am and be totally honest about it.'

The next morning, as Vanessa entered the *GN/Datumline* office she came in partway through a conversation between earlier arrivals chatting as their computers went online.

'. . . even so, how did Rochester intercept the shipment like that?' Pru was saying.

'He had people watching our vans and followed them,' said Rhona. 'That's what the Director thinks.'

'But she doesn't know for sure,' said Steve, adding in a bitter undertone, 'She doesn't seem to know much about fucking anything right now.'

Hearing the Director derided and the strong language made Vanessa pause.

'Maybe Rochester's getting inside information from somewhere,' Gavin said conspiratorially. He caught sight of Vanessa and suddenly grinned. 'Like our office slut, here. She was his pet spy once.' He lunged out and caught a pinch of Vanessa's close-trimmed pubic pelt and drew her to his side. 'Well, Spy, do you admit it?'

She was used to this sort of treatment from Gavin. As he was perfectly entitled to do, he often tickled her bottom as she passed him or else came up behind her at the water cooler and cupped her breasts and tweaked her nipples. She enjoyed the attention in a slavish way even though she classed him personally as too blokish for her tastes.

Vanessa tried to make a joke of the accusation. 'That's right, Sir, I report to him everyday. I've got a secret camera up my fanny and a transmitter in my hat.'

He shifted his grip to slide a finger up her vaginal passage. 'I don't feel anything.'

'That's because it's a very small secret camera, Sir.'

The rest chuckled while Gavin said in mock exasperation: 'Well, the spy slut would say that, wouldn't she, just to put us off.' But he kept his finger hooked inside her and she had to stand there before them. 'Remember she's the reason everybody's getting searched. They think Rochester's going to try to force somebody to smuggle a gas bomb into the place up their bum or pussy hole, like he did you, eh Spy?'

Vanessa shivered. That was not a joke. A few months earlier Rochester's agents had taken her and Kashika prisoner in her own flat, where Rochester had used a laptop video link to operate an electric torture device to try to force her to obtain incriminating evidence against Shillers by smuggling a spy camera into the building concealed in her vagina. The attempt had failed but the memory was painful.

'Yes, Sir,' she admitted.

'And now the guards are getting pissed off frisking us and we're getting pissed off for them doing it to us and it's all your fault.'

'I'm searched as well, Sir,' she pointed out.

He gave her soft flesh a pinch. 'But you enjoy it because you're a sex slut.'

Vanessa blinked the tears from her eyes. 'Yes, Sir.'

'Let her go, Gavin, you've had your fun,' Pru said.

With a shrug Gavin withdrew his by now sticky finger and sent Vanessa on her way with a slap on the bottom.

As Vanessa seated herself at her desk she knew none of them seriously believed Gavin's accusation any more than he did, but she was tainted by her past association with Rochester which gave him all the excuse he needed for having some fun at her expense. That she could live with. She was more worried about the doubts Steve had expressed about the Director's competence. Nobody ever questioned the Director's actions.

The office settled down to work. Unfortunately Gavin would not let his spurious accusation rest. Throughout the morning, when Vanessa passed anywhere near his desk, he greeted her with a call of 'Hello, Spy!' or 'Fetch me a coffee, Spy,' or 'Show us your pussy, Spy, I want to see this camera of yours!'

She had to obey, of course, even peeling her love lips wide to expose her clitoral valley to his scrutiny.

'Have you lost it or is it up your bum?' he asked, which produced a snigger from Steve and weary sighs from the others.

That lunchtime Zara was attending a meeting and the office was half empty. Vanessa was working on a piece for *Datumline* and was too absorbed to notice Gavin and Steve had left their desks and had worked their way round behind her. The first she knew anything was amiss was when Steve grabbed her, pinning her arms to her sides. As she opened her mouth to protest a band of

54

broad transparent adhesive tape was pulled tight across it, wedging between her teeth and cutting into the corners of her mouth.

'Can't let you raise the alarm, Spy,' Gavin said, wrapping the tape reel tightly round and round her head, over her back hair, until her mouth was sealed under half a dozen layers of tape. Then they pushed her face forward over her desk, pulled her arms behind her back and taped her wrists. Another few turns went round her ankles and she was helpless.

They pushed her down onto her knees. Steve took a handful of her hair below the tape band and forced her up against the side of her desk, scooping up her breasts as he did so they rested on its top trembling like pale pink jellies, and then bent her head back so she had to look up at them. Her eyes showed wide and fearful over the crisscross bands of tape that sealed her mouth. Gavin had a plastic ruler in his hand that he swished though the air.

'We don't like spies, do we, Steve?'

'No, we don't.'

'This is what we do to spies . . .'

The ruler swished down across the tops of her resting and upraised breasts. There was a whack and fluid smack as plastic met yielding flesh. Her mammaries flattened and bulged outward for a moment, then rebounded resiliently.

Vanessa's eyes bulged, misting with tears as the sharp pain burned into her milk glands, and she shrieked through the tape closing her lips. Gavin grinned at her distress and swiped the ruler down again and again. Vanessa tried to squirm aside but Steve held her in place. Gavin began to alternate his blows, sending some skimming across the desktop to smack into the forward bulges of her breasts, driving her hard and blood-suffused nipples deep into their soft fleshy cushions. Through bleary eyes she watched the rosy blush spread across her orbs as their upper slopes turned a deeper shocking pink, capped by cherry-red nipples. Her tears dripped off her cheeks, splashing onto her hot raw shivering flesh, their stinging salt adding to her misery.

She knew it was just a silly game. They were burning off energy and taking out their frustrations on her. They wanted to see somebody suffer for the doubt and uncertainty they felt and who better than a slavegirl?

Gavin only ceased his assault when both her raggedly heaving breasts were scarlet and Vanessa was sobbing miserably.

'Now, let's see what you've been hiding from us, Spy,' he told her.

Dragging her to her feet, Gavin heaved her across his shoulder. Meanwhile Steve went to the office door and checked the corridor, which at this time of day was usually quiet.

'Clear!' he said, waving Gavin on after him.

With Vanessa draped over his shoulder so that her burning, throbbing breasts hung across his back, Gavin jogged along to the door of the toilets that Steve was holding open. As she was carried through she saw Steve slap a notice on the outside of the toilet door: OUT OF USE.

They went to the end stall, put her down facing the toilet and lifted the lid. Cutting the tape round her ankles they spread her legs wide, jamming her knees against the outer rim sides of the bowl, then used more tape in loops and figure eights to bind them to the toilet seat. A longer loop went completely around the pedestal of the toilet bowl, binding her ankles to the cold white china. They cut free her wrists, pulled her arms round in front of her and made her bend forward, pressing her palms on the rear of the seat. More tape bound her hands to the plastic ring so she could not pull free.

Anybody looking in through the stall door would see her bent forward with red breasts dangling free and her bottom and pubic pouch presented for inspection while bands of tape crackled and shone about her knees, ankles and wrists. She twisted her head round as far as she could to look pleadingly at her tormentors.

'Now, lets see if you've really got anything naughty up inside you,' Gavin said.

Steve held up the ruler for Vanessa to see. She shook her head in alarm. The men grinned.

While Gavin peeled back her labia, Steve thrust the ruler up inside her vagina as far as it would go. Vanessa whimpered as it filled her, but at least its ends were rounded and did not cut.

'Bloody deep cunt she's got,' Steve observed as over half the ruler disappeared between her sex lips. 'You could hide anything up there.' He stirred it around vigorously making her wince and tremble. He pulled the ruler out, now shiny with her juices.

'No camera in there,' he reported.

'Try her bumhole.'

Vanessa froze. They could not force the ruler up there. That would hurt.

But Steve said: 'I've got the probe,' and held up a bundle of unused pencils he must have liberated from the stationery supply. They were taped together to form a long yellow wooden rod with ribbed sides.

As Gavin pried apart her buttocks Steve forced the makeshift probe through her anal ring, greased as always, and into her rectum. Again he stirred, making her whimper, but finding nothing in her flushed-out passageway.

He withdrew the probe. 'Nope, she's clean. Not even any crap.'

'Perhaps she's not a spy at all,' said Gavin in mock dismay. 'Maybe we should release her.'

Vanessa whined and nodded in desperate agreement.

'Or maybe we should give her a spanking anyway for wasting our time,' Steve suggested.

'Yeah, I like that idea better . . .' Gavin agreed.

They used the still-wet ruler on her behind as they had her breasts. Crisp meaty smacks reverberated within the stall as her bottom flesh jumped and shivered and went from pink to mottled and barred burning crimson. With her knees and ankles taped to the sides of the toilet bowl she could not evade the blows and the full force rippled through her buttocks. She yelped and snivelled and tossed her head about, her tears flowing afresh.

Finally Steve stayed his arm. 'What do you think of that for a bum? Two rosy apples or what?'

'Nice,' Gavin agreed, stroking Vanessa's simmering flesh. 'I suppose we should let her go now.'

'Or we could screw the arse off her.'

'Better!'

Steve made use of the conveniently presented bronze eye of her anus to sodomise her, thrusting hard and fast into her hot tight rear, adding a few slaps on her sore flanks as he did. Being who and what she was, despite her snivels of pain her anal ring was clamped tight about his pumping shaft before he was done, trying to hold him inside her. Gavin chose to use her equally well-positioned pubes, splitting her cleft with his straining cock and setting her breasts swaying and jigging as he plundered her depths. He squeezed and slapped them as he shafted her, adding pain to the fire of her helpless slavish passion.

When they were both done with her they wiped their cocks clean on her hair and then walked out. They ignored her plaintive whimpers to be released, leaving her taped to the toilet, sore and aching, with their sperm and her juices trickling down her thighs.

It took Vanessa half an hour to twist and wriggle herself free of the clinging tape, pulling her hair as she unwound it from her mouth and about her head. A few people used the toilets while she struggled but she was not disturbed. She sat gingerly on the bowl, favouring her sore bottom as she wiped herself clean and discharged the rest of her assailants' sperm from her passages.

Waiting until the room was empty she left the stall and went to the sinks, splashing her face with cold water and then dabbing her sore breasts and bottom with damp paper towels. As she did so she considered herself in the mirror. He cheeks were flushed and eyes a little red from the tears but she didn't look bad for a girl who had just undergone bondage, a double beating and forced sex with two men she did not particularly like. She'd been casually and callously used as a sexual plaything without regard for her feelings. Despite, or perhaps because of this, she'd had a minor orgasm of her own. In all it had been a typical slavegirl workout.

The next morning Gavin and Steve hardly spared her a glance. They seemed a lot more cheerful as they went about their work.

After some thought Vanessa went to see Zara. Kneeling before her in her office she explained.

'The Director ordered me to keep the girls' morale up, Mistress Editor, but it looks like they're handling this better than the regular staff. I need to do something that will help them as well. They're wondering why, with all the company resources, the search for the Canary girls is not getting anywhere. They're also frightened of Rochester's reputation as a hard man. I've already had some trouble with them in the office. It might get out of hand if we're not careful. And they're . . .' She found it hard to say '. . . they're beginning to doubt the Director's competence.'

Zara looked at her seriously. 'Go on.'

'There are two things I want to do. The first is to inform. The older chains and the older staff know more about the background to Rochester's slave business and might understand the scope of it, but the newer ones won't. Even though I worked for one of Rochester's papers I don't know it all, except that he was filthy rich and had fingers in a lot of pies. And that was only what was public knowledge. His slave business is something else and I realise I know next to nothing about it.'

Zara nodded. 'So what do you propose?'

'What I want to do is write a full investigative feature for *GN* about Rochester and his organisation, Mistress. How big it is, where it's based, how it recruits girls, how he runs it, the lot. Maybe that'll help put it in perspective.'

Zara smiled grimly. 'That sounds rather like the sort of thing he sent you here to write on us.'

'Yes, Mistress, I suppose it is. Maybe I want to return the compliment. But I think it will help. People are getting frightened because they haven't got the facts and that breeds rumours. I think it's best to know your enemy.'

Zara looked thoughtful for a minute then nodded. 'Yes, go for it. Everybody should know what we're up against.' She turned to her computer and tapped away on the keyboard for a few seconds, then downloaded a large sheaf of files to a memory stick, which she handed to Vanessa. 'Right, that's everything we have on Rochester's slave business. But don't let it leave the office. The access password is UTTERBASTARD. Think you'll remember it?'

Vanessa smiled. 'Yes, Mistress. I'd no idea you had so much material on him.'

'You don't think we've been fighting him all these years without finding out a few things, do you? This is essentially what the Director's agents will be using to track down Canary Chain. I just never thought of dirtying *GN* by doing a feature on him. We write about honest, bound, beaten and well-screwed girlflesh, not slimy bastards. It lowers the tone. But perhaps now is the time to get down and dirty, because he certainly won't play fair. Right, get your recorder.'

'Mistress?'

'You can start by interviewing me. That'll give you something to get started in the right direction. The deep background detail you dig out yourself.'

In a minute Vanessa was back with recorder in hand. 'First, Mistress, I think my readers will be wondering why finding out where Canary Chain have been taken is not going to be easy, when we know who's taken them.'

'That's because Rochester's operation is not designed like ours,' Zara said. 'Unlike our company headquarters and established regional facilities, he moves his girlflesh operation around between different locations. Literally he trucks girls about by the hundred. If a special event is planned his clients are informed, probably by coded e-mails and texts, where to go. Regular deliveries to large private sex parties are simply made by different routes from the nearest temporary slavegirl "warehouse", so they are hard to intercept . . . unlike ours, as we've found to our cost. By the time we discover where his girls are being kept they've moved on. A few times in the past we've had a lucky break and mounted raids in time and freed a few of his girls, but only a small fraction of the total we think he has. That's why we dare not make a pre-emptive raid to free the Canary girls on the wrong property. It would only raise the alarm and Rochester would immediately cover his tracks.'

'Does Rochester manage his slavegirl business personally, like our Director, Mistress?'

'As far as we know he takes a very close interest in his girls, but at the same time he's careful never to have any provable personal link so he cannot be compromised. We think most of the time he does his business via secure video link from any one of several properties he owns around the country, and he moves between them often enough. He can control pretty nearly anything he wants that way.'

'As I know from personal experience, Mistress,' Vanessa said with feeling, thinking of Rochester's face in the laptop as he tortured her by remote control.

'Yes, you know it, Vanessa, and we believe you,' Zara said. 'But could you prove it in court? Only you ever saw his face. Even his hired thugs didn't know who they were working for. It would be your word against his. He almost never actually meets with his girls in person so they have no idea who they're working for.'

'Almost never, Mistress?'

'On a few occasions he has a particular girl sent to him for use in a private dungeon in one of his houses, but she never knows where she's been taken or who uses her. He's very careful to be masked at all times and doesn't give away anything that might identify him. He's just "Sir" or "Master" to her. After he's had his fun, if you can call it that, she's returned to the general stock.'

'That seems a very specific detail, Mistress, when the rest of your intelligence is so general.'

Zara looked impressed at her deduction. 'Yes, it is very specific. And for a good reason . . .' She hesitated. 'Perhaps there's somebody else you should talk to.' She picked up her phone and dialled an internal number.

'Hello, Trevor, it's Zara. I wanted to ask a favour of Cindy. I've got my slave reporter here . . . yes, Vanessa Buckingham . . . Cindy's a fan, is she? Well, I'm glad she likes her stuff. Anyway Vanessa wants to do a piece on Rochester's business to try to let everybody understand what we're really up against, so people can get a sense of proportion and kill some of this wild speculation that's going round. I know it might be painful but I wondered if she could talk to Cindy about her experience for background research? Nothing verbatim and no photos. I really think it would help, but only if she's happy to do it ... yes? Well, that's great. Can you come down to my office around lunchtime? Right, see you then.'

She put the phone down and turned to Vanessa. 'When you meet Cindy be very patient with her. She's a slave, but she's not a true Shiller girl. You'll understand ...'

Vanessa saw what Zara had warned her of as soon as Cindy and her master entered the office a couple of hours later.

Cindy was a slim, innocently pretty girl with slightly elfin features, deep brown shadowed eyes, and dark urchin-cut hair. Her neat breasts rose to pointed brown tips and her deep-cleft pubic mound was quite bare. About her neck she wore a heavy studded collar. Trevor Russell, her master, was a large amiable-looking man with a deep resonant voice. He carried most of Cindy's leash wrapped about his hand so she was on a tight rein.

There were plenty of naked girl pets on leashes around the building. Apart from house chain girls, business guests often brought their pet slaves with them to dine in Shiller's exclusive and very discreet restaurant. But Cindy was different. The other girls were confident in their submission, biddable but at ease, even proudly flaunting their ringed and harnessed bodies. Cindy had the air of a beaten puppy and her shadowed eyes had a haunted look to them. She walked with a slight hunch to her slender shoulders, her eyes darting about her nervously before returning to her master with a look of relief. She responded instantly to the slightest tug of her leash, moving perfectly to heel. When Trevor sat in the chair Zara offered, Cindy crouched down at his feet in a tight huddle, her eyes flicking quickly over Vanessa and Zara before looking up at her master again.

He patted her head. 'Good girl,' he said reassuringly.

His manner appeared caring, Vanessa thought. But how did that square with Cindy's crushed demeanour?

'Hello, Cindy,' Zara said gently. 'How are you?'

'I'm very happy, thank you, Mistress Zara,' Cindy said in a clear but meek voice. 'My master is very good to me and I love him very much especially when he punishes me.'

Vanessa blinked at this unexpected declaration which was almost childlike in its phrasing. It was delivered in a rush of words that sounded both sincere and yet desperate. Was she an extreme pain slut? Cindy had a pink blush on her bottom that suggested a recent mild spanking, but that was practically part of a slavegirl's uniform like her collar. Except for her eyes she looked perfectly fit and healthy.

'I know you do,' Zara said. 'Now this is Vanessa, my slave reporter on the *Girlflesh News*. Your master says you like her articles.'

Cindy looked at Vanessa properly for the first time and her face briefly lit up in a pretty smile. 'Hello, Vanessa, I'm pleased to meet you. I love your hat. My master lets me read your work.' She added quickly: 'He's very good to me.'

'Hello, Cindy,' Vanessa said. 'I'm glad you like my writing. In fact I was wondering if you could help me with a new article. It's about Harvey Rochester's slave business. I understand you know about him.'

Cindy's face clouded and she bit her lip. Trevor stroked her hair. 'It's all right, Cindy. You can tell Vanessa everything.'

Cindy took a deep breath. 'I didn't know it was . . . him. Not till later, after I'd been rescued. Not till after my master told me. He . . . Rochester . . . hurt me. I deserved it, of course, because I know I'm just a miserable masochistic slut of a slave and I deserve to be treated like that, but he still hurt me. I tried to please him. I did everything he said but he still wanted more.'

'I know,' Vanessa said quickly. 'He's hurt me as well. Now we're trying to stop him hurting other girls.'

'You mean Canary Chain?'

'Yes. And all the other girls he has. I want to tell everybody else in the company what he's like so they understand. And what you tell me might even help bring him down. So I know it's hard, but I'd like to hear your story.'

'You can speak absolutely freely, Cindy,' Trevor said. 'I think you should tell Vanessa your story.'

She looked up at him. 'If it would please you, Master.'

'It would. From the beginning.'

A little of her beaten puppy manner seemed to leave Cindy as she spoke, hesitantly at first but with growing confidence.

'I was eighteen when it started. I'd moved away from home. My dad was long gone and my mother had met this other guy I didn't like. But it was fine because I had a job and shared a flat with some other mates. I found a boyfriend. The sex was great. I was having a good time.

'Then one of my friends showed me this questionnaire thing about sex and lifestyle. There was a competition as well. I . . . can't remember what the prize was. Anyway, I filled it in, more as a joke really. I'd tried a bit of light pervy stuff with my boyfriend, tying up, spanking, that sort of thing, and I quite liked it. I wrote it down and sent it off. Inside a week I got an offer to go to some "research laboratory" to be tested. I thought it was weird but they paid my expenses. They wired me up and showed me pictures. Some were just everyday things or odd patterns. It was so boring I dozed off at times. But in between were pictures of people having sex and doing S&M stuff. I thought some of it was sick . . . but afterwards I couldn't get it out of my mind.

'They asked me if I wanted another session and I did. The tests got stranger. They put things inside me and started giving me electric shocks. It was all to test my reactions to intense stimulation, they said. But even though I hated some of it I wanted more. I didn't know why. I just kept going back. In the end they were strapping me down and making me have sex with other girls and screwing me for real and it hurt and I felt dirty but I had to have more. Then they said there was somewhere I could go and work with others like me.

'I gave up my job and my friends and my flat and let them take me. It was a country house, I think, but I don't know where. There were a load of girls like me there and they treated us like slaves. But it was all very disciplined. We even had a sort of uniform. We wore red collars and red high-heeled shoes with locks on the ankle straps and a chain-link pattern on them. They were silly things to wear with the sort of things we had to do. The heels were always breaking. But we still had to wear them. We also had red painted nails and nipples and lots of lipstick. We paraded like that every day before our shift standing to attention like we were soldiers. There was always a camera watching us. Sometimes our masters got a message from elsewhere if a girl didn't look neat enough and she was punished.

'And people came to the house, usually wearing masks, and we had to do whatever they wanted us to do. Not that we had any choice. Some of it was amazing and some frightening but I couldn't escape and wasn't sure what I'd do anyway because I missed it when I wasn't doing it even though I knew it was wrong. I was like a junkie, high on pain and sex and feeling I was a filthy slut.

'Then one day the camera at the parade stayed on me for a long time, looking at me from all angles. Then I was taken out of the line and told I'd been chosen to serve "The Boss". That's what our masters called him. I was stripped and hooded and put in a tiny cage and driven a long way. When I was taken out again it was inside a sort of cellar or dungeon, full of gadgets. And there was a man in a mask that covered his whole face except his eyes. And he did everything the guests did to me but much worse . . .'

Cindy paused to sniff and wipe her eyes. Trevor stroked her head again. She continued with a shudder: 'I tried to please him . . . I would have done anything if he had just stopped hurting me . . . but he was never satisfied. I think he liked watching me cry and beg. Even when he wasn't using me there were cameras on the walls watching me, even when I sat on the toilet, one of those squat types, I think he was watching me.'

'And you never saw his face or knew his name?' Vanessa asked.

'No, he never took his mask off. I know because I was never blindfolded. I think he liked watching my eyes when I cried. When he let me speak I had to call him "Sir" or "Master". He did smell a bit of cigar smoke, I remember.'

'How long did he keep you?'

'About a week, I think. There were no windows, no clocks. Then he got tired of me and sent me back. Except it wasn't to the same house. The girls had been moved somewhere else. But I didn't care. I was just glad to be out of that dungeon . . . except that I missed him as well. It was crazy but I still wanted to please him . . . so he'd stop watching me . . . and tell me just once that I was good . . .'

She hung her head and started crying softly. Trevor said: 'Good girl. It's all over now.'

'You've told me everything I need to know,' Vanessa said quickly. 'Thank you very much, Cindy. That's been a great help.'

Cindy smiled shyly through her tears.

Zara showed the pair of them out and then returned to her chair and looked solemnly at Vanessa. 'Not long after that we raided the house and freed Cindy and the

67

girls. The rest were returned to ordinary life with the cover story that they had got mixed up with some cult. One or two genuine natural submissives were taken into chains. But not Cindy, of course.'

'Rochester really broke her will, didn't he, Mistress?' Vanessa said, feeling the anger rise inside her.

'Yes. Combined with the conditioning she had received. She's become an addict to pain and servitude. She can't face any other life. She's having psychiatric help from one of our specialists, of course, but I'm not sure if she'll ever recover fully. She certainly couldn't survive free on her own at the moment. She's lucky she has found a kindly master and an environment where she can be herself . . . or at least what she's become.'

'Master Trevor's voice sounds a little like Rochester's, Mistress.'

'Yes. I think that's what drew her to him. Subconsciously she's still trying to please the man who hurt her so much and broke her spirit, trying to win his approval by proxy.'

Vanessa shuddered, sick at the thought of what had been done to Cindy. It was the very opposite of what she had experienced when her resistance had been skilfully broken down by Shiller trainers allowing her to discover her true nature.

'Now I understand why you hate him so much, Mistress,' Vanessa said. 'And why you were so suspicious of me when you knew I worked for him.'

'I'm glad to say I was wrong about you,' Zara said with a smile. 'But one day, Rochester will pay for what he did to that girl.'

Silently Vanessa made the same vow. Aloud she said, 'It seems as though he uses a similar method to our Human Response Laboratory to recruit girls, Mistress.'

'He stole the idea from us,' Zara said. 'But where we only select potential natural submissives and allow them to bloom, his laboratory conditions girls who just have a mild interest in BDSM and turn them into addicts. They make more interesting slaves that way. Also they appear to give up their normal lives voluntarily, which is less likely to arouse suspicion than if they simply go missing.'

Vanessa turned off her recorder. 'I have enough to be going on with for now, Mistress. I'll show you my first draft in a few days.'

'This morning you said you had two things you wanted to do to help boost morale. What was the second one?'

'I must clear it with the Director first, Mistress, because I'll need some help, but I'm sure you'll want to cover it for *GN*. The staff all need a distraction, especially the security personnel. Everybody resents them for doing their job. They need a reward and a chance to put their training to good use. So I thought we could give them one.'

Five

About ten the next morning, when Vanessa drove her Mini up to the outer car park gates of the Shiller building, she was not alone.

Sitting next to her was Sandra. In the back seat were Daniele 14 White and Laura 9 White. They were all dressed identically in long dark-grey belted trench coats with the collars turned up, wide-brimmed grey felt hats pulled down low, and dark glasses. Glued to their upper lips were drooping black moustaches.

Pru from the *GN* office was standing by the gate kiosk recording the scene on her camera. A pair of gate guards, informed that there would be a security exercise but not of its exact nature, looked in through the Mini's open side windows, grinning broadly. 'And who do you think you are?' the first said, trying to maintain his official poise.

'Vee are a travelling band of international tax inspectors here to examine your bookings,' Vanessa said in a gruff and very cod-eastern European accent.

The guard struggled to keep a straight face. 'Are you men or women?'

'Vee are men, of course,' Vanessa assured him. 'Can you not see our moustaches?'

'Only these look like tits to me,' he said, reaching in and pulling open her coat to reveal her bare breasts. On the other side of the car his companion did the same to Sandra.

'You are quite wrong,' Vanessa said unabashed. 'They are merely highly developed pectoral muscles resulting from overexertion carrying too many heavy tax files.'

'Oh ... I see,' said the guard. 'My mistake. Well, you'd better get on with it then ...'

As they passed under the barrier he could be heard chuckling as he said into his radio: 'You might want to check out the contents of the red Mini ...'

They were stopped again at the gate that controlled access to the lower level of the car park. Rhona was standing by this gate also armed with a camera.

'Good morning, "gentlemen",' the guard said, looking in at them as severely as he could manage in the circumstances.

'Good morning, gate guard,' Vanessa said. 'Please be letting us through as we have urgent business to attend to.'

By now they had their legs carelessly splayed and coat fronts parted to expose stocking tops and their pantyless and unmistakably feminine genitalia.

'May I point out that you don't appear to have the usual wedding tackle that goes with those 'tashes,' the guard said.

'Our lack of male organs is simply the result of a misfortune with a document shredder we mistook for a photocopier,' Vanessa assured him. 'Oh my, did we feel foolish that day, I can tell you!'

'Of course,' said the guard, stifling unmanly giggles, 'I should have thought of that myself. Well, you'd better go down, then ...'

The gate slid aside and they drove down to the lower level. A squad of a dozen security guards were waiting for them. Standing a little to one side were Gavin and Steve, also holding cameras.

Vanessa and her companions clambered out of the car, tottering slightly on black high heels.

'Hold it right there, "gentlemen",' said Mister Horton, the burly chief of building security, brandishing a hand scanner while keeping a commendably straight face. As they closed in around the girls the men became aware of tinny muffled voices interspersed with electronic beeping that seemed to be coming from the girls themselves.

'What's that then?' Horton asked suspiciously.

'Vee hear nothing,' Vanessa assured him. 'You must be suffering from tinnitus brought on by too much shouting.'

'You'll have to take those coats off right now!'

'This is no way to treat respectable gentlemens!' Vanessa protested.

'Listen, "sonny",' Horton said, 'if I tell you to strip you strip!'

Reluctantly the girls shrugged off their coats, revealing they had nothing underneath but black stockings and matching suspender belts. The guards searched the coat pockets and checked them with their scanners, but found nothing. The strange sounds continued to permeate the air around the girls, but it was hard to pinpoint the source.

'And your hats,' Horton said.

These were examined but contained nothing out of the ordinary.

'Lets have a look at those shoes . . .' No result. 'Suspender belts and stockings . . .' The same. 'Glasses . . .' Nothing.

The girls were now standing in a ring of grinning guards wearing only their collars and their ridiculous moustaches, which were starting to peel from their lips. The strange noises continued.

'I demand vee have our clothes back so vee may be properly attired as gentlemen should,' Vanessa demanded.

'So you still claim to be men . . . only you're not exactly shaped like men,' Horton pointed out.

'Our reduced waistlines are the result of a strenuous diet vee have been on,' Vanessa said.

'So why were you wearing stockings?'

'Just because vee are tax inspectors does not mean vee cannot be a little kinky, no?'

Horton bent closer to her stomach. 'Do you know there's someone talking out of your pussy?'

'That is a lie! I have no pussy! I was hung like a donkey before my unfortunate accident!'

Horton rammed the scanner loop aerial into her cleft. The machines beeped madly.

'So what've you got up there then?'

'Your machine is merely responding to latent static electricity in our pubic hair due to the removal of our nylon stockings.'

'I have reason to believe that you are women in disguise!' Horton said, reaching out and tearing off Vanessa's false moustaches.

'Curse your fiendish perspicacity!' Vanessa cried. 'Our cunning disguises have been penetrated! Run!'

The girls scattered with the laughing guards and Gavin and Steve in hot pursuit.

They dodged between cars and round supporting pillars, their breasts bouncing, bottoms jiggling and bare feet slapping on the concrete. But inexorably the guards closed in on them. One by one they were grabbed and forced up against the walls, grinding their bottoms against the hard concrete, or flattening their breasts as they were bent over the bonnets of cars. Enthusiastically pawed and manhandled, with much squeezing of tits and pinching of bottoms, their arms were pulled round behind them and wrists cuffed. Their flailing legs were pinioned and ankles likewise cuffed. Expanding ball gags forced into their mouths stifled their screams of outrage.

Josh and Harry finally managed to corner Vanessa at the far end of the car park.

'Right, let's see what you've been trying to smuggle past us, girlie,' Harry said with a delighted leer.

'You'll never catch me, chauvinist guard dog pigs of a corrupt capitalist oppressive organisation!' Vanessa shouted defiantly.

They grabbed her and twisted her arms behind her and pushed her up against a pillar and slapped her bottom hard, leaving handprints. After cuffing her wrists they spun her round and pried her lips wide so they could stuff a ball gag into her mouth to stem the flood of insults. Then they squeezed her breasts and twisted her nipples until she cried and stopped kicking and they could secure her ankles. Finally they dragged her back between them to join the others.

Bound and gagged but still wriggling, the four intruders were hoisted shoulder high and taken down in the lift to B3. Emerging onto the slavegirl level Horton called out: 'Make way! Highly suspicious and possibly foreign intruder sluts coming through for interrogation. Make way . . .'

Trailing a growing tail of curious giggling slavegirls after them the guards carried the prisoners to The Mall.

This was a mews lined by a double row of small cell-like rooms, each with large low windows that were in fact one-way mirrors sheltered by striped awnings. Opened up, they formed tiny shops selling off-duty slavegirls small goods. With windows closed and curtained, the cells could be used by slavegirls wanting to enjoy some private sexplay, while others had girls enticingly on display bound to various restraining devices for use by members of staff.

Now two adjacent larger cells were conveniently ready to receive the intruders. The partition between them had been removed, forming one long room with two viewing windows. Arranged in a row along it were four sturdy wooden tables. Each was fitted with semi-circular hinged neck and wrist cuff hoops. At the foot of each table rose two side posts with chains and ankle cuffs hanging from them. Beside the tables were racks of probes, restraints and assorted punishment devices.

The four white-collar girls were carried inside the interrogation suite, the doors were closed behind them and they were dumped on their backs on the tables. The guards uncuffed their ankles, pulled their legs wide and lifted their feet upwards, then re-cuffed them to the tops of the posts. Now their bottoms and exposed pubic pouches overhung the ends of the tables. As their legs were spread and pussy lips parted slightly the mysterious muffled voices and beeping sounds became louder. The guards lifted the girls' shoulders sufficiently to free their arms, pull them out and bend them back and secure them with the hoop clamps. The final larger middle hoop went across their necks.

Vanessa twisted her head to look to her left and right, seeing Sandra, Daniele and Laura secured as she was, their breasts still heaving from their struggles. In the viewing windows, which looked like mirrors from this side, she saw their slightly misty images reflected: a row of four pairs of 'V' spread legs, with pubic clefts and anal mouths exposed at their bases. Beyond the windows she could just make out the faint shadows of the crowd of watching girls.

A sense of relief came over Vanessa. She was gagged and helpless. Now the playacting was over. All she had to do was respond as came naturally and savour the pain and the pleasure of being a Shiller girl. She imagined what the onlookers were seeing and let herself become one with her chain sisters . . .

'Now let's see what you were carrying,' said Horton. 'Open 'em up, lads.'

From the equipment racks the men took out dinner plate-sized oval metal hoops lined on the inside with a dozen coil springs terminating in hard rubber hooks with rounded tips. These they positioned between the girls' spread thighs so the ovoids framed their genitals and bottom clefts. They stretched the springs and dug the hooks between their labia pulling their lovemouths painfully wide, making the girls whimper as they exposed the crinkled pink mouths of their vaginas. As they did so the strange vocal buzz and beepings became louder still, and it could be seen there was something hidden in their dark moist depths. More hooks opened up their well-greased anal passages, pulling them into odd asymmetric forms despite their desperate clenchings. There also seemed to be something plugged within their rectums.

The guards-turned-amateur gynaecologists produced long slim metal tongs and reached into the inviting and helplessly gaping passages, probing their secrets despite the girls' squirms, and carefully extracted the glistening contents.

First out of their rectums were wads of soft black compressed foam rubber that expanded to form larger balls with a string fuse on the top and the word BOMB painted on it in white letters. The men laughed and held up their finds for the watchers outside the windows to see. Meanwhile from the captives' vaginas were drawn out small pliant items wrapped in plastic bags that were revealed to be tiny novelty cameras that squirted water when squeezed. Rolled up inside condoms and stuffed higher up their rectums were tiny soft-cover diaries bearing the inscriptions CODE BOOK: TOP SECRET. Finally at the top of their vaginal passages the guards discovered the source of the noises and the scanner alarms. They were slim-line mobile phones wrapped in condoms dialled to the speaking clock.

Amid much laughter these items, still warm and glistening, were laid out in front of Horton. 'This is a highly suspicious collection and will be closely examined. Meanwhile I condemn these spies to a good thrashing and a screwing by all security staff as compensation. Have fun, lads . . .'

As the girls whimpered the staff moved eagerly to obey. The spreader hoops were unhooked, paddles and lashes were taken out and the men lined up two to each girl, standing on either side of her parted legs. They swung in alternation, each having a buttock to themselves and overlapping on the girls' bulging pubic mounds with their wet and still gaping clefts. The girls yipped and squirmed and gurgled, tears running down their cheeks as their bottoms and vulvas turned to a rosy crimson. The curling tips of lash thongs and rubber paddle blades penetrated their labial valleys and licked and slapped at their clitorises, which were budding and swelling and rising to meet the onslaught. Dribbles of lubrication ran from the lower ends of their clefts over their anal mouths, to be splattered by the rain of blows. The girls' hips began to jerk in desperation as they offered themselves up in surrender and sacrifice to spare them more pain.

The guards began to drop their lashes and paddles along with their trousers. As one rammed his cock into vagina or anus as he pleased, his companion used his blade or thongs on the girls' breasts, setting them bouncing and wobbling. The girls' eyes bulged at this dual assault and they clenched at the shafts reciprocating within their passages to suck every last gram of pleasure from them.

One by one the men came inside their chosen victims, accompanied by chain girl cheering from outside the windows. They swapped with their fellows who had been lashing the girls' breasts. When the first group of guards had had their fill, they zipped up and went off to relieve their fellows. The girls' dripping vulvas and weeping anal mouths were flushed clean. In minutes the second wave arrived and took up the lashes and paddles afresh . . .

Vanessa, Daniele, Laura and Sandra were not released until every guard in the building had used and abused them, some even coming back for seconds. Aching but well satisfied, Vanessa hugged and thanked the other white-collar girls and then they all tottered outside to receive the appreciation of their sisters in the Mall.

A little later, back in Zara's office, Vanessa saw the front page of the special edition of *GN* covering the incident already being assembled. It was headed: ALERT SECURITY GUARDS FOIL MYSTERY INTRUDERS, and contained several pictures of their capture and 'interrogation' and images of the 'sophisticated espionage' devices recovered from them.

'Well done,' Zara said warmly. 'That was a piece of nonsense we all badly needed.'

The issue also featured an announcement by the Director that as the likelihood of a direct attack had now passed, and as the security personnel had shown such alertness in preventing this incursion by 'mystery intruders', from tomorrow they would step down to regular levels of building security.

That night in her flat Vanessa lay in her bed with an icepack between her legs feeling sore but content. Everything had worked as planned. It had given the resented guards a good time at the expense of the Director's personal chain and brought everybody together. Choosing Steve and Gavin to be special photographers recording her humiliation would not harm office harmony either. Now she was counting the days until Kashika returned. She had done her best to bring some solace and relief to others and now she wanted somebody to comfort her and make her believe they would get Canary Chain back safe and well. They could beat Rochester . . . they had to . . .

She drifted off to sleep with fragments from the last few hectic days swirling round in her head. A jumble of images surfaced and faded away . . .

The bums and boobs of naked girls appeared with

formulae and graphs drawn all over them. They multiplied into a whole column of naked girls all looking like Cindy with rifles over their shoulders marching into a blood-red sunset ... click-clack, click-clack ... Now there was something slithering in the grass by their feet ... it had Rochester's face. How he'd love to get his hands on her. A gagged Kashika was shaking her head but Rochester could not hurt her because he didn't seem to have any arms and his mouth was stuffed with money. Hungrier for money than he was for revenge, and she was just one girl and he needed lots more to keep earning. A page from *Datumline* cut up like a circuit board. Vanessa was running and running, looking for something she could not name, but it was like wading through treacle and she was squatting down and hundreds of squirming rubber toys were pouring from both her orifices as though she was giving birth. Now Rochester was howling in rage, spewing the notes from his mouth as he choked and snarled. What did they not search, what did they not, what did they ...

She woke with a start, gasping for breath, fumbling for the light switch, wanting to lock the idea into reality before it melted away like the memory of a dream. She struggled to hold it all together. Did it make sense? Yes! There it was. The way to end it once and for all.

Six

Vanessa knelt on the green leather of the Director's desk in the Director's private office, arms folded behind her back and knees wide in a display of respect and submission. It placed her pussy at the eye level of anybody sitting in the desk chair. Only one person ever used that chair, of course. At this moment Shiller was leaning back in it with brow furrowed and fingers steepled as she considered the plan Vanessa had just set out.

A living sculpture stood against one wall. It was the kind of art you only found inside Shiller offices. An athletically built naked black girl in a green collar was posed on a glass plinth. She appeared to be frozen in the act of throwing a spear of plastic sculpted to resemble a slender javelin of ice. She was held in place by several intersecting segmented panels of thick clear plastic that rose from the plinth. They slotted together to form a three-dimensional grid that clamped about her body through holes and slots in the plastic. A clear moulded plastic mask was fitted over her face, closing her eyes and mouth. The only movement about her was the slight rise and fall of her chest and the tiny tremble of her stubby dark-chocolate nipples. She was quite immobile and exposed both to the eyes and hands of any who cared to examine her. Yet Vanessa knew without asking that right now she felt only honour and pride at being on display in the Director's private sanctum.

As she waited nervously, Vanessa realised the desktop under her was faintly mottled by the excited exudations of the many girls who had knelt in this place before her, displaying themselves as she was to their mistress and owner. It was an inevitable slavish reaction to the aura of power she commanded. But none of her predecessors, Vanessa suspected, bore a proposal that meant so much to the company.

'What you suggest is logical and ingenious,' Shiller said at length. 'Which is just what I have come to expect from you.' Vanessa felt a swell of pride. 'Once again seeing a situation from the chain girl perspective has given you a special insight. But are you fully aware of the risks?'

'I'm prepared to take them if this will put an end to Rochester's operation once and for all, Director,' Vanessa replied, trying to sound calm and confident. 'It has to be me. It won't work any other way.'

She had been awake half the night refining her idea and trying to anticipate all its consequences and possible weaknesses. She had come into the office early and checked back issues of *Datumline* to confirm her memory was correct and what she would need existed. Then she had requested this personal meeting with the Director. In essence it was a simple plan, but she knew so many things could go wrong.

'There will be risk to others as well,' Shiller pointed out. 'It's a great deal to ask of them.'

'I know what I'll be asking of them, Director. But I know they'll want to take the risk as well.'

'But will they agree out of love and friendship for you, perhaps?'

Vanessa felt a flush of embarrassment. 'A little, perhaps, Director. But I hope, I know, more for love of their chain sisters and this company . . . and hatred of Rochester and all he stands for. They know this cannot go on. We have to win or we lose everything. That's worth taking risks for . . . unless we find Canary Chain first.'

Shiller sighed. 'I have not released this information yet. We have already raided two suspect addresses, but Rochester's girlflesh operation had already been cleared out. If the Canary girls were being kept there we missed them. At least we believe our actions were not detected by Rochester so there will be no reprisals against the girls. But at the moment we have no other firm leads.'

'And even if we do rescue them, we're only back to where we started, Director. Rochester will just try something else. He has to be stopped once and for all.'

There was a long pause during which Vanessa feared she had spoken out of turn. Then Shiller nodded. 'Sadly you are quite correct, Vanessa. Therefore we will enact your plan. Finish any outstanding work for *GN* this morning. Then go down to B3 and have your collar and rings removed and dress as appropriate to your new executive position. I will assign you a private office and a personal assistant. They will be ready this afternoon. You have unlimited funds and may call on whatever technical and logistical support you need. I will have a memo sent out to this effect to all relevant departments.' Shiller turned to her computer screen and began reading. After a moment she looked back at Vanessa with a quizzically raised brow. 'Well, go on then, Vanessa, get started.'

Vanessa shook herself out of her daze. 'Yes, Director, thank you, Director. I won't let you down . . .' She scrambled off the desk and made for the door.

Still feeling a little dizzy at the speed of events, Vanessa went to see Zara.

'I'm going to be working on a special project for the Director,' she explained. 'I'll finish up this morning but then I'll be out of the office for the next few weeks. It might get complicated and I don't want people asking questions or bothering me.' She took a deep breath, about to explain in detail, but then settled for the simple: 'Basically I'm going to see Rochester get screwed so he's off our backs once and for all!'

Zara blinked, then smiled, leant forward and kissed her. 'Good luck,' she said.

Vanessa's new office was a medium-sized room on the floor above the *GN* office.

As Vanessa, uncomfortably dressed and collarless, entered it early that afternoon she saw desks set out with phones and computer terminals, executive swivel chairs, a day couch, pin boards and empty shelving. From behind one of the desks rose a slim, attractive mid-fortyish woman in a grey two-piece, her hair in a bun and round metal-framed spectacles perched on her nose. She was exactly the sort of person one could not possibly imagine working for a company that traded in slavegirls.

She inclined her head to Vanessa. 'Good afternoon, Miss Buckingham. I am Angela Wilton, your personal assistant.'

'Good afternoon, Mistress . . .' Vanessa began automatically, but Angela interrupted.

'Excuse me, Miss Buckingham, but the Director was quite specific that you are in charge and I am to serve you, and I like to be correct.' She smiled, suddenly looking younger than her years. 'I've had the privilege of working for this company for over twenty years, and have been on the Director's personal staff for five. Perhaps this will make it clear . . .'

She raised her skirt, revealing slim thighs. She wore no underwear. Beneath a neatly trimmed delta of pubic hair the deep cleft of her vulva was decorated with three gold rings.

'Oh . . . I see,' said Vanessa.

Angela lowered her skirt again and brushed it down. 'Yes, Miss, I once wore a white collar as well so I know what you're feeling. But the Director was most specific

. . . and I still enjoy following orders. She also told me you are trying to bring down Harvey Rochester. To do that I will help you in any way I possibly can.'

Vanessa blinked at her new assistant's almost old-fashioned politeness. Perhaps some of the Director's assured manner and precision of speech rubbed off on her closer staff

'Thanks for that . . . Angela.' Cautiously Vanessa sat down in the chair by the second desk and looked about her. 'Right, what have I got here?'

'You have a terminal with the usual internet facilities plus full security clearance and access to every department and subsidiary company in the Shiller group, Miss Buckingham. Any requests or directions you give through this system will automatically carry the Director's authorisation. What do you wish to do first?'

Vanessa took a deep breath. 'Well, there's a bunch of things to get going as soon as possible. I've got to talk to a couple of technical companies, Keller Wilson Systems and Robotikine, about certain items I want made or modified, and track down the latest address for the front company Rochester uses for recruiting girls and get hold of the forms they use. Then there's finding the addresses of all the houses Rochester owns. Also I need to find a professional porn photographer. Then there's some niche fashion research that may lead to a bit of computer hacking and possibly even breaking and entering. And I need an address to stay where I can receive mail. Also looking up sewer drain layouts in local council planning department records offices, or whoever keeps those things, across several counties. Oh, and there's the matter of arranging a little cosmetic surgery. That should keep us busy for a while.'

'That's an interesting set of requirements, Miss Buckingham,' Angela said with a smile. 'But we are not alone. You can call on anybody you need to assist, private agencies or company staff. Even off-duty chain girls if they're best suited.'

'Can I really?'

'Recovering our girls safely has top priority, Miss, and you have been entrusted with the task. In theory you have the resources of the entire company at your disposal, which means several thousand staff, twenty principal subsidiary companies and combined assets to the value of several hundred billion pounds. When the Director gives somebody her trust it is total.'

Vanessa gulped. 'I don't think I'll need all of that. Maybe I'd better tell you the plan in detail so we can work up a list of what I need and why and then we can see what comes first . . .'

As Vanessa explained her objectives Angela took careful notes. When she was done, Angela said solemnly: 'It's an ingenious plan, Miss Buckingham, but I think you're taking a considerable chance. There are so many things that might go wrong.'

'But you agree it's the only way of ending this war between us and Rochester once and for all,' Vanessa said. It felt important that Angela believed in it too. After all she was only the second person Vanessa had told in detail and she needed reassurance that it made sense.

'Oh, I do, Miss. I just think you are very brave to take the risk. It confirms everything I've already heard about you. The other girls said you had a special quality. I admire you so much for what you're trying to do . . .' Her pale cheeks had coloured. 'May I . . .' Quickly she moved round from her chair to stand before Vanessa. She went down on her knees and kissed Vanessa's feet, then, with a glance up at Vanessa's face as though asking permission, rolled back Vanessa's skirt.

Though required to dress about the office, Vanessa had decided that at least she could do so knickerless. Angela smiled as though in approval, ducked her head between Vanessa's thighs and delicately kissed her pussy lips.

'You can ask anything you wish of me, Miss Buckingham,' she said quietly. 'If you ever need any relief or pleasure I can provide then do not hesitate to ask.'

Vanessa felt thrilled and embarrassed in equal measure. 'Thank you, Angela,' she said, stroking the older woman's hair. 'I think, with your help, I'm going to make this work.'

Containing her smile of pleasure Angela resumed her seat and became the professional secretary once more. 'As I see it the cosmetic adjustments clearly must take priority, Miss. I can put everything else in hand while you are undergoing the alterations.'

'The trouble is I don't know how available any of these things are,' Vanessa said. 'I only read about them in back issues of *Datumline*. I know the enlargement procedure is expensive, but I have to use it to save time.'

'As I said, Miss, money is no object.'

'Well, I suppose that helps. Then there's the skin treatment and the special contact lenses. But I haven't had a chance to find out where I could get hold of them yet.'

Angela had been studying the list carefully. 'Actually, Miss, I think you can get everything done at the Chattlewell Clinic, which is only half an hour away. They can call in any additional specialists that are required.'

Vanessa blinked. 'I've never heard of them. They're not like the Alves Clinic, are they?'

Angela smiled. 'No, the Alves is a place for clients to have fun playing at doctors and nurses. The Chattlewell is a genuine professional cosmetic practice with the highest standards. They've performed many procedures for our clients and are totally familiar with handling the needs of slavegirls.'

'But will they able to do it all soon enough?'

'As Shiller's owns a controlling interest in their firm I think I can guarantee swift service. I can call them right now if you wish.'

'Angela, you're a treasure. Please . . .'

Angela dialled a number and had a brisk interchange with the person on the other end during which she methodically listed Vanessa's requirements. There was a pause, then she said: 'Thank you, that will be fine . . .' made a note in a desk diary, put the phone down and turned to Vanessa. 'You are booked in at the Chattlewell Clinic tomorrow morning, Miss Buckingham. If the consultation is satisfactory they will operate within a couple of hours. The enlargement treatment of course requires a general anaesthetic so you are advised not have a meal tonight and keep your fluid intake down to a minimum. They say you should be out again within a couple of days.'

Vanessa took a deep breath, unused to the speed at which power and influence could be used to achieve a desired result. Last night she had a dream, today it was already being turned into a reality. It was a little frightening. *I just hope I can keep my nerve*, she thought. 'What about the rest of the list?'

'We can initiate most of it this afternoon, Miss. I'll monitor progress while you're in the clinic. I can call in on you to keep you up to date and pass on any fresh instructions.'

'That sounds good.' Absently she rubbed her neck where her collar had been. It felt uncomfortably naked.

Angela touched the black fabric band around her own neck. 'Wear a choker when you can, Miss. A broad firm one. It helps you pretend it's still there.'

'Do you ever get over having been Shiller girlflesh?' Vanessa asked.

'Never, Miss. And I wouldn't want to.'

The Chattelwell Clinic resided behind discreet black wrought railings and a discreet brass plaque and an even more discreet black door just off Harley Street. As Angela had promised, they were totally familiar with handling the needs of slavegirls. Within a very short while they'd made Vanessa feel at home.

She hung naked inside a gingerbread-man-style cutout within a thick Perspex panel set within a tubular gimbal-mounted frame that was in turn mounted on a wheeled base. Clear plastic restraint bands passing through slots in the Perspex about the edges of the cutout bound about her body from ankles to neck and held her firmly in place. Her name and patient number had been written on a plastic band and were taped across her forehead. Already missing her collar, it felt good to have a label securely attached to her once more. Her mouth was plugged by what looked a little like an overlarge baby's ring dummy, with an expanding inner flange too big to expel from between her teeth. Somebody hooking their finger through the ring could lead her around, making it substitute for a collar and leash.

As soon as she had signed the consent forms she had been ordered to strip and was secured in the frame, presumably like many slaves girls before her. It was something of a relief. Her head was buzzing with the decisions she had made over the last twenty-four hours and the responsibilities for it all weighed on her shoulders. Now she was being treated like a slave again and all she had to do was obey and accept the decisions of others.

Her consultant and surgeon, Mr Radleigh, had examined her thoroughly and was now describing what they were going to do to her. By his side taking notes was a smart, pleasantly full-bodied nurse in a dove-grey uniform. Radleigh had been totally professional and his credentials were impeccable, but Vanessa could read the natural excitement in his eyes as he took pleasure in lecturing his helpless patient.

'This is what we'll be injecting you with,' he said, holding up a vial filled with a heavy pinkish jelly-like substance. 'Essentially it is synthetic body fat that will not be rejected by your body's immune system. It will be injected under high pressure via a computer-controlled depth and alignment system using ultra-fine needles. This method allows us to modify your natural contours with great precision without distorting them unrealistically.' He took out a marker and began drawing arcs of dots on her breasts. 'We shall inject it into the natural fatty tissue that underlies your milk glands here . . . and here . . . to build up volume and lift . . . then a little under your nipples to increase their prominence in proportion.'

He reached up to her nose and added a dash on each nostrils. 'We'll use small internal contoured plastic inserts here to flare your nostrils slightly. These may be removed if required at any time.' He drew dots over her lips. 'Add a little extra fullness here . . . and on your cheeks . . .'

He spun and flipped the frame on its gimbals, turning Vanessa around and then on her head. He started drawing on her bottom that was now conveniently presented to him. 'Then we'll add some weight and extra roundness to your buttocks . . . and a little on your hips to balance . . .' He spun her round so she was facing him once more but upside down. Now her newly clean-shaven pubes were at his eye level.

'And to maintain proportion a little plumping up of your labia majora . . .' he explained as he drew on the outer lips of her vulva. 'With this method the recovery process is minimal. The needle marks and any slight residual bruising will fade within a few days and there is no adjustment or settling in as with traditional implants. While you're on the table I'll also close up and skin-glue your labial piercings. The skin, hair restyling and deep depilation Miss Belling will take care of tomorrow, assuming you've made a normal recovery. We'll also arrange for a lens specialist to call round.'

He stood back and looked at Vanessa's inverted marker-dotted form with satisfaction. 'Nurse Kelly here will be your personal attendant throughout your stay. She'll monitor your progress and take care of anything you need.' He checked his watch. 'Right. That will be all for the moment, Nurse. You can call back for this patient in half an hour . . .'

Flashing a quick knowing smile at Vanessa, Nurse Kelly left the room.

Radleigh moved closer. Vanessa saw him unzip his flies and free a hardening erection, its single slit eye seeming to be stabbing towards her. He reached down and twisted the ring and pulled the dummy from her mouth. Grasping the sides of her imprisoning frame to steady himself he thrust his stiff cock in to take its place.

She gobbled and sucked automatically, pleased to be able to slavishly satisfy the basic need of a man in a position of power over her. She was helpless, he had the time and her mouth was available. It was all very simple.

As he thrust steadily into her gullet she felt him rubbing his face into her groin. He was not kissing her pussy lips but rather luxuriating in the texture of their soft, rubbery pliancy, exploring their many folds, lathering his face with her lubricating juices. It was a curiously reserved response to her most feminine organ and unexpectedly sensuous.

But all too soon he was spouting down her throat and she was swallowing, trying not to let any dribbles run up her nose.

When he was done he pulled out of her and pushed the dummy back into place. She would go to the operating table with the taste of her surgeon's sperm in her mouth.

* * *

Vanessa became aware of a deep dull ache in her breasts, buttocks, vulva and face, partly masked by painkillers. She opened her bleary eyes to see Nurse Kelly sitting by her bedside. Around her was the well-appointed comfort of her private room.

'It all went as planned,' Kelly said reassuringly. 'Want a sip of water?'

Vanessa grunted. She still had the dummy in her mouth. Kelly touched a button that raised the head of the bed, twisted the ring of the dummy and pulled it free. She fed Vanessa water from a beaker through a drinking straw and then replaced the dummy.

As her head cleared further Vanessa realised there was a soft cool ring under her hips to ease the pressure on her bottom. She looked down at herself. A light sheet covered her from the waist down, but her breasts were bare. They were mottled in pink blotches and tiny pinpoints of blood and felt heavier. They certainly stood up more prominently than before.

'They're lovely,' Kelly said. 'I was just admiring them when you woke up.'

She tried to touch her new breasts but found she could not move. Her arms were bound to her sides by a broad strap above her elbows that passed across her chest under her breasts. Her wrists were cuffed and linked via short chains to garter-like bands about her thighs. Her legs were spread and ankles cuffed wide to the raised frames running down the sides of the bed.

'We try to keep regular patients from lifting their arms too much immediately after breast surgery, but they don't always listen,' Kelly explained. 'The trouble we've had with some models you wouldn't believe. It's easier with you slavegirls. We just keep you strapped in place. You're no trouble at all. Do you want to see your face?'

Vanessa grunted again. Kelly held up a hand mirror. Again her skin was mottled and pinpricked in places, but she could see the changes. Her nostrils now had an added sensuous flare to them, her lips were fuller and cheeks slightly rounder. Her features now hinted at a dash of exotic African ancestry, except for her pale skin. And that would soon be taken care of.

'How about downstairs?' Kelly asked.

Vanessa nodded.

Kelly pulled down the sheets to expose her groin and angled the mirror. The lips of her bare pubic mound were now distinctly plumper, making her cleft seem even deeper.

'I think you could call that pouting,' Kelly said. She smiled mischievously. 'Almost kissable . . .'

When Vanessa was feeling stronger Kelly uncuffed her ankles and helped her to the bathroom, leading her by her dummy ring. Her wrists remained chained to her garter bands, but she did not need to use her hands for anything. Kelly sat her on the toilet and wiped her clean afterwards. Then she washed her, returned her to her bed and re-cuffed her. Later she brought a light meal in and spoon-fed her. While her dummy was out Vanessa did not attempt to speak and Kelly did not encourage her. There was no need. Vanessa simply enjoyed the luxury of her confinement.

That evening Angela called in as arranged. Kelly took out Vanessa's dummy, while leaving her strapped to the bed as before, and then left them discreetly alone. *Only Shiller women could hold a business conference like this as though it was perfectly normal*, Vanessa thought with pride.

Angela admired Vanessa's new breasts and pubes. 'There was nothing wrong with your natural shape, Miss Buckingham. But I do like these.'

Vanessa smiled, flattered by the praise, but tried to sound businesslike. 'As long as they do the job.'

From her bag Angela produced a colourful questionnaire. 'I have obtained one of the current Deedas Research forms to fill in, Miss. That's the company fronting as a psychological research institution Rochester is using. Their nearest facility currently listed is just outside Guildford.'

'"Deedas"?' Vanessa queried.

'A little joke I think, Miss. It's an anagram of "De Sade".'

'I get it. Anyway, well done. That was quick.'

'Thank you, Miss. I simply sent some off-duty girls out to search the usual places they appear: youth hostels, clubs, mailshots through small newsagents. They are always anxious to recruit more stock.'

'Well, I'm going to help them out there. Have we got an address to use?'

'A flat one of the managers in accounts lets out, Miss. It's vacant at the moment and quite comfortable so you can take it over for as long as you need. Have you chosen a suitable alias for yourself?'

'I think "Debra Kane" for modelling purposes and the more prosaic "Josie Gribbleson" for everyday.'

'That suggests plenty of scope for aspiration, Miss,' Angela agreed, noting the two down. 'I have the mobile phone you asked for so we can assign it to "Josie" for contact purposes.' She unfolded the form and studied it. 'This begins with innocuous enough questions but gradually gets more personal and intimate as it progresses, including sexual experience in some detail. There are also a lot of boxes to tick. Apparently if you return this fully completed you get a free "sensual lifestyle profile" and you are also entered into a draw with a prize of a holiday in the Caribbean.'

'A "sensual lifestyle profile"?'

'A lure to the next stage of the process, Miss. Specially designed for young women who are unsure of themselves, their relationships and direction in life.

Those would be the kind Rochester would target. Preferably with few close friends or strong family ties.'

'That makes sense. Well, I think they'll find Debra/Josie fitting into that category.'

'For the purposes of assessment, as they put it, they ask for photographs to accompany the completed forms. I assume so they do not waste their time on unattractive women.'

'That'll have to wait until after tomorrow. You can take a casual snap of me when I get back to the office and send it off then. I want Josie to get onto their radar as soon as possible.'

'Yes, Miss. If you're not too tired, I can help you fill the rest in now.'

'It won't make you late getting back home, will it? What about your family?'

Angela smiled. 'It's good of you to ask, Miss, but there's just my daughter, and she fully understands I may have to work unusual hours over the next few weeks.'

'It sounds as though you get along well together.'

Angela smiled proudly. 'We do, Miss.'

'So this questionnaire would never have hooked you.'

'There was a time when it might have done, Miss,' Angela admitted. 'But Director Shiller found me first. The company's been like my family for years.'

The next day Vanessa woke feeling perfectly clear-headed. Radleigh came round to examine her and was happy with her progress. The mottling and pinpricks on her skin were already fading. She was taken off the painkillers. Her skin was sore and there was a lingering ache where she had the injections but it was nothing she could not live with. It really had been as rapid and simple as he had promised. It was wonderful the quality of service an unlimited budget could buy. The next phase of her transformation could begin. It was going to be a busy day . . .

Vanessa was strapped to a couch with her legs pulled up and spread wide and bound to stirrups. Dark safety goggles covered her eyes and the large dummy was still plugged into her mouth. Of course she did not need the restraints but that was not the slavish way.

Her exposed groin was cupped by a tinted plastic dome, through an aperture on the apex of which the lens of a small computer-controlled medical laser mounted on a hinged arm was directed at her pubes. She winced as she felt a fleeting wave of tiny hot pinpricks passing across her tender flesh.

Miss Belling and her assistant, also goggled, stood over the controls watching on a monitor the progress of the treatment. Vanessa's newly plumped vulva and anal mouth filled the screen, overlaid by a dense pattern of tiny red crosses that were turning green one by one. Every cross marked a hair follicle that was being zapped out of existence with surgical precision.

The last cross turned green and the laser shut down.

'All done,' said Miss Belling cheerfully, raising her goggles.

She swung the laser and safety dome back from Vanessa's groin and stroked Vanessa's pubes.

'There, as smooth as a baby's bottom. And I guarantee you'll stay that way for at least three months. Now we'll see about the rest of you . . .

Vanessa stood upright in a shallow tiled tray like the pan of an open shower stall. Her arms and legs were pulled out wide and held by thin cords about her wrists and ankles to two steel posts. A ball gag that left her lips exposed had replaced the dummy and her clinic label had been temporarily removed from her forehead.

Miss Belling and an assistant were working on her. Each was clad in plastic aprons, gloves, booties and masks. They were using artists' airbrushes to carefully coat every square centimetre of her body with a fine brown mist. It was not a mere spray-on tan but a deep penetrating dye that she had been assured would last for several weeks.

Inside an hour the normal pale tint of her flesh had been replaced by an equally natural-looking warm coffee tint. Her lips and nipples were darkened in proportion while the skin over her breasts, buttocks and pubes was left slightly paler, giving the illusion of a swimsuit shadow. The deepening in shade was about what she would have shown from getting a strong suntan, except this now looked to be her natural colour.

'I understand you wanted a few tattoos,' Miss Belling said, holding up a set of stencils. 'What about these?'

Vanessa made her selection with nods and grunts, relishing the strange dichotomy of her situation. She was both their pampered client yet at the same time a helpless company slave and living canvas for their craft. It made the process so much more exciting and briefly pushed her concerns to the back of her mind.

A spray of heavier-coloured dyes laid down a pattern of chain links round her left upper arm, a column of oriental characters supposedly conferring good luck went over her right buttock, a small butterfly appeared on her lower stomach and a snake soon coiled about her right ankle. That should make Josie Gribbleson appear suitably unsure about what she expected from life.

When they were done they ran UV lamps over her body, curing and setting the stain so it would not smudge or run. She would be this colour until it grew out of her skin.

An hour later Vanessa sat strapped to an otherwise conventional barber's chair while Larry, Miss Belling's associate, worked on her hair. He was using a variant of the skin dye that would penetrate and feed her roots for a month or more. Again Vanessa wondered what this miracle cosmetic treatment was costing and again she told herself not to worry about it. Her hair was skilfully cut, dyed black and re-styled, making the most of its natural curl. Her eyebrows also were thickened and darkened. In combination with her new skin tone she was by stages becoming another woman.

It was late afternoon when the specialist optician called in on Vanessa in her room. He was a thin bespectacled fiftyish man introduced as Mr Johnson. He probably had a fuller technical title than optician but Vanessa never learned it. He seemed at ease attending a naked woman strapped to a bed, which prompted the question: what sort of lenses had he fitted to other slavegirls? Perhaps her requirements seemed very tame by comparison. Still he had brought with him what Vanessa had ordered, which was all that mattered.

With Nurse Kelly looking on he checked her eyes were healthy and confirmed her sight did not need correction. Then he fitted her with the thinnest, most flexible set of contact lenses she had ever seen.

'Twenty-eight-day super gas-permeable hypoallergenic monofilm-tinted optically neutral contacts,' Johnson explained as she blinked and rolled her eyes. She could hardly feel anything. 'At the end of that time they simply dissolve away. I'll leave you with a second set and applicator. During that period there's no need to remove them for cleaning. Apart from cosmetic applications they can provide additional UV and particle protection for people in harsh environments.'

It was because of that application that she had come to read about them in *Datumline*. What was it about being with a naked gagged slavegirl that made some people want to lecture her, she wondered? Was it to cover their own embarrassment or the pleasure of having a truly captive audience?

Johnson showed her the result in the mirror. You could not tell she was wearing contacts and her hazel eyes were now a deep brown.

Angela visited her again that evening with her progress report.

'It really is an amazing transformation, Miss Buckingham,' she said, looking her up and down and then peering closely at her face. 'I think anybody who knows you well would see close up that it's still you. But at a casual glance or from a distance you'd pass for another woman.'

'That's about what I was aiming for. Do I look hot enough to interest Deedas, do you think?'

Angela pursed her lips. 'Miss Buckingham, you know you don't have to ask that. You were hot enough before, now you're even more so. I'd say European with a dash of perhaps North African or Middle-Eastern blood. Very exotic.'

'Well, as long as they think so.'

That night, after seeing to her needs in the en-suite bathroom and re-cuffing her to her bed, Nurse Kelly left Vanessa uncovered instead of leaving so she could take a long lingering appreciative look at her. Then with a smile she began undressing.

'I know what your sort are like after a few days without a screw,' she said as she stripped. 'So I like to ease the pain. Of course I don't take advantage of all my patients like this, but I know with slavegirls it doesn't count. If somebody had wanted you to stay celibate they'd have sent you here in a chastity belt. Do you have a special owner? Don't worry, I won't pry . . .'

She dropped her knickers over a chair and stood poised grinning with her hands on her hips and legs wide. There was a touch of the sturdy Valkyrie maiden about her. She had muscular arms, large breasts with full red nipples, a distinct belly, a thick full pubic bush and strong stocky legs. Her skin was clear and smooth and she carried herself with pride.

'This is the best chance a girl like me can have copping off with a looker like you . . .'

She bent down to take something out of the bottom of the bedside locker and Vanessa saw her pale chubby buttocks trembling slightly. She rose again with a large strap-on dildo in her hands.

'Think you can take this up you?'

The sight of Kelly's naked body was already making Vanessa's newly plumped nipples swell painfully hard while she felt the familiar slippery heat suffusing her labia. The dildo only increased her desire. For the last two days she had been aroused a few times but also preoccupied. Now true need returned. She grunted and nodded, lifting her hips.

'You really are a gorgeous slut, you know that,' Kelly declared.

She strapped on the dildo, clambered onto the bed and knelt between Vanessa's spread legs. She pinched Vanessa's nipples, lifting her breasts and fingered her swelling clit. When Kelly had cleaned her up in the bathroom she had been totally professional during the intimate personal contact. Now she was enjoying playing with her helpless patent.

Vanessa whimpered as her still sensitive flesh was roughly handled.

'Oh, you like this, don't you?' Kelly said happily. She positioned the head of the dildo between Vanessa's pouting and swollen love lips. 'Look at you, already dribbling on the sheets. Naughty girl . . .'

She leaned over Vanessa and took hold of her shoulders, her big breasts swaying free, her hard nipples brushing across Vanessa's own enlarged mammaries.

The rubber shaft slid into Vanessa's eager vagina. She needed this so badly . . .

Kelly rode her forcefully, using all her strength, making the bed shake, ramming the shaft hard up into her sopping sheath, making squelching sounds as it sucked and ground inside her. Under her Vanessa squirmed and gasped in delight, submitting herself to Kelly's powerful dominance. This was all she really wanted to do. She did not want to play undercover detective or plot and scheme. She just wanted to be used and loved . . .

After they had come, Kelly lay on top of her for several minutes in silence, eyes closed, breathing heavily, her large sweaty breasts flattening Vanessa's own. Finally she opened her eyes and smiled down at Vanessa. Bending forward, she kissed the label stuck to Vanessa's forehead.

'You slavegirls are the best screws ever,' she sighed happily. 'God, I want to go again already . . . but maybe the other way round . . .'

She unclipped Vanessa's ankles and rolled her over in the bed and refastened her on her front. Kneeling between Vanessa's spread legs she cupped and rolled her buttocks.

'You've an amazing bum-cleft now. The darker skin makes it look even deeper than it is. And your cheeks are so round and yummy but they don't sag at all. Hmm . . . would anybody mind if when you go back home tomorrow they were a little red?'

Vanessa shook her head.

Kelly used her double-up uniform belt to spank Vanessa. And it stung and burned and sent ripples though her new fleshier buttocks and it felt wonderful. Then Kelly rammed her dildo, still slick and shiny from Vanessa's vagina, through her anal ring and hard up into the depths of her bottom. And she rode her rear until they both came again.

'That was fantastic,' Kelly said softly as she pulled the covers up over them and laid her head beside Vanessa's, kissing her neck and stroking her new mane of curling dark hair. 'Still I wish I knew why you wanted all this done. You looked pretty fucking good to me when you came in.'

If you really want to know I did all this for the sake of a man I hate, Vanessa thought to herself.

The next morning, just before Angela was due to collect her from the clinic, Vanessa stood in front of the full-length mirror in her room and considered her new reflection. Three days ago at about this time she had been kneeling on the Director's desk full of her wonderful plan. Now she was virtually a different woman.

Secretly she had always wished for slightly larger breasts but had dismissed the thought of unnecessary cosmetic surgery as vain and wasteful. Well, now she had them and more, but ironically not out of vanity.

Perhaps the surgery had made her body more sensitive – or she was turned on by her new appearance – because her dark-brown nipples were swelling shamelessly before her eyes. For the first time she realised how the extra fullness in her breasts and hips also made her waist look slimmer by comparison. God, her laser-bared pubes really were perfectly smooth and pouting. She turned side on and stuck her hips forward. The swell of her mound now showed over her thighs. And, as Kelly had proved, her new rounder fuller buttocks were eminently smackable.

She thought of how Rochester would have seen her last, the image of her caught by the camera of his laptop placed at the foot of her bed: looking up between her spread legs at her pale spreadeagled and bound body, seeing her dark-haired vagina plugged with his torture dildo and her pink nipples on her trembling breasts clamped with electrodes and over and beyond them her tear-filled hazel eyes.

Well, all that was gone. He'd never recognise her at a single glance now. But what about a second? Had she judged it just right? If she hadn't then it might all fail. And if she had, of course, then it meant she was going to truly suffer. But that was a price she was willing to pay.

Seven

Vanessa could not go back to her own flat in her new guise so she moved into the temporary flat that served as Josie Gribbleson's postal address. It was comfortable enough and Angela had brought everything she needed from her own flat, but it was still not home. She wanted Kashika to return and assure her everything would be all right. But even that prospect was tainted by the thought of what she would have to ask of her afterwards.

The next day she drove to the office. Her Mini remained in the company car park and she used a hire car. They had no proof Rochester's agents were still keeping watch on traffic entering and leaving Shiller tower any more than they might be watching her flat as they had in the past, but they could not take the risk.

Vanessa's discomfort was intensified by the continuing sense of bareness and exposure about her neck. She missed the comforting weight of the collar that assured her she belonged to something important. Taking Angela's advice she had tied a choker band in its place and that helped a little.

The security guards peered at her with interest as she entered the gates but they had their orders and passed her through without comment. She missed their usual banter, especially as she had more bust to ogle and fondle now.

It took an effort of will not to go down to B3 and strip as normal. But she pressed the lift button for the sixth floor and her new office. It wasn't natural for a chain girl to walk round the Shiller building clothed but she had to get used to her new character. Her one concession to normality was that she was still not wearing any panties. As she strode along she felt the air excitingly cool against her naked pubes. Depilation was one thing she'd keep up after this was all over.

There was another reason for ascending rather than descending. She did not want to show her new face about B3 for the chain girls to see while it was still possible her plans might have to change. For the moment they were safer left in ignorance. She made a mental note to get a regular check on the mood of the girls from Sandra.

Angela was waiting for her. 'Good morning, Miss Buckingham. May I say you look every inch the smart young businesswoman.'

'Thank you, Angela. But I'd rather be stripped and collared.'

'I would rather that as well, Miss,' Angela said with a smile. 'But we must all do our duty in these times.'

'OK, how's everything going?'

'First, you have an appointment to see the Director. She said to send you up as soon as you got in.'

'I suppose she wants to see what her money's been spent on.'

'I rather think it's to assure herself that you're well, Miss.'

It felt unnatural to walk into the Director's office clothed and uncollared. She could not even clamber onto the Director's desk and display herself properly with her skirt on. Vanessa did the best she could by going down on her knees on the rug in front of the desk and bowing her head.

Shiller considered her for a moment. 'Take off your clothes, Vanessa.'

It was such a relief to strip. In a minute she was standing naked with her legs spread and hands clasped to the back of her neck while Shiller walked round examining her. With cool careful fingers she tested her breasts, bottom and pubes and looked intently at her face. Her touch made Vanessa tremble with joy. She would happily stand there all day if it meant getting this much attention from the Director. With a flush of emotion she realised how badly she wanted the Director to find her new body attractive. If she liked her enough perhaps one day she would be permitted to serve her personally . . .

'You were right to make these changes,' Shiller said at length. 'It adds essential credibility. Is everything else going to plan?'

'Yes, Director.'

'The regular investigation team have made no further progress in tracking down Canary Chain. I believe your plan may be our only hope. Keep me informed of your progress or if there is anything further that you need.'

Elated by her approval, Vanessa gathered up her clothes and bowed herself out.

Back in the office Angela updated Vanessa on the progress of the technical programmes. The modification work at Robotikine was proceeding to plan. Vanessa made a personal call to Keller Wilson Systems to confirm a detail of the specifications for the specialised devices she had ordered from them. The manager, knowing she spoke for Shiller, sounded painfully eager to please and promised everything would be done exactly as she wanted. She rang off feeling a little dizzy with power. So that was what having the weight of a big company behind you felt like.

'If you're ready, Miss, I have a camera for your picture to accompany the Deedas questionnaire,' Angela said.

'Oh yes, that's got to go off today.'

Vanessa posed against a blank wall and flashed a few smiles while Angela clicked away. They chose the best image and Angela printed up a small copy and attached it to the completed questionnaire.

'I have also arranged for a session with Martyn Nevis the day after tomorrow, Miss,' Angela said. 'He's the professional photographer you asked for.'

'Great. What sort of stuff has he done?'

'He has worked with several of our clients who wanted records of their girls performing in novel situations, Miss. I have some samples . . .'

She called up a slideshow of images. From basic glamour shots they worked up through sex toys to playful bondage and finally naked collared girls chained to the walls of mock dungeons, crouched in cages like dogs, or secured in stocks being whipped and then entered by well-endowed men.

Not so long ago her instinctive reaction to such images would have been disgust at the degradation of the women or at the very least a kind of resigned despair that men liked such things. Now she couldn't help putting herself in the models' place and getting turned on by imagining what they were feeling.

Out of curiosity she asked Angela: 'What do you think about pictures like this?'

'If I knew the girls are just doing it for the money or being pressured into performing then I would feel desperately sorry for them, Miss. Nobody should be forced to do anything that they felt truly debasing. But if they find that as exciting as I would have done when I was their age, and truthfully still do, then I wish them joy. If there were more happy slavish submissives free to be themselves, and would-be dominants educated as to how to use them properly and fairly, there would be less oppression of their straight sisters.'

'Unfortunately there are always people like Rochester.'

'Yes, Miss.'

'Right, well, I think the lower end is the sort of thing Josie's getting into. Ripe material for Deedas.'

'Mr Nevis understands you want several portfolios of still images. He can also distribute them via the internet to other outlets if you wish. Potentially they'll be all round the world.'

'That should make her background seem convincing enough.'

An hour later Angela took a call and passed on the news to Vanessa. 'One of our researchers thinks she has found a match for the shoes, Miss. She's sending the details . . .'

An image of red high-heeled shoes with a lockable ankle strap and silver chain motif appeared on her screen, along with the model name: 'Crimson Shacklz'.

'That looks like the type,' Vanessa agreed. 'Can you send that to Trevor Russell's terminal so Cindy can confirm?'

A few minutes later the answer came back. 'Cindy says they are definitely the shoes she wore, Miss,' Angela said. 'The sole manufacturers, no pun intended, are "Heelz High", a small company based in Bradford.'

Vanessa felt a thrill of excitement. 'Right, we start phase two. Getting into their records . . .'

Around midday Sandra breezed into the office, bare and beautiful as always.

'I just wanted to take at look at the new you I've been hearing about,' she said. 'Oh . . . wow!' she exclaimed as she took in Vanessa's transformation. 'You really went to town. Hot stuff . . . ohhh . . . and new boobs.' She skipped forward, straddling Vanessa's legs and plucking at the front of her blouse. 'Can I have a peek?'

Vanessa pushed her away laughing. 'Maybe later. I've got work to do. Say hello to Angela, my invaluable assistant. Or maybe you've met before . . .'

'Sort of. Hello, Mother,' Sandra said brightly.

'Hello, dear,' Angela replied.

Vanessa gaped at her foolishly. 'You're . . . Sandra's mother?'

'Well, why shouldn't she be?' Sandra said. 'Most people have one, you know. And where do you think I get my sweet submissive nature, not to mention my fantastic sexiness, from anyway?' She went and sat on Angela's lap and kissed her. Angela seemed perfectly at ease having her lovely naked collared daughter sitting in her lap with her arm about her shoulders.

In the months she had known Sandra, Vanessa had never thought to ask about her background. Now it made sense.

'Sorry, of course,' Vanessa said, recovering herself a little. 'I can see the likeness. I just didn't think about your family . . . I mean you just seemed to belong here.'

'Thanks,' Sandra said. 'We both do.'

Vanessa said sincerely: 'Angela, you have a lovely daughter.'

'Thank you, Miss. I think so too. I was so proud of her being taken straight into White Chain. Very few girls are. Now you must run along, dear, we have work to do.' She sent Sandra on her way with a pat on her rump.

Sandra paused at the door. 'Remember I'm booked to check out the rest of those alterations asap,' she said cheerily.

Vanessa tried to focus on her screen but her mind kept drifting off, trying to accommodate this new revelation.

Seeing slavegirls as isolated free-spirited individuals following their own destiny was one thing. She'd come to accept that. But turning it into a family affair made her feel uneasy. Was this the system she was trying to preserve? One that permitted a daughter to follow in her mother's footsteps into commercialised slavery? Sandra, whom she had been harnessed beside and had shared Mister Winston's cock with, and Angela who had knelt at her feet and kissed her pussy so submissively? Was this sick? Yet Sandra and Angela were two of the nicest people she had ever met. She took a mental deep breath. They were adults and seemed to know exactly what they were doing. If a desire for submission really was genetic then why should she be surprised? Perhaps the bottom line was that if working for Shiller could make them both so happy and inspire their loyalty then it was worth fighting for.

Martyn Nevis was a greying wiry man in his mid-fifties and thoroughly professional. As it seemed with everybody associated with Shiller's secret world, he did his job well without asking questions.

He guided Vanessa expertly through a long sequence of nude glamour poses, regularly changing props, backing and lighting to suggest several different sessions. She pouted and simpered, cupped her breasts enticingly, stuck out her bottom, spread her legs and peeled her pussy wide. There were no other models in the shots. She had decided that Josie had not yet gone that far.

Nevertheless Vanessa enjoyed showing off her new body. Perhaps the changes had been liberating. It was something a year ago she would never have imagined doing, and despite her experiences as a chain girl she had felt nervous at first. But she soon warmed to the task.

Her ebullient mood might also have been due to the thought that Cherry Chain would be coming home the next day. She imagined Kashika looking at the images as she had viewed her own amateur shots of her.

By the time it came to the bondage and sex-toy shots she was getting seriously excited, which was good for the quality of the pictures but hard for her. Eventually, as she knelt doubled over on a bed with her bottom in the air, a vibrator plugged into her vagina, her knees

109

spread and her wrists tied to her ankles, she could stand it no longer. She wiggled her bottom at Nevis who was shooting right up into her groin.

'Please . . . I need a fuck now!'

'Sorry,' he said. 'My rule. I never screw with my models.'

Damn him for being a man of principle, Vanessa thought in frustration.

Vanessa returned to the office late that evening still feeling frustrated. Sandra was there chatting with Angela. It was as though they had both been waiting up for her.

'How did the porn shoot go?' Sandra asked brightly. 'Is Debra Kane hot enough for Deedas?'

'OK, I think. See for yourself . . .'

Nevis had given Vanessa a digital disc of her session. They put it into the computer and mother and daughter perused her poses.

'I think you are very attractive and enticing and just what Deedas is looking for, Miss,' Angela declared after a few minutes.

'What Mum means is that you've got a hot body,' Sandra translated. 'Which I still want to road-test.' She turned and hugged and kissed Vanessa, as she did so sliding a hand up under her skirt into the hot humid furrow of her buttock cleavage in the frank way of chain girls.

But despite her unrequited need Vanessa drew back, leaving Sandra looking puzzled.

'Why have you never made love to my daughter, Miss?' Angela asked. 'I understand you have been close but never intimate. I know it's troubled her. Does she fail to please you in any way?'

Only in Shiller's could such a question be asked in such circumstances, Vanessa thought. 'No, she's lovely,' she assured her truthfully. Then she had to think. Why

110

had she never slept with Sandra? 'I suppose it's that I thought she was indecently young-looking when I first saw her, back when I believed she was a forced sex slave. I've never quite got over it.'

'But you know better now, Miss,' Angela said. 'And you know she adores you.'

'Come to that, why haven't you screwed my mum?' Sandra said. 'She's no teenager but she's still pretty damn fantastic and you know she's hot for you.'

Vanessa looked at the pair of them, both offering themselves so freely. *What is this thing some Shiller women see in me*, she wondered. And just why was she holding back? She smiled. 'You're right and I want both of you . . . I'll just get a few things . . .'

'If you look in the bottom drawer of your desk, Miss,' Angela said, 'I think you'll find all you need there.'

Vanessa looked. There was a double-ended dildo, a spanking paddle and a collection of binding straps.

'Angela, you are the perfect secretary,' Vanessa said.

'I try to give satisfaction, Miss.'

'Then clear the desk, strip off and bend over next to your daughter . . .'

'With pleasure, Miss . . .'

Vanessa bound them side by side with their inner ankles strapped together and outer bound to the desk legs. She strapped their wrists together in front of them and pulled their arms over the desk, making them bend across its top, and secured their wrists with longer straps to the front legs of the desk. Two fine sets of buttocks and vulvas now presented themselves to her. For a moment Vanessa's head swam with a dizzy sense of power. Mother and daughter were utterly at her mercy. Their most intimate orifices were open for her to use as she wished. It was a loving surrender of total trust and the greatest compliment they could pay. Yet why should it surprise her? She had assumed a position of responsibility and control in the company. Angela and Sandra

111

were loyal company slaves. It was natural that she should enjoy them.

Angela did still have a great body, of which Sandra's was a delightful echo. She also still had the responses of a chain girl, as Vanessa found when she paddled her bottom while stirring her fingers in her daughter's hot wet pussy slot. Then she reversed the arrangement. When both bottoms were tanned and rosy she slipped one end of the dildo into herself and thoroughly reamed out the hungry lovemouths of mother and daughter in alternation until they all came.

Office sex had never felt better.

Afterwards she lay across them, hugging and kissing their soft fragrant bound bodies. 'You're both lovely,' she said dreamily. 'I needed that. Thank you . . .'

'We're here whenever you want us, Miss,' Angela said. 'You have a huge burden on your shoulders and should take every opportunity to relax.'

'But we know you won't be thinking of us tomorrow,' Sandra added. 'We understand . . .'

It was true. The next day Vanessa woke with a light heart knowing that Cherry Chain would be coming home that afternoon and she would see Kashika again. Of course this time would not be quite like their previous reunions.

She had warned Kashika by e-mail that she would look different but the frantic activity of the last few days had left her with no time to go into details. She knew Kashika would understand why she had undergone the procedures but she also hoped on a purely personal level that she liked the result.

The day started well when she found a letter from Deedas Research on the doormat of her temporary flat that morning. The speed of their response suggested they were still anxious to recruit despite having twelve extra Shiller girls working for them. But then Rochester

112

would be foolish to give up any source of new stock. She took it into work to show Angela.

She was a little concerned that their intimacy of the previous evening would be a problem but Angela was her usual efficient self.

'They seem to have been impressed by your response to their survey, Miss,' Angela said, reading over the letter that accompanied Vanessa's personalised 'sensual lifestyle profile'.

'I knew listing Josie's occupation as waitress/model would help,' Vanessa said. 'Putting those two together always suggests something juicy.'

'I think perhaps your photo and the wide range of sexual experiences you listed for Josie may also have had something to do with it, Miss,' Angela suggested dryly, reading on. 'Your "profile" supposedly shows Josie to be a "sexually liberated and adventurous personality type of unusual character", and they are inviting her to participate in a further special course of research into "the psychology and physiology of sexual responses" as they put it. There's a number to call to book an appointment.'

'Which is really an excuse to get Josie into their labs so they can start turning her into a sex slave.'

'Of course, Miss. As a sweetener all participants' travel expenses are paid plus they get a second entry into their holiday competition.'

'I might win it yet,' Vanessa chuckled. 'I'll give it a couple of days before calling them. I don't want to seem too eager. And everything else has got to be in place before I start getting seriously involved with them.'

Vanessa wanted to meet Kashika as soon as Cherry Chain arrived back at Shiller Tower, but she knew she could not afford to do so. Instead she had asked Sandra to bring her up.

She could picture the Cherry girls being unloaded

from their transport truck down in the basement car park. They would be neatly gagged, cuffed and chained in ranks. They would be taken down in the big goods lift to B3. There they would be marched along the high street to the training yard. One of the trainers would check the reports of their conduct while they had been away, review any comments by their customers, advise them of any change in B3 routine, and then they would be dismissed and unchained, free to do what they wished like soldiers going off duty after a parade.

Other chain girls would then greet them and they would go back to their dormitories or wander along the Mall or maybe go for a swim in the pool in the tiny garden park. She so wanted to be there with them and meet the girls she had come to know better than any other chain. Instead she had to wait.

It was nearly an hour after Cherry Chain returned when Sandra ushered Kashika, naked and collared, through the door of her office. The surprise on her lovely face when she saw her was clear.

'I'll take a coffee break, Miss,' Angela said diplomatically. 'I'm sure you wish to be alone . . .' Arm in arm, mother and daughter left together.

As soon as the door shut behind them Vanessa ran to Kashika and kissed and hugged her. 'God, I've missed you!' she said fervently, feeling tears pricking at the back of her eyes.

Where normally Kashika would have responded with uninhibited passion of her own, Vanessa noticed a slight but distinct hesitation before she kissed her back.

'I've missed you too,' Kashika said, gazing into Vanessa's new brown eyes uncertainly. She took a step back, looking Vanessa up and down. 'Sorry, but all this takes some getting used to.'

Vanessa understood her feelings. Sandra had been able to take a more light-hearted view of her alterations,

but she was not as close to her as Kashika. To her this
was very personal. She would have felt the same if
Kashika had done anything so drastic to her perfect
body.

'I know this is all very weird, but I had to do it,'
Vanessa said, squeezing Kashika's hands and wishing
she had a magic wand to wipe the doubt from her
lover's eyes. 'And I will explain everything. You can
come home with me tonight. Well, not home exactly, I
can't go there, but it's a nice flat. Then we can talk
properly. There's a lot I've got to tell you. Meanwhile
take the Cherry girls my love and say I wish I could
spend some time with them but I'm seriously busy.
That's true enough. Until then can you all please trust
me that this is for the best.'

'Whatever happens we all trust you,' Kashika said.
'Always.'

They made love in the bed of Vanessa's temporary flat.
It was tentative at first, with Kashika taking time to
explore Vanessa's new body. But gradually Vanessa
sensed the tension in her lover's body ease a little. When
the intensity of kisses between their literally hot wet and
pulsing vulvas finally drove them both to joyful orgasms, Vanessa knew an important hurdle had been
cleared.

Afterwards, lying sweaty but content in her lover's
arms, Kashika made an intimate inventory. 'The boobs
are nice, the bum good and the smooth pussy very
good!' she declared. 'You must keep that.'

'I was going to,' Vanessa giggled.

'The hair is like changing tints. That's not so hard to
live with. Just don't go blonde on me.'

'I won't.'

'The eyes are nice but not you.'

'They're not permanent,' Vanessa assured her.

'Good. The skin is very convincing. It's almost like

115

my colour so I can't really complain. But I like to see how different we are when we lie together, you wrapped around me. We're not the same, which is how I want it.'

'It'll grow out after a few months.'

'I'm glad. The face is still you. I can see that. But I hope you'll have it changed back afterwards.'

'I will. The nose rings can be easily removed and they can suck out the synthetic fat the same way they put it in. I think all the points they injected it into are stored on a computer at the clinic. The wonders of modern cosmetic surgery. I hate to think how much it cost. But you understand why I had to do it.'

'You have to infiltrate Rochester's organisation and try to find our girls. I'll support you in any way I can, you know that.'

Vanessa chewed her lip. 'That's good . . . because it's a bit more complicated than that. I'm going to have to ask for your help . . . in a big way. This is what I'm going to do . . .'

Kashika listened in rapt silence as Vanessa explained her plan in detail. When she was done she said: 'It's very dangerous.'

'Everybody keeps telling me that. But I still think it's the only way. And it won't exactly be a picnic for you either.'

'That doesn't matter.'

'It does to me. I hate to have to ask but I must cover every possibility.'

'I understand. Of course I'll do it, you know that.'

Vanessa hugged and kissed her. 'Thank you. I knew you would but I was dreading this moment.' She took a deep breath. 'And now I'll have to tell the other Cherry girls.'

'Don't,' Kashika said firmly.

'What? But I must.'

'No, it's safer if they don't know anything. Nobody should know anything they don't need to, then it will all

116

seem perfectly natural. I know they'll volunteer anyway. We already have, remember? I'll tell them afterwards it was my decision. We'll only have one chance. This is too important to get wrong.'

Eight

Seeing Kashika was a joy and knowing she had her support lifted Vanessa's spirits, although their time together was limited. Kashika went home to visit her family and Vanessa had her project to manage.

The first of the commissions from Keller Wilson was ready and would be despatched for her to try out. The second was being tested in prototype form and then they would move on to producing the first batch of a hundred units. Meanwhile she was invited to watch a demonstration of the modified devices at Robotikine and to supply certain personal samples. She made a flying visit and was impressed by what she saw.

Derek Shepherd assured her the augmented control units would be ready on time. He was clearly surprised and deeply curious about her altered appearance but accepted her simple: 'Please don't ask, it's complicated,' with good grace. *After this is over I really must make sure all these people who have helped get proper recognition for their efforts*, Vanessa thought, especially as they would probably never know the real purpose to which their creations would be put.

Back at the office Vanessa returned to her planning of a carefully managed break-in to Heelz High. *I'm arranging the burglary of a fetish footwear company near Bradford*, she thought wryly. *Now that's not something I ever imagined doing*. Then Angela suggested a simpler solution.

'Why doesn't Shiller's simply buy the business, Miss? The existing Heelz High staff and management can be kept on but it will give us all the access we need and avoid all this subterfuge.'

'But the cost,' Vanessa protested.

'Is trivial by Shiller standards, Miss. You must stop worrying about that. In fact it's not a bad investment. As long as no word of our takeover reaches Rochester it is the simplest solution. I'm sure the Director will approve. It is vital to your plan.'

Shiller approved the suggestion without hesitation. The legal and contracts departments were put into top gear and a generous offer, with full employment guarantees to the workforce, was made to Heelz High the next day. They were a small company and it did not take them long to deliberate. The offer was accepted.

'Thank you, Angela,' Vanessa said, when the acceptance was confirmed. 'You really are invaluable.' The look on Angela's face showed delight without the need for words. 'And with that in hand I think it's time I responded to Deedas' invitation . . .'

She spoke to a Miss Graves, who was delighted that 'Josie' was willing to participate in further research, and together they agreed an appointment for her to call on them the day after next, accommodating her part-time hours as a 'waitress'.

As Vanessa rang off she thought that Miss Graves had sounded almost painfully pleased at her call. Perhaps she had a quota to fill. If Rochester had taken to kidnapping Shiller girls as replacement stock then the Deedas operation might be wound up and Miss Graves and her fellow workers be out of a job. What sort of employment could former slave recruiters find anyway? Hard to list as skills on a job application . . .

She became aware of Angela looking at her and shook herself out of her little reverie.

'The first step into the lion's den, Miss,' Angela said solemnly.

119

'Hopefully the lion won't know I'm in his den yet. And there's still a lot to do before I take a step further. First I've got to go shopping for Josie's wardrobe. Want to give me a hand?'

'I'd love to, Miss. May I also suggest we obtain a large map of the South of England for the wall, together with some coloured map pins? If all goes well we should soon have some locations to start plotting. We can already put up Rochester's home addresses and the known sites of his slave facilities. It will be a way of charting our progress.'

'That's a great idea. And we can also add Deedas Research . . .'

The Deedas Research facility had its offices on the edge of a commercial estate outside Guildford. It was simply one rather bland detached unit among many, with a row of office windows and a lot of blank wall suggesting workshop or storage space beyond, and quite anonymous apart from its modest sign. Vanessa had no doubt it was secured on a short-term lease and it could be packed up and moved on at short notice.

She had arrived by train and then taxi, as she didn't think 'Josie' would drive a car. Relying on public transport made her seem more dependent on others. It also meant there was no need to carry a driving licence. Everything else she had with her bore the name Josie Gribbleson.

In character as Josie she was wearing a denim jacket and ankle-length skirt over a low-cut white blouse that made the most of her enhanced cleavage. On her feet were three-quarter length leather boots, and she carried a shoulder bag. Her nails were all varnished deep red. Her aim was to look presentable but with a hint of restrained glamour. Josie knew she looked good and while not particularly well off was not cheap. She was reasonably well educated but perhaps currently feeling insecure and a little confused.

Vanessa took a deep breath and pushed open the door of the main entrance.

Deedas' modest outer office was sparsely decorated with a few potted shrubs, and a couple of bland pictures. On the wall behind the reception desk hung an array of what appeared to be framed certificates with lots of scrollwork and flourishes. Nicely reassuring and professional, Vanessa thought.

A smart thirtyish woman in blouse and grey skirt rose from behind the desk to greet Vanessa.

'I'm Josie Gribbleson,' Vanessa said. 'I've got an appointment.'

'Of course, Miss Gribbleson, we spoke on the phone,' she said warmly, shaking Vanessa's hand. 'I'm Jane Graves. So pleased to meet you. Thank you for taking the time to help us. I'm sure you will make a valuable contribution to our research.'

'Your form did say you'd cover my expenses, travelling and so on?' Vanessa asked, trying to sound a little ashamed at raising the matter of money.

'That's quite correct,' Miss Graves said smoothly. 'Naturally we wouldn't expect you to be out of pocket. Do take a seat . . .'

Vanessa sat in front of the desk while Miss Graves resumed her seat. She steepled her fingers and looked seriously across at Vanessa.

'As our letter explained, we at Deedas Research investigate the psychology and physiology – that is, the physical reactions – involved in sexual activity and emotions. We're tying to understand why women react the way they do in certain situations, what the boundaries of so-called normal behaviour are, or perhaps prove that there are no true boundaries. To do that we have to test the responses of a large number of subjects, especially ones like yourself who have a range of sexual experience. This may involve you viewing extreme sexual imagery or participating in tests and role-playing

121

experiments of an extremely intimate nature taking in a wide spectrum of sexual practices. Of course we won't make you do anything you're not happy with, but you have to know what taking part in our research might mean. Are you happy with that?'

It all sounded perfectly reasonable, Vanessa thought. No wonder they had sucked in so many innocent victims. And Josie was next on the list.

'Yeah, I'm OK with that,' she said.

'That's fine then.' Miss Graves took out some forms from a drawer. 'We'll get the paperwork out of the way first.' She handed over a simple duplicate claim form. 'If you'd just like to sign there then I can pay you your expenses when the session's over. You don't mind it in cash, do you?'

'Cash'll be fine,' Vanessa said quickly, signing "Josie Gribbleson" with a flourish she had been practising all week.

'Good . . . and there's your copy. Now this other form is a bit longer . . .' It was four pages of fine print with many sub-clauses. 'Half of it's really for bookkeeping. We have to justify our funding too, you know. The rest says we'll treat your participation with total confidence, your name or identity will not appear in any studies we publish, we have the rights to use any images we take of you for further research, you confirm you're a volunteer and indemnify us from any emotional reactions you may get as a consequence of the research. That's only a safety clause for people of a nervous disposition. Silly really, because we wouldn't have those sort of people coming to us, but the lawyers insist we have it.'

Vanessa smiled and signed. 'So what happens next?'

'Well, now I'll take you through to meet our principal researchers, Doctor Banks and Doctor Lister. This way . . .'

She escorted Vanessa through a door, down a short corridor to another door bearing the sign: LABORATORY

3 RECEPTION. It opened onto a small windowless interior room. An unexpected wash of soft background music came to her ears.

The room, which was formed of light partition boarding, was antiseptically white-painted and lit by fluorescent tubes. A couple of other doors led off it. A horizontal mirror was set into one wall that she recognised, though Josie probably would not, as one-way glass. On the opposite wall was a row of pegs. The other walls were decorated with medical charts depicting the organs of the body and a long height chart. It was furnished with a plain desk and a few utility chairs. A strip of broad yellow tape had been stuck to the floor in a line running from one side of the room to the other passing in front of the desk.

Sitting behind the desk were a man and woman in white lab coats. Both wore glasses, name badges and studious expressions. In front of them were laptops, a camera and electronic notepads.

Their appearance went with the charts on the walls and the other props. It was all for show of course. But, Vanessa had to admit, it was effective and oddly comforting.

The pseudo-scientists rose and greeted Vanessa warmly. Banks was a fifty-something man with greying temples while Lister was a lean sharp-featured blonde woman a few years younger.

'See you later,' Miss Graves said cheerfully, closing the door behind her.

Banks beamed at Vanessa. 'Before we begin, Josie, may we say how grateful we are to you for participating in our study.'

'Yes, we really are most grateful to you, Josie,' Lister added.

Their show of gratitude, probably genuine in its underhand way, warmed Vanessa. 'Thanks. But I hope you can help me as well.' She bit her lip, looking

123

embarrassed. 'Look, I've done some modelling, right? Glamour work and that sort of thing. I needed the money.'

'That's nothing to be ashamed of,' Lister said reassuringly.

'Yeah, but it sort of got beyond that.' She reached for her bag. 'Can I show you? You won't be shocked or anything?'

'I promise you that nothing you can show us will cause any offence,' Banks said, and Vanessa believed him.

Vanessa got out a selection of prints from her photo session and spread them on the table. Nevis had headed them up professionally with his studio details. 'My model name is Debra Kane,' Vanessa explained. 'Anyway, you see the sort of things I've done. They get sold over the internet. But a while ago my photographer said I could earn more if I did some bondage poses . . . then a bit of spanking. Then he got me to start having dildos shoved up me . . .' She bit her lip again. 'The thing is, I liked some of it, even though it hurt. I felt I shouldn't but I did. Now that's a bit sick, isn't it? And I want to know why.'

It was easy to sound genuine. She was only retelling her own confused feelings when she had been introduced to the strange and wonderful world of pain and submission.

'Let me assure you it isn't at all sick,' Lister said with almost cloying sincerity. Unexpectedly Vanessa felt her heart lift. 'Finding you enjoy practices such as bondage or corporal punishment is not as rare as most people think. Many studies show that at least a third of women have tried such things and three to five percent do so regularly. You're not alone and certainly should not feel ashamed. You're not one in a million, you're one of a million.'

Put like that it sounded very reasonable, though Vanessa had no idea whether those figures were true.

But Josie would be reassured. She smiled hesitantly. 'That's nice to know. I was beginning to worry.'

'In fact your willingness to experiment with novel sexual practices and to admit you found them pleasurable shows unusual self-confidence,' Banks said, heaping on the praise. 'That's going to be a great help to us in future tests. I think you're going to be a very special and valuable subject, Josie. Many women are unnaturally inhibited, too frightened to admit their secret desires. You're certainly not one of them, but what we find out from you may help them.'

'Well, I've never been exactly shy,' Vanessa admitted. 'I suppose that helps.'

Banks looked at Lister thoughtfully and she nodded back. 'In fact I think you're ready for Stage One,' he said.

'Most of our volunteers don't reach this stage so soon during their first interview,' Lister agreed.

'What's Stage One?' Vanessa asked.

'It's a double test. We have to have a full physical record of your body to have a reference point for our tests.' He held up the camera. 'Just pictures, no needles or anything.' He held up his notepad and activated the stopwatch function. 'The second part is your response time to a particular request. So without thinking about it we'd like you to strip off right now so we can see your reaction.' He started the clock.

'Everything off please, Josie,' Lister said briskly.

Vanessa blinked, then took a deep breath, stood up and began peeling.

For a few seconds she felt a pang of unease, but as she shed her clothes it lifted. Even before scheming strangers she was happier naked. 'I don't have any knickers on,' she admitted with an apologetic smile as she undid her skirt.

'Very sensible,' Lister said.

The familiar thrill of exposure grew in her loins. She had better control that and not look too eager.

125

When she stood naked before them Banks stopped the clock and noted the time down. 'Good, now clasp your hands behind your neck and turn sideways,' he commanded and she obeyed. 'Now, keeping your hands clasped, walk across the room and back following the line of the tape . . .' Vanessa did so. 'Good. Now can you jog across and back . . .'

With her breasts jiggling and bouncing, Vanessa obeyed. *This is a simple but very effective trick*, Vanessa thought to herself, feeling pleased at her perception.

'Good, well done,' Lister said, as though she had performed some remarkable feat of dexterity, making a note on her pad.

Vanessa was aware her nipples were standing up and her bare pussy was tingling and pouting. She hoped they'd put it down to naïve excitement.

'Now we're most concerned about confidentiality and your complete anonymity,' Banks said. 'So while you're here for tests we'll want you to wear a number. Nobody else here will know your name but Miss Graves and us. That's how you'll appear on all our files and records. You'll just be test subject number . . . what's the next one available?'

'An easy one for us all to remember,' said Lister, opening a small flat cardboard box and pulling out some red and black discs of soft plastic. 'Number 77!'

'From now on think of yourself as number 77, Josie,' Banks said smoothly. 'I'm sure you understand we don't want the personal to get in the way of our tests. That means you can respond as comes naturally because while you're here you're not Josie Gribbleson but Test Subject 77. What are you?'

'Test Subject 77,' Vanessa said quickly.

'That's the idea. We'll even call you that from now on. And that's what will appear on your reference photos and any other images we need to take during our tests. Because we might be recording from different cameras we'll put a few stickers on you so they show from every angle . . .'

Vanessa stood by the desk with her hands still clasped behind her neck while they applied the self-adhesive number discs to her forehead, left shoulder, right hip and over her left buttock. She felt a lift as she was numbered once again. It was not as good as her collar but it was better than nothing.

'This'll be the routine every time you come here,' Banks explained. 'Strip off and put your numbers on. You'll need to be naked for the tests because of the sensors we have to put on you so it's much more convenient that way.'

'Now stand in front of the chart, Subject 77,' Lister said and Vanessa obeyed.

They photographed her from the front, sides and back. She stood firm and straight, feeling rather proud to be showing off her new body.

'That's very good,' said Lister. 'That's all we need. You may lower your arms now . . . but keep them folded behind your back.'

Vanessa obeyed, adopting a basic meek posture that concealed nothing. There was no necessity for her to stand like that but it got her used to obeying their commands. She was being made their subject in more ways than one.

Lister glanced at her fellow 'doctor'. 'I think we can go to Stage Two.'

'I agree,' Banks said. 'Subject 77, Stage Two involves recording your responses to some pictures we're going to show you. Some will be ordinary pictures and some sexual, so we can compare the two and find your normal level of response. Do you understand?'

'Yes, I think so . . .'

'A simple "Yes, Doctor" or "No, Doctor" will do.'

'Yes, Doctor.'

'This way then . . .'

They took her through a door into another corridor lined on both sides with boldly signposted doors. They went through the first on the left that read: SENSORY RESPONSE CHAMBER. The signs were a nice touch, Vanessa thought, and so cheap to put up.

In this room the lights were a dim red. It contained only a contoured semi-reclining couch with an array of wires and other fittings round it and a large plasma screen. The soft background music was also playing in here.

'Lie down, Subject 77,' Lister directed. 'Arms and legs spread a little and place your head on the rest.'

She obeyed. There was a small plastic-backed absorbent paper sheet on the seat of the couch. The headrest was padded and contoured and cupped the back of her head. Then they began pulling Velcro fabric straps across her wrists and ankles.

'For this test it helps us if you can keep still,' Lister explained. 'That's what makes your experience with bondage so valuable to us. Some women might have a problem with this but you won't.'

Crap, Vanessa thought to herself. *You're doing it to get me used to you strapping me down. Submission 101.* Still it was nice to feel restrained. Aloud she said simply: 'No, Doctor.'

Broader straps went across her waist and thighs. Then they stuck electrodes to her temples and chest.

'These will measure your brain activity and heart rate, 77,' Banks said. 'They help build a picture of how you react to images you see on the screen.'

With her temple contact in place he pulled a strap across her forehead between the wings of her headrest. Now she could not turn her head aside. 'We want to make sure you stay focused on the screen,' he said. He pulled out a hollow ovoid rubber plug trailing wires from behind the headrest. 'Now this will measure your rate of salivation and jaw tension. Open wide, 77 . . .'

Vanessa automatically obeyed and he pushed it into her mouth, fastening it in place with adhesive strips that went across her cheeks. *And it also gags me*, Vanessa thought, *but all in the name of science, of course. These guys are good.*

Lister had a couple of wires with sticker pads and ends made out of fine spring loops. She rolled loops over Vanessa's semi-hard nipples and stuck the wires in place on sides of her breasts. 'These will measure your nipple erection, Subject 77, which is a simple sign of your state of arousal.'

Of course she could not object to any of this now, not that she would, but Josie might be a little less sanguine. She could only try to look bemused and a little uneasy.

Banks held up a thick rod of clear plastic with a rounded snout trailing a bunch of coloured wires. The surface of the rod was studded with silver electrodes while inside could be seen tiny circuit boards and microelectronic components. A short rod with hooked ends was slotted through a ring on its base.

Vanessa widened her eyes at the sight of it in genuine apprehension. But strapped down as she was she could make no protest. Then her fear was replaced by a sudden thrill of anticipation.

'This is a special vaginal probe, Subject 77,' Banks explained. 'It measures your true sexual responses. Some women lie about what they find stimulating out of embarrassment or from cultural pressure, but you can't lie to this. You said you've used dildos before so this should be no problem . . .'

He bent down between her legs while Lister parted her labia to expose the mouth of her vagina. 'Good, you're already lubricating,' he said. 'Well done, 77, that makes it much easier . . .' She felt a lift at his praise. The probe slid up inside her with little resistance, leaving its base rod exposed. 'We don't want it popping out so we'll just hook this to your thigh straps . . .' He hooked the rod ends to the bands holding her thighs parted. 'There . . . all done.'

Now the probe was held fast inside her.

'You'll be shown a rapid repeating sequence of images, Subject 77,' Lister explained. 'The control system will detect which ones stimulate you the most and discard the rest. With each repetition we can focus in more accurately on what you find arousing. This will provide valuable data for later experiments. You don't have to do anything, just respond as comes naturally.'

They closed the door, the lights dimmed and the background music grew louder but she could not make out any particular tune. Then the screen came to life.

In rapid succession, so no image stayed in place for more than a second, Vanessa was shown a tree, a flower, a classic nude oil painting, a factory chimney, a vertically erect penis, a teddy bear, a tiger in a cage, an empty cage, a naked woman in a cage, hanging chains, a whip, a woman caressing hanging chains, a street scene, a woman's caned bottom, an ape, a woman's cuffed hands crossed over her breasts, a banana, a penis side-on . . .

On and on they went, the commonplace mingled with the erotic. Some of the images had similar outlines and were positioned similarly on the screen, like the banana and penis, so it took a moment to distinguish them. Occasionally there was a fleeting flicker on the screen and she was not sure if she had missed something. Gradually the quantity of sexual images increased. Some were simple nude shots but others featured female bondage.

The common images left her more or less cold and inevitably the sexual ones were more arousing. Automatically she clenched on the probe inside her as they appeared. They seemed to be unusually hot, though she could not say quite why.

The cycle began again with fewer everyday images. As it did so the pace of the background music picked up.

She was aware that her nipples were rock hard and her pussy was pulsing and dribbling onto the paper sheet. She was trying not to show too much interest this quickly but it wasn't easy. The pictures were teasing out her true nature. She could not help responding to them . . . or was the stimulation coming a little ahead of the image? Was she doing it or was the probe filling her vagina cuing her?

But it was getting harder to think straight. She was sweating and breathing heavily, chewing on her gag, clenching on the probe, tugging at her cuffs and feeling the thrill of their resistance. The images had become a montage of flesh and metal that seemed to fill her mind: cuffed women, caged women, caned women, stiff pricks . . .

Then the knot in her loins exploded and her juices spurted out round the probe plugging her spasming vagina.

The next thing she knew the screen was dark, the lights were brighter and Banks and Lister were standing over her limp body looking down at her.

'You are going to be a very valuable subject to us, 77,' Banks said.

Yes, and I bet I'd also be a valuable sex slave, Vanessa thought dizzily. *Too bad I already belong to somebody else.*

Vanessa still felt a pleasing ache inside her when she got back to London that afternoon and related her experience to Angela.

'So it was a successful trip, Miss,' Angela said.

Vanessa grinned. 'You might say I saw, I came and I even got my expenses paid.'

'And you're satisfied you found out how Deedas operate, Miss?'

'It's a simple but effective con. They kid you that you're taking part in vital research. They make you feel

131

good about being used like a sexual guinea pig. I just wonder if it's worth the cost and effort.'

Angela turned to her calculator and began tapping in figures. 'From what you describe I can roughly estimate the cost of building rental, construction of sets, as we might call them, props and so forth. Assuming reuse over five years ... processing say five girls a month ... regular work for fees on our scale but with no money going to the girl ... minimal upkeep ...' She turned back to Vanessa. 'Each girl could pay off the cost of Deedas entrapping her in six to eight weeks. From then on what she brought in to Rochester would be almost pure profit.'

'And she would be at least a partially willing slave with no trafficking trail or string of foreign agents to worry about,' Vanessa added. 'Willing slaves cause less trouble and have a wider appeal to customers. So it *is* all worth their trouble. It's sick but you have to hand it to them that they do it well.' She beamed. 'I'm looking forward to my next session.'

Angela was looking at her doubtfully. 'So would you say you had a good time, Miss?

'Yeah, I had a really great time ...'

Then she bit her lip. It had been too enjoyable. Even though she had known what was happening and had been playing along a lot of the time, that wasn't natural. She frowned, concentrating, trying to recall those doubts she had felt that had been blown away by her orgasm. *Pull yourself together, Buckingham, and start thinking with your brains and not your pussy.*

At length she took a deep breath. 'Invaluable, lovely Angela, thank you for putting me back on the rails. I was getting carried away and Deedas have been screwing with my mind. Now arrange an appointment for me with Dr Gold at the Fellgrish Institute tomorrow. I know he can be tetchy and doesn't like visitors but tell him it's top priority and the Director will know it if he doesn't see me. Tell him he might not have his test girls to play with for much longer if he doesn't!'

A little awed by this sudden show of masterful determination, Angela said in a happy meek voice: 'Yes, Miss. At once, Miss.'

The next morning Vanessa was in a low, slab-like building with a façade that mingled red brick with tinted glass and polished steel, located in a science park off the Henley Road just outside Oxford. It was the home of Shiller's own slave-recruiting centre, the Fellgrish Institute Human Response Laboratory. The vital difference with Deedas was that here they did not brainwash women into becoming slaves.

Doctor Gold was as she remembered him from her last visit a few months earlier when she had written an article for *GN* about his work: short, balding, bespectacled and white-coated with a perpetual air of slight distraction. He was virtually a caricature of a scientist, except that unlike the fakes at Deedas he was the genuine article.

He blinked as she stood before him in his office. He was seated behind a large black-topped desk that was less cluttered than she recalled. He did not stand, of course, since even though she was clothed and on a special mission she was still a company slave.

'I see you've altered your appearance, Miss Buckingham. Interesting. All part of this secret project, I assume. But you have no collar on and you're fully dressed. If you must interrupt my work at least have the decency not to remain clothed so I can see what other changes you've made.'

Knowing it was the easiest way, Vanessa quickly stripped off her business suit. In a minute she stood before him naked with her hands meekly clasped behind her back.

Gold gazed at her new form approvingly. 'Very nice. Perhaps even an improvement.' He swivelled his chair round and slapped his knee. 'Now sit here and tell me your problem.'

Doctor Gold enjoyed his work. As he had explained to Vanessa last time, in how many other occupations could he, a long way from being young and handsome, have an attractive naked woman sit on his lap and allow him to play with her pussy?

As he was doing to Vanessa's right now. While he toyed with her new smooth plumper sex lips her clit responded with its usual enthusiasm. It made it hard to keep her voice steady but she knew Gold could listen and finger her at the same time.

'I've been investigating Deedas Research, Master,' she explained. 'They use methods a little like I saw you using here, but I think they're adding something that messes with your mind. My feelings went up and down like a yoyo and I enjoyed myself far too much . . .' His fingers twirled about her clit and she shivered '. . . even allowing for these alterations and the slut I know I am.'

'Hmm . . .' Gold mused. 'Describe the process and setting in detail . . .'

Vanessa did so as well as she could. By the end Gold was nodding and Vanessa had made a wet patch on his trousers.

'Yes, they undoubtedly were playing with your emotions. Subsonic, subaudio and subliminal imagery, I should think. Oh, my, you've left a stain. I shall have to punish you for that. Bend over the table . . .'

She did so, flattening her breasts into fat pancakes against the cool desktop. He pulled her arms out straight and wide, reaching across to the front of the desk. Metal cuffs extended up out of the top and snapped about her wrists. Gold bent down, spread her legs and she felt more cuffs pop out of the sides of the footwell and secure her ankles.

'It's a new executive model from Shiller's furnishings division,' Gold explained, stroking her now neatly presented bottom. 'What do you think?'

'Ingenious, Master,' Vanessa said. 'You were saying about a lot of subs . . .'

'Subsonics: sounds below the level of human hearing but to which we do respond on an unconscious level. The right frequencies can induce feelings of apprehension. When suddenly turned off, the psychological response is a flush of relief that might be mistaken for pleasure. Timed correctly they could be used to modify a person's response to certain events.'

He pressed a hidden switch and a slim drawer slid out from the side of the desk. It held a selection of canes and spanking paddles. Gold selected a paddle and swished it through the air experimentally.

'Subaudio, Master?'

'Not quite the same thing. Audio messages concealed within other sounds. The theory is the brain may unconsciously absorb and respond to them. But it's quite controversial.'

He swiped the paddle across Vanessa's bottom, making a crisp smack. Vanessa gasped.

Gold ran his hands over her buttocks. 'Firm muscle overlaid with a pleasing quantity of fat and resilient elastic flesh producing a satisfying ripple on impact,' he said with satisfaction. He delivered a few more strokes from different angles, watching her bottom shiver and clench in pain. 'Are your eyes watering, girl?'

'Yes, Master . . . ahhh . . . Subliminal, Master?'

'The flicker you saw on the screen. Simple images or words inserted amongst other imagery but visible for too little time to be read easily but which may enter at a subconscious level.' He felt the heat in Vanessa's buttocks, changed the angle of his paddle and swiped up into the cleft peach of her sex.

Vanessa gave a little sob of pain. 'Mind control . . . Master?'

'Oh no, no, no!' Gold said, emphasising his negative with more smacks to her pussy. 'None of these

135

techniques by themselves can do that. At best they can only colour and warp mood or emotion, not totally control it. You could not use them to make a person perform an act totally at odds with their character. That is sheer fantasy.'

He tested Vanessa's cleft and found it wet enough for his needs. Opening his flies he freed a sizable erection, grasped her hips and entered her.

Vanessa grunted as he filled her, squeezing hard on his shaft. 'But could they reinforce the feelings . . . uhhh . . . of subjects who are already . . . receptive . . . when all used together . . . Master?'

'Turn a partial submissive into a true one, you mean?'

'Yes . . . ahh . . . Master.'

'Perhaps, if the environment is also carefully controlled. I'll have to check up on that. But it's always dangerous to attempt to twist the mind, girl. At least now you know what is being done you can allow for its effects.' He leaned over her bound body and began to thrust harder. 'What a pity I never had you in my lab. I'd have kept you here for weeks.'

Nine

A fully briefed Shiller accountant had been put in place at Heelz High where he was able to examine the company's customer records. After a few days in his post Vanessa received a call from him.

'I've definitely tied in regular sales of "Crimson Shacklz" to Derringham, one of Rochester's suspect front companies, Miss Buckingham,' he told her. 'I assume when they receive it they probably break it up for distribution by internal mail service to their various mobile holding centres. We can't follow the goods any further from there.'

'Well, it confirms the link. Thank you.'

'But that's not the only reason I called, Miss Buckingham. We've received a new order for Shacklz from Derringham just a few minutes ago. That's ahead of schedule, judging by the usual pattern of orders.'

'And is it larger?' Vanessa asked anxiously.

'Twice the previous size.'

Vanessa's heart gave a little leap. 'That's great. Have you enough in stock to fill it?'

'Just, Miss Buckingham. Though there wouldn't have been if I hadn't asked them to start on a fresh batch as you requested. The manager is now wondering how I knew this new order was going to come in.'

'Let him wonder. Acknowledge the order and tell Derringham it'll be despatched in a week. Then get the goods to Keller Wilson today.'

'I'll deliver them myself, Miss Buckingham,' he promised.

Vanessa put the phone down and turned to Angela. 'The order's come through and it's doubled.'

Angela smiled. 'That's wonderful news. You were quite right, Miss.'

'I just hope I'm right about all the rest.'

Vanessa shared her nights with Kashika in the temporary flat at every opportunity. She wished she could go down to B3 and see the other girls but it was best she did not. Kashika had passed on her love and explained Vanessa was busy with a special project, though she was careful to be vague about the details. They were sad not to see her but accepted this explanation like good Shiller girls.

Both Kashika and Sandra reported the tension was growing in B3 amongst all the chain girls as the month Rochester had specified ticked away a day at a time. They knew if Canary Chain were not rescued soon two of their number would be selected to replace them. They were being brave about it but it was clearly telling on their spirits.

From reports Vanessa had seen she suspected there was little chance of finding the Canary girls in time. Shiller's agents had compiled a lengthy list of likely locations from which Rochester operated his slave business, which she had in turn plotted on her map. But they were utilised on a random basis and, like the Shiller HQ, there was always enough traffic passing through them to make it impossible to tell what if any was slave related. They might raid several addresses simultaneously but if they did not find the Canary girls they would only alert Rochester and risk him punishing the Canary girls as he had warned. Any rescue bid had to work first time. Like Vanessa's own plan.

Keller Wilson completed their work quickly and efficiently and the shipment of 'Crimson Shacklz' was sent on to Derringham. Keller Wilson also reported that the associated units were tested and fully functional. They were nearly ready but would Rochester's people unwittingly play their part?

Vanessa travelled to Guildford for her second session at Deedas Research with a greater sense of apprehension than she had her first time. Then she had been uncertain of what to expect. Thanks to Doctor Gold she now knew the tricks they were playing on her mind, which seemed somehow far dirtier and more intimate than anything they might do to her body. But Josie would not be aware of this and she could not afford to let it show. Somehow she would have to convince herself to respond naturally. She must let her instincts take over. They had done everything to establish their dominance over her from the start. She must simply let them think it was working.

In fact it was not as hard as she had feared. Josie was a potentially valuable commodity to Deedas and their operatives were anxious to make her feel comfortable with what she was doing.

Miss Graves met her at reception with a familiar and welcoming smile. 'Hello, Miss Gribbleson. Prompt once again. We do appreciate that. Doctor Lister and Doctor Banks were just talking about you.'

'Were they?' Vanessa asked innocently. 'What about?'

'They didn't go into details, of course. That's confidential. But I understand they were very pleased with your first session. An excellent subject, they said.'

'It was all so weird I wasn't sure,' Vanessa admitted with a suggestion of embarrassment. 'I mean what I did was . . . well, a bit gross.'

'I'm sure it was perfectly ordinary behaviour for a Deedas subject,' Miss Graves assured her. 'They were not shocked in the least. We're used to what other people might think of as unusual. That's what we're here to explore . . . with your help and women like you.'

'Oh. How many others are there?'

'I'm afraid that's confidential, like all your details.'

'Will I ever meet any of them?'

Miss Graves smiled. 'Maybe, at a later stage in the testing schedule. You might also share the holiday prize. Remember each time you come here you get another entry into our competition.'

Would the chance of two weeks in the sun really induce women to subject themselves to such intimate experiments? Vanessa wondered. Perhaps. People had been known to do far worse for less. And it was all supposed to be in the name of science . . .

Vanessa signed her travel cost claim form and Miss Graves showed her through to Lab 3 Reception.

Banks and Lister were waiting for her as before. Once more the background music was playing softly.

'Good Morning, Subject 77,' said Banks. 'Remember the routine. Clothes off and numbers on . . .'

'Yes, Doctor,' Vanessa said obediently.

Once again she stripped before them. Did she imagine the music changed slightly as she did so while a flush of pleasure filled her, or was it the normal thrill of exposure and delight in being naked?

Leaving her clothes on the hooks she came over to the yellow line in front of the desk with her hands clasped behind her neck. Lister stuck the numbers on her body in the same places as last time.

'As you did so well in your first tests, 77, we think you're ready to move to Stage Three,' Lister said. 'Not many subjects advance that fast.'

'Thank you, Doctor,' Vanessa said automatically.

'You did say you frequently used vibrators, didn't you?' Banks asked.

'Yes, Doctor.'

'Then this should be simple. Last time we measured your responses to erotic images and found what sort of things excited you. Today we want to measure your rate and level of arousal when your erogenous zones are specifically stimulated. We shall also assess your capacity for achieving multiple orgasms. You won't have to do anything except respond naturally. This way . . .'

They ushered her through into the narrow corridor and opened a door that was labelled impressively: EROTOGRAPHY.

Inside was a white-walled room with a large solid lab bench in the middle with three stools beside it. Around the edges of the bench top were set out some electronic control boxes and a lot of coiled wires. In the centre of the bench was a rectangle of black foam rubber matting. Arrayed about this, rather like miniature scaffolding, were several laboratory test stand supports with metal rods rising from heavy bases. Slotted onto the rods were adjustable pivoting arms with three-fingered screw-clamp jaws of different sizes. Like the outer room, this was also filled with the soft seductive background music.

'Up on the table and kneel on the mat, 77,' Banks said.

Vanessa used a stool to climb onto the bench top and knelt on the matting on her hands and knees. From this position she saw the bases of the test stands were firmly screwed to an array of boltholes sunk into the bench top.

'Once again it's important that you do not move about so we can get accurate readings,' Lister said. 'Just spread your hands and knees a little . . .'

It was laboratory bondage. The clamp arms were swivelled about and locked off and the rubber-sheathed jaws were closed about her wrists, elbows, two each side of her neck with rubber fingertips meshing to hold her head steady, two each side of her waist to brace her, one each about her knees and ankles. A pair of the larger clamps that might in a real lab be used to hold large retort beakers were swung in from either side and slid under her to close about the roots of her heavily

141

pendant breasts, squeezing them gently but inexorably into slightly more rounded balloons of flesh. A stand was positioned between her legs and screwed down. She felt hard rubber fingers clamp about and pull wide her labia, letting the air flow through her clitoral valley.

'Open wide, 77,' Lister said and she pushed the so-called mouth plug sensor between her lips. 'We want to know exactly how you respond to the stimulation.'

Vanessa suppressed a perverse shiver of delight as she was gagged. It was so good to be restrained again and let them bind her helpless body and baffle and flatter her with their pseudo-scientific double talk. She must just enjoy the game.

Lister positioned a clamp arm in front of Vanessa's face and carefully closed it about her chin. Now she could not turn her head but had to keep looking straight ahead, fixed in a posture more usually associated with canines on a stand at a dog show about to be examined by judges.

They taped a spray of electrodes to her chest and temples and then added a few more to her labia for good measure. She had no idea if they actually recorded anything but they were good props.

Somebody else entered the room. Vanessa's eyes swivelled round as far as the clamps permitted. She saw it was a skinny younger man with tousled hair and large glasses dressed in a white lab coat. He was carrying a small box and did not appear surprised at the sight of Vanessa kneeling naked on the bench clamped in place.

'I've got the stimulator pack that you wanted, Doctor Banks,' he said.

'Thank you, Tom. Open it up so we can begin the test on this subject.'

The box was opened out of Vanessa's line of sight. She could feel them working around her. Then something was pushed up under her breasts. What felt like small soft greased rubber suction cups were pressed up to surround her nipples. The activity moved down to her hindquarters. Things were clamped to the stands.

'Add a bit of oil to the Subject's orifices, Tom,' Banks said. 'They must be properly lubricated.'

'Both of them, Doctor?'

'Both. Number 77 is a highly responsive subject and quite capable of taking dual orifice stimulation.'

'Yes, Doctor.'

Flatterer, Vanessa thought, fighting down another shiver of delight. At least they were going to do it properly.

Vanessa felt a nozzle pushed up into her vagina and pump out a squirt of oil. It was pulled out and reinserted in her anus to pump out a second squirt.

'What size stimulators, Doctor?' Tom asked.

'A vaginal four and rectal three.'

Vanessa felt a fat phallic object being slid up inside her vagina and secured in place. A slightly slimmer device was pushed deep into her anus and clamped into place.

'Brink me the flask, Tom,' Lister said, 'I want to find out how much discharge she puts out during the course of the experiment.'

'Here it is, Doctor.'

Out of the corner of her eye Vanessa saw him hand over a tall slender glass tube with a graduate scale marked down the side and a funnel plugged into the top.

Lister positioned the tube on the mat with the funnel mouth just under Vanessa's groin. They were going to catch the juices that dribbled out of her as she was brought to orgasm. This was getting freaky.

The ersatz-scientists moved round to the side of the table to stand in front of the controls.

'Test each stim unit,' Banks said.

The cups about her nipples sucked and buzzed briefly and sensuously, making Vanessa shiver. Then the device in her anus buzzed, which gave her a dark happy thrill.

Lastly the vaginal vibrator cut in and she clenched her passage tight about it. They could play about with any part of her they wanted.

'Subject responding normally,' Lister reported. 'How high should we start?'

'Level four, I think,' Banks said.

'Timer running, levels set . . . activate.'

The cups sucked hungrily at her nipples, making her feel like a cow being milked. Then they began buzzing as well. Her nipples swelled within the cups so hard they hurt. Suddenly the cups went dead, leaving her for a few seconds feeling a terrible sense of loss. Then the probe in her rectum came to life, vibrating and pulsing inside her, sending shivers up her spine. Then it cut out. A moment of lustful freefall and the vaginal probe cut in and she clenched on it happily, savouring its intimate buzzing pulsations inside her hot wet passage. But too quickly it died. Then the nipple cups started up again.

And so the sequence repeated. A rolling wave of stimulation rippled through Vanessa's body, round and round, building in strength. And it felt so good. And why shouldn't it? This was what she loved.

Yet a part of her knew they were playing on her expectations with the sequence of stimulation. They were controlling her pleasure, chopping it up into neat segments and it was not natural. She was being made to come to order. And she could not fight it . . .

Vanessa shuddered, bit on her mouth plug and came. The clamps held her steady and kept her in position. She sagged gracefully into their inflexible embrace. All the devices plugged into her went dead.

'Subject 77 has achieved first orgasm,' Lister said. 'Can you measure the discharge when it's finished dripping, please, Tom?'

'Yes, Doctor.'

'Five minutes' rest before restarting,' Banks declared. 'Water the subject, Tom.'

'Yes, Doctor.'

Tom pushed the straw from a plastic squeezy bottle through a hole in Vanessa's mouth plug and she sucked on it greedily. He grinned at her need, took out a damp cloth and wiped her face over, then gave her sweaty breasts and flanks a quick wipe down. She tried to smile back.

Nice work if you could get it, Vanessa thought dizzily. How much did being a fake lab technician at Deedas pay? Or maybe he was an innocent stooge simply following orders while thinking he'd landed the wet dream of all jobs? If they could lure girls in to be sex guinea pigs why not naïve young men to help look after them? It might make the operation seem more credible.

After five minutes the test started up again and Vanessa surrendered herself to pleasure.

After her fourth orgasm in an hour Vanessa was beginning to tire, which Lister noted.

'I think the subject may be reaching her limit for this session,' she said.

'We'll try one more cycle with electro stim,' Banks replied.

The nipple cups started to suck and buzz and then they stabbed her tumescent thimbles of flesh with a rapid series of electric shocks. They were not severe but they make her flinch in her lattice of clamps and brought tears pricking at the corners of her eyes. Then the anal vibrator cut in and added its electric needles to the sequence. Vanessa whimpered even as her anal ring clenched tight about the shaft. Was she trying to push it out or hold it in? The vaginal probe was the worst and best of all. As it stabbed into her she gave a muffled shriek and bit hard on her mouth plug. She imagined she could hear her juices dripping into the measuring flask.

Inside five minutes they had forced one last orgasm out of her.

As Vanessa sagged limply in her clamps she heard Banks saying: 'Tests sequence complete. Note that even in a state of exhaustion, Subject 77 responded well to electric impulses supplementing the tactile output of the basic stimulator units. She is highly responsive to sexual stimuli and is easily aroused.'

Lister moved round to look Vanessa in the eye. Vanessa had to blink away her sweat to focus on her.

'That means you're very useful to us, 77,' Lister said with apparent sincerity. 'We can make tests on you that we could not make on many other women. You will be helping us increase our knowledge of sexual responses which will be of great benefit to human knowledge.'

Screw a masochistic slut hard enough and she comes, Vanessa thought. *That's all you need to know*.

A little unsteadily Vanessa walked back out into the main reception. Miss Graves looked up from her computer screen. 'Finished already, Josie?' She called up a diary page. 'Can I book you in again for next week?'

The thought of coming back to Deedas suddenly seemed irresistibly appealing, and despite what she'd just been through she felt the familiar tingle glow in her loins.

'Of course,' Vanessa said with more eagerness than she had intended.

On the way back to the office Vanessa tried to analyse her response.

Why was she looking forward so eagerly to the next session? Of course she knew she had to go and it was easier if she found some pleasure in it, but her gut feeling had still been unexpected.

Was it that her life at this moment was so fragmented and full of concern and responsibility that the thought

146

of playing Deedas' games for a few hours like a slave was actually a relief? *Receiving comfort and succour from the enemy are you, Buckingham?* Always a risk when you worked undercover, of course, and she knew it was necessary . . . but should she be enjoying it quite so much?

Fortunately Angela's progress report for the day briefly wiped the concern from her mind.

'The last of the maps you wanted have been located, copied and distributed, Miss. The necessary items of public works and utility service equipment have been purchased and are held ready close to the targets. Robotikine have reported their devices have passed the final tests and all the modifications are integrated. The control units and detector kits are also ready.'

'That's great,' Vanessa said, looking over the typed notes.

'And this package from Keller Wilson arrived for you by courier, Miss.'

Vanessa opened it up and examined its contents closely. There was a pillbox of four red capsules and a pack of carefully moulded slivers of clear plastic with tiny metallic flecks in them. It was unlikely that such innocuous-looking things had ever before been transported with such precautions, she thought. Carefully she fixed the items in place. They were all she could have hoped for.

'It's hard to believe they can do what they claim, Miss,' Angela said, admiring the result as Vanessa displayed them.

'According to Keller Wilson they can. Whether they'll ever get the chance is another thing.'

'It will all go to plan, Miss.' Angela checked through her lists. 'I think all the preparations are made.'

Vanessa blinked. 'Really all?'

'Yes, Miss.'

'Then I'll report to the Director.'

* * *

147

Shiller listened intently as Vanessa related their situation.

'There are the volunteer staff to find and train to operate the detector units, of course, but both Robotikine and Keller Wilson say they're very easy to use. We can always draw on their specialists for advice at short notice if we need to. Regular truck crews are on hand to take care of transportation. Any strong-arm stuff will be handled by security. I think we're ready, Director.'

'That's good, because we have got no further in tracking down the Canary girls. Tomorrow I shall make the draw for the chains who will replace them and the next day they will be sent away. It won't be easy, deceiving the girls even in this small way, but I know it must be done.'

'I'm sorry, Director. But I couldn't see any other way.'

'Of course. Don't concern yourself about it. You still have the harder task. And I'm very proud of you for undertaking such a project.'

'I couldn't have done it without Angela's help, Director.'

'Yes, she's as valuable and dedicated in the office as she was as a collared slave. When you have any doubts remember it is for the continued happiness of people like her that we are doing this. As I must do myself.'

Vanessa did not attend the draw, which the Director carried out in front of the assembled chains in the training yard. Sandra told her about it afterwards and she read Zara's report for *GN*.

It was very simply done. The Director had the names of all the chains written on tightly folded slips of paper in a glass bowl, including those working in regional centres. If they were chosen they would be replaced by another chain and brought back to London. She stirred them about and picked out two.

The first was Dahlia chain. The second was Cherry.

Vanessa knew it would be Cherry, of course, since that slip of paper had been taped to the bottom of the bowl for the Director to pick out. It was safer for the Dahlias, who really had been picked by chance, that they believed the Cherrys had as well.

The hardest thing was saying goodbye to Kashika. She thought she should spend the night with her chain sisters and Vanessa agreed, so that afternoon they snatched a brief couple of hours together back at the flat.

As they clung together in the bed, after they had exhausted their passion through desperate lovemaking, Kashika tried to be light-hearted.

'It's not as though I'm going to the guillotine, you know. It is a far, far better thing I'm doing, which is being a sex slave, which I love. It might be a little rougher than usual but I can manage. I'll have the others with me. We'll survive and we'll come home again.'

'You know what's going to happen,' Vanessa said, feeling too guilty to joke in return. If it were not for her Kashika would not be going at all. 'At least, what might happen,' she added.

'I know and I'm prepared,' Kashika said. 'If your plan ends this war then it's all worthwhile.'

'If it works.'

'It will, I know it.'

The next day marked one month since the Canarys had been kidnapped, and was the day their replacements were due to be handed over.

From early in the morning Cherry and Dahlia chains waited nervously down in B3. A truck was held on standby. The hours dragged by. Vanessa fretted and wished she could be with Kashika and the other Cherry girls. But she had to stick to her plan now. It was six o'clock when a text was sent to Shiller from a mobile phone.

TO: FG SHILLER

YOU WILL DELIVER TWO REPLACEMENT CHAINS OF MERCHANDISE TO THE DISUSED BARN YOU WILL FIND AT THIS LOCATION AT 8 PM TODAY.

(An O/S map reference followed which was found to be a small wood on the Berkshire Downs east of Swindon not far from the M4.)

THE VEHICLE SHALL BE PARKED IN THE BARN AND LEFT UNLOCKED. THE CHAINS SHALL BE SECURED WITHIN BUT UNCOLLARED. THE TRUCK CREW WILL DEPART FROM THE VICINITY AND NOT RETURN TO THE VEHICLE FOR A MINIMUM OF 6 HOURS. ANY ATTEMPT TO OBSERVE THE COLLECTION OF THE MERCHANDISE OR TRACK ITS SHIP-MENT WILL INVALIDATE THE EXCHANGE AND LEAD TO THE PENALTIES ALREADY SPECIFIED. IF THE REPLACE-MENT CHAINS ARE OF SUITABLE QUALITY THEN THE ORIGNAL CHAIN WILL BE LEFT FOR COLLECTION TOMOR-ROW NIGHT AT A LOCATION TO BE SPECIFIED BY THIS METHOD.

SIGNED: R

Rochester had left sending the instructions to the last minute. It would take at least an hour and a half to reach the location. He was making sure they had no time to arrange undercover surveillance of the delivery site.

The directions contained one hopeful sign. Rochester wanted the girls sent uncollared. That Vanessa had been expecting. And if she had anticipated that then maybe the rest would follow.

But one small triumph did not negate her despair at being unable to go down and see the girls off. Sandra did and said everybody was very brave but there were a lot of tears. Then it was a just a matter of waiting a day.

Vanessa thought she had rationalised her fears over the Canarys' captivity, convincing herself that they would cope and come back defiant. After all, that was how she and most others in the company had got through the last month. But at this moment Rochester had three of their chains in his power, one containing her lover.

What if she had been wrong?

It was a terrible night.

The next morning Shiller called Vanessa to her office.

'You will want to talk to the Canary girls as soon as they return?'

'Yes, Director. I must know they were handled as we expected. If they were, we can set everything rolling.'

'The girls must first be security scanned,' Shiller said. 'I do not put it past Rochester to have planted some sort of spying device on them. Then our doctors will examine them. There will be no debriefing until I know they are well.'

'I only need to talk to one of them, Director. Julie 5, if possible. I know her. If it went the way Cindy described then we can go.'

At eight that evening another text was received. This gave the location of a hut in the Ashdown Forest in East Sussex. A Shiller van and a security car were despatched to check it out. Just after ten they got the news that the Canary girls had been recovered safely. The news briefly diverted Vanessa from thinking about what Kashika was going through.

The next morning Sandra gently ushered Julie 5 Canary into Vanessa's office.

The last time Vanessa had seen Julie she had been bright-eyed and bursting with life. Her hair was a silvery blonde, her complexion creamy pale, her waist tight and the nipples that capped her taut breasts prettily pink. About her neck she wore a yellow collar and she went about as cheerfully naked as all Shiller girls.

Physically she was much the same, save that there were a few cane cuts across her breasts, deeper scarlet and purple mottling on her buttocks, and her pubes looked red and swollen. But those things Vanessa knew would heal and would trouble a slavegirl far less than an ordinary woman. The subtler signs of the ordeal she had been through were the shadows under her eyes, which flicked nervously from side to side, and the slightly hunched, hesitant way she walked, so different from her normal bouncy stride.

Julie blinked in surprise as she saw Vanessa, struggling to adjust her mind to the changes.

'Vanessa?' she said uncertainly. Then she smiled in wonder and ran forward and hugged and kissed her passionately. 'Oh . . . it's so good to see you . . . so good to be back home.' And she cried softly on Vanessa's shoulder.

Without being asked, Angela got up from her desk and went out with Sandra, leaving them alone.

Vanessa sat Julie down, got her a drink of water and a tissue, and waited until her tears had abated.

Finally Julie took a deep breath and smiled, looking a little more like her old self. 'I'm sorry, it's just . . . you know.'

'You don't have to apologise. After what you've been through you're entitled.'

Julie forced a smile and tried to sound offhand. 'Well, it could have been worse. The hijack was the most frightening bit. But once we'd recovered they told us about the deal and that if we cooperated we'd be sent back in a month. It's not as though we had any choice . . .' She gave a little brittle chuckle '. . . so we just opened our legs and treated it like normal work.'

'That's what we all hoped you'd do.'

'It wasn't too bad most of the time as long as we behaved. We had to keep quiet about where we'd come from in front of their clients or we'd get a thrashing, of course.' She touched her cane-marked breasts and red pubes. 'Most of this was a goodbye present from our guards. They could be harder than the clients, though a few of them were also pretty shitty. The living quarters were crap as well, but we survived. And now we're home and I'm so happy! But . . . is it true you gave Rochester two chains to get us back?'

'Yes. Dahlia and Cherry.'

Julie's face fell. 'Not . . . Kashika?'

'She volunteered. They all did. Every single chain.'

Julie gulped. 'Oh . . . wow . . . that's so . . .' She wiped her eyes, sniffled and smiled proudly. 'That's so wonderful of them.' Then she looked Vanessa up and down once again. 'But what about you? What have you done to yourself?'

'I'll explain later,' Vanessa said. 'Just say it's all part of a plan to put Rochester out of the slave business for good and get Cherry and Dahlia back. But to make it work I've got to know a few things about what happened to you. I wish I didn't have to ask so soon but it's really important.'

Julie took a deep breath. 'Of course. What do you want to know?'

'Did they keep moving you about?'

'Yes. In big trucks and sometimes articulated lorries, I think. Not that we ever saw the outside of them, but that's what they must have been.'

'Did you ever see Rochester?'

'No. We guessed he was behind it, of course, but we never saw him and nobody mentioned his name. Sometimes one of the masters said "The Boss" wanted something done, but that was all.'

'Were there cameras watching you?'

153

'Oh, yes. Wherever we were we had to parade once a day and there was always somebody with a camera looking us over.'

'And what did they make you wear?'

'Well, their own collars for a start. All red. They cut our collars off when they kidnapped us.' She fingered her yellow collar that had JULIE 5 CANARY stamped into its side. 'This is a replacement. The Director actually had them ready with our old numbers on. She knew we'd be missing them. It feels good to be the right colour again.'

'What else?'

'Red lipstick, nail varnish, nipple paint, padlocked high heels. Everything matched.'

From a drawer Vanessa pulled out a pair of Crimson Shacklz and put them down in front of Julie. 'Like these?'

'Yes, exactly. Where did you get them? They took ours off before they sent us back. Are they important?'

Vanessa smiled, feeling hope swell inside her. 'They are going to help us screw Rochester once and for all!'

Ten

'A month ago I promised you that only if there was a prospect of freeing our girls from Rochester's clutches would I allow an exchange to be made,' Director Shiller said. 'The day before yesterday Cherry and Dahlia chains bravely went off to win the release of their sisters and last night, as you know, Canary Chain were returned to us. And we welcome them back . . .'

Briefly the yard rang with cheers and applause.

It was the afternoon following Canary Chain's return. The Director, Vanessa and trainers stood on the dais before the naked girlflesh crowd who were congregated in the training yard. In the front row, surrounded by a huddle of close supporters and comforters, were the Canary girls. Like Julie they bore the marks of their captivity and looked pale and tired.

When the applause died down the Director continued.

'But I also said that it would happen only once. Before another month passed this bitter rivalry between Rochester and myself will be ended for good, one way or another. You may have been wondering what steps have been taken to do this or to track our girls down. I hope you have read Vanessa 19 White's article in *GN* explaining the problems with unravelling Rochester's slave business. We could perhaps rescue a few of his captives and close down some of his branches, but that would not bring down the entire operation, nor would it prevent Rochester starting again elsewhere. And while he holds our girls effectively hostage we cannot risk making anything less than a swift and decisive move.

'However we have not been idle. A plan has been under intensive development for the last few weeks that I hope will bring Rochester down for good. Until this moment I have not been able to tell you about it for reasons of security. But now the exchange of chains has been made you deserve to hear about this plan, because you may also be asked to play a part in its execution.

'The concept was Vanessa's own and she has been working on it with my full support and the backing of many company staff and technical associates. Now I have asked her to explain it to you. Because above all this situation affects you, our loyal girlflesh stock, and you will be part of its solution. Vanessa . . .'

Vanessa had been standing at the back of the podium with the trainers dreading this moment, but Shiller had insisted she should speak to the girls personally. There was a stir as she stepped forward. Some of the girls had recognised her press hat but had been puzzled by the clothed and darker-skinned form beneath.

She removed her hat. 'I really am your slave reporter Vanessa 19 White . . . well, Brown, now as you can see . . .'

There was a scattering of laughter that encouraged her to go on.

'I was transferred to management to work on this and told to wear clothes but not my collar, when I would rather have been stripped in the *GN* office or down here with you. But like this makeover it had to be done and, as you'll learn, I had to keep out of the way until now. The chains sent to Rochester to replace Canary could not know what I was up to in case they gave something away by accident or under torture. But now, I hope, it's going to be finished very soon and I, and the company, need your help.'

She turned to a table that had been set up beside the dais. Odd shapes lay on it concealed by a dustsheet. Vanessa wanted to show them some tangible result for all the effort that had been expended. She pulled the sheet off and mutters of wonder and puzzlement went up from the watching girls.

'As you can see there's some rather special equipment to operate and work to do that may require a lot of patient waiting around, which I know slavegirls are good at. Then, if it all goes well, you'll have to move quickly to support other staff and our security teams. When it's over Rochester will be finished and never bother us again, his slaves will be freed and we'll have Cherry and Dahlia back safely!'

The yard erupted into wild cheers.

'So . . . who wants to help me?'

Julie 5 stepped forward. 'I volunteer, Vanessa.'

And then the rest of her colour sisters stepped forward. 'We volunteer.'

Then all the girls were stepping forward. 'I volunteer . . . I volunteer . . .'

The wonderful glow the memory of the girls stepping forward had given her faded the next day as Vanessa went down for her third session at Deedas.

Until now she had been worrying the trap might spring before she was ready. Now she desperately wanted to make it happen to save Kashika even a minute of unnecessary suffering.

How long must she wait? According to Cindy it had taken ten visits to hook her securely before she had been taken on to the next phase. But that had been a few years ago. The process might have been refined since then. Did they make allowances for individual responses to the treatment or did they follow a fixed schedule? If she was right and they were short of girls they might fast track her. She did not want to waste any time but neither must she appear too eager.

'This experiment will test your determination, physical reactions, response to external stimuli and sexual

157

endurance, 77,' Banks told Vanessa as she once again stood naked except for her number stickers in the lab reception room. 'It's a challenge and normally we would not try this on a subject so soon, but you are clearly special.'

Was that mere flattery or was it true? 'Thank you, Doctor,' she said.

'First we'll fit you with some new equipment,' Lister said.

Several items were set out on the table in front of the two fake scientists. Vanessa had been eyeing them with interest.

Lister took up a thick rubber-coated ring. It trailed two sets of wires with sticky pad contacts. She opened a catch and the ring hinged open into two halves.

'This is a device you'll become familiar with during the next cycle of testing, 77,' she explained. 'It's a remote transmitter of brain function, heart rate and respiration. It means you can move about freely and we can still collect data. Lift your hair out of the way . . .'

Lister clipped the device round Vanessa's neck and attached the contacts to her temples and chest.

And of course it's only coincidence that it resembles a slave collar, Vanessa thought to herself. But it did feel good to have its weight round her neck.

'Hold out your hands and make fists, 77,' Banks commanded.

He had a pair of silver metal balls in front of him. He split them open to reveal padded interiors with semicircles cut out of the edges opposite the hinge. He clamped the balls over her hands, the scallops closing about her wrists. Small spring catches clicked shut.

'It's important that you do not touch yourself at any time during the test,' he explained. 'That might invalidate the results.'

By taking away the use of my hands, Vanessa thought. It represented another degree of control over her. She felt hot anticipation seeping through the folds of her labia.

This time they went a little further down the corridor and turned in through a door marked ENDURANCE TESTING CHAMBER.

It was a warm square unfurnished white room with rubber matting on the floor, which was covered by a grid of bare metal wires. Set low down on a rectangular black panel in the middle of each wall was a small LED array mounted above a large black rubber vibrator jutting up at an angle of about thirty degrees. Around the base of each vibrator was a ring of metal studs. Small video cameras were mounted high up in two corners of the room with their lenses angled downwards. Beside them were speakers droning out more soft background music.

Vanessa felt a perverse thrill as she took this in, which might of course have been entirely natural.

'We want to determine how important sexual gratification is to you in a more interactive situation,' Lister said. 'Once again you will be given the opportunity of reaching orgasm as many times as you can. Our remote sensor collar will tell us when you climax. But this time you will have to work to achieve satisfaction.' She indicated the vibrators jutting out of the walls. 'These will be switched on and off in a random pattern. You may only use an active unit. When they are active the lights over them will flash and you can use them to pleasure yourself. When the lights change the bases of the phalluses become electrified. Just enough to give you a little sting. Then you must move on to another one. Do you understand?'

It was a lovely little perverse game. 'Yes, Doctor.'

'You may have five minutes' rest for refreshment after each orgasm. We expect you to get thirsty, but that is also part of the experiment. Straws supplying water are built into the phalluses. You may drink from them only when they are safe. If you do not suck from them a buzzer will sound and the floor becomes electrified. It will also shock you if you stand still for too long or are not using a phallus when one is active. After each stage we will add an impediment to make it harder for you to pleasure yourself. Do you understand?'

Vanessa gulped. 'Yes, Doctor.'

They shut her in.

Vanessa looked around her at the ring of blatantly erect phalluses. She'd have to go down on her hands and knees and back onto them doggy-fashion. How degrading. And then drinking from them and tasting herself! It was wonderfully sick.

Banks' voice came over the speakers. 'Test begins.'

The light over one of the phalluses flashed and it began to pulsate green. Before Vanessa could react a buzzer sounded and she felt a pricking in the soles of her feet. With a yelp she skipped across to the phallus, twisted round, squatted down to open her thighs and expose the swell of her pubes and rammed her haunches backwards, impaling herself. The vibrating head of the phallus slipped easily between her lips and up into her passage.

For a few moments she worked her hips happily back and forth, setting her breasts swaying in time. Then the light turned red and the vibrator died. Still caught up in the rhythm she pushed again. The ring of contacts about the base touched her wet sucking love lips. A stabbing pain shot through her pussy and she jerked herself off the rubber phallus with a yelp.

Instinctively she went to rub her cleft but her ball-encased hands were no comfort. There was a buzz and the floor stung her feet even as the vibrator on the far side of the room lit up green. She scrambled over to it and impaled herself once again.

She was allowed half a minute of pleasant shafting and then it turned red. She got off quickly, looking round for her next safe haven. The vibrator to her right was flashing and she almost threw herself upon it.

After ten minutes' frantic activity in the warm room the sweat was beading her brows and gathering in her cleavage and bum cleft. Her pussy was tingling in sympathy with the vibrating shafts it had swallowed and her thighs were beginning to ache. Her nipples were standing out like organ stops and there were crisscrossing trains of drips across the dark matting floor where her pussy had dribbled as she dashed from one rubber cock to another. If she had been allowed to stay still she would have already orgasmed.

Instead she was hardly being given time to think, let alone come, responding automatically to the signals being thrown at her via coloured lights, sore feet or smarting pussy. But now her growing need could not be denied much longer. She had to relieve the lustful tension inside her. She was boiling over.

In desperation she plugged herself onto the next phallus and stayed there, working her hips frantically, her breasts jiggling. The light turned red. Jolts of electricity sparked and stabbed at her sucking, clenching pussy lips. But by now pain and pleasure had merged within her as only a slavegirl could make them. With a gasp she came and then sagged to her knees, the vibrator still inside her, her body twitching with little shocks.

The punishment ceased. Over the speaker Banks said: 'Well done, 77. You may rest and drink now.'

On her hands and knees she pulled herself off her rubber stud and shuffled over to a phallic water fountain and sucked hard, not caring that she was tasting her own juices, only aware of how wonderfully fresh and cool the water was and how good resting felt. How kind of them to let her lie still . . .

What was she thinking? She struggled to clear her post-coital haze.

161

She was being conditioned. The warmth of the room was part of it as well, helping to soften her up. That was what the test was really for. A green light was good. It meant having a cock up inside her or sucking on one for sustenance. A red light meant pain and fear. A buzzer meant she must move quickly. Now she was responding to a voice from on high as though it was bestowing divine largess when it was just allowing her water and a rest. How many repetitions would it take before she got hot at the sight of a green light or looked for a cock to suck? She was being turned into Pavlov's pussy.

Would it work as quickly on a non-slave? She had no idea. Deedas' questionnaires must have helped them select girls with a higher than average liking for sex. If they had also chosen those whose profiles suggested lack of self-confidence or a sense of direction in life then that made them potentially vulnerable to this sort of treatment. And she was probably more responsive than most. But she knew who she was and where she was going. That would protect her . . . wouldn't it?

Lister came in. 'Stand up straight, 77. Hands behind your back . . .'

She had a pair of screw-fixed nipple clamps. From them dangled spiked lead weights. She screwed the clamps to Vanessa's still swollen nipples. The weights rested against the lower curves of her breasts, the sharp points pricking her flesh. Without the use of her fingers there was no way she could remove them.

Lister said: 'Ready to go again?'

She could say no. She could walk out on them. At least she could protest that it was too painful or simply too freaky and perverse, dream holiday or not. That's what Josie probably would have done. But she had to keep going.

'Yes, Doctor.'

The spiked balls hung free from her nipples as she went down on her hands and knees to take the enticing green vibrator into her. But as she worked herself back and forth they began to swing up and down, jabbing her swaying breasts. When she had to scuttle between phalluses as the red lights flashed they jumped and jabbed even harder. Crescents of little pinpricks were forming about the full underswells of her breasts. But she had no choice but to keep ramming herself onto the vibrators.

Did the pain help or inhibit? With a masochist that was not easy to say. She might be trying harder to reach orgasm and end it or to make it hurt more and intensify her pleasure. All she knew was that her nipples felt as though they were going to burst and her pussy was swollen and raw.

She orgasmed two minutes sooner than she did the first time.

As she sucked at her phallus like a baby at a bottle, Lister came in again. She was carrying a pair of cuffs connected by a bungee cord.

'That was very well done, 77,' she said. 'Now sit up and stretch your legs out.' Warm praise paired with brisk commands, associating pride with obedience.

Vanessa obeyed. Lister fastened the cuffs about Vanessa's ankles. She had been in effect hobbled.

Lister left and the test restarted. But now Vanessa was forced to shuffle on all fours between the vibrators. There was no time to struggle to her feet hindered by her hobble. Groggy with the heat and effort she was now responding to the lights and buzzers like a puppet. But her balled hands did not grip the floor well and she slipped and fell onto her face a couple of times, mashing her heaving breasts onto the wire grid overlaying the matting, which then shocked her as punishment for her clumsiness.

Her hair was now sodden with sweat and sticking to her shoulders. Sweat dripped off her clamped nipples, stung her anus and ran into her red and swollen cleft, which added its own effusion to the drops that fell to the floor. The close hot room stank with her sweat and bodily juices.

But she could not stop trying to screw herself onto the vibrators. An orgasm was the way to end it, the only goal she had. She was getting too tired to care about pulling herself off the vibrators when the lights turned red. The jolts of pain helped. She was simply a mobile vagina trying to get its fix of rubber cock and wishing they would spout inside her like real cocks did and cool her down. Nothing else mattered but making that pleasure bomb explode one more time . . .

'Stop drinking, 77, sit up and open your mouth,' Lister was saying and Vanessa obeyed. Her pussy was pulsing and dribbling messily.

Lister pushed a ball gag into Vanessa's mouth. 'This is the last phase. Spread your knees . . .'

Vanessa did so. Lister parted her sticky labia and clipped something to them. Vanessa looked down at her flushed and swollen cleft. In the pink and red valley there now rested a small metal ball studded with stubby spikes. From its sides extended a pair of arms with clips on their ends that were now fastened with painful tightness to her inner labia, holding the ball nestling in the mouth of her vagina. As long as it was not disturbed it did not prick her. But no vibrator could get past it and with her hands encased as they were there was no way she could take it off.

'Now you only have one orifice you can use,' Lister said. 'We want to test how important gratification really is to you.' She left the chamber, closing the door behind her.

Was she really going to sodomise herself just to chase one more orgasm, Vanessa wondered? Wasn't that too demeaning for anybody, let alone to please a bunch of fake scientists performing a sham experiment?

The vibrator lights began to flash. Vanessa squirmed onto her knees, turned her rear to the wall and pushed the buzzing, pulsing rubber shaft still wet from her last encounter up into her bumhole.

It felt so good . . .

Vanessa found herself sprawled face down on the floor with her bottom in the air. Her aching juice-lathered pussy with its clamped lips and tormenting ball plug was pulsing feebly while the head of a phallus was still lodged in her anus. She was utterly spent. That had to be Josie's limit and hers. She did not want to know if she could have been pushed to screw her body or mind any further.

She became aware of Banks and Lister standing over her.

'That's really excellent, 77,' Banks said. 'You have a remarkable capacity for pursuing pleasure despite discomfort. This is providing us with very valuable data. You have done a great service to science. Well done.'

And for a brief moment she really believed it.

At reception Vanessa contrived to look a little awkward as she said to Miss Grant: 'I'm, you know, free for a couple of days next week. If you want me . . .'

Miss Grant smiled. 'Well, I'm sure the doctors can fit their star subject into their experimental schedule somewhere.'

A warm glow filled her heart. She was a star.

The trip home on the train gave her time to think again.

She decided it had been a good perverse slavish workout and she'd shown them what she, or rather Josie, was made of. It was foolish not to admit that she enjoyed being used as a laboratory test animal, even though she knew it was all just a front. Was she responding too readily to the stimulation the tests involved? No, it was quite natural. As submission and a love of forced usage came naturally to her it was not surprising she wanted more when it was offered so enticingly. She was not getting hooked, whatever tricks they were playing on her. Since she knew the truth, they were not going to catch her like they had poor Cindy.

That night Vanessa took Julie 5 home to her temporary flat.

Most of Julie's chain sisters were on compassionate leave visiting their relatives and recovering from their captivity. Julie did not seem to have any close relations she wanted to be with so Vanessa had invited her back. She liked the Canary girl and wanted to be sure she was getting all the help she needed. As they were both still sore and drained from their respective recent usage they spent most of the time simply sleeping in each other's arms with the familiar ease that came to slavegirls used to the joy of resting on warm resilient naked female flesh. But in the early hours they woke and talked.

'I think the worst part about it was knowing they didn't care about us,' Julie said. 'The guards, I mean, not the customers. We put on a show for them as we were told and I don't think they realised what was really happening. But managers and guards were real shits. Here we know we're important to the company. There we were treated hardly better than animals. I don't mean in a play way, that can be fun, I mean for real. But at least we only had to put up with it for a month, not like their regular girls. They kept us away from them but from what we saw they looked pretty sad but sort of resigned to it, as though they had to do it and couldn't imagine anything else. I wanted to tell them it could be so much better.'

'I don't know if they keep the treatment up that they use when they're recruiting,' Vanessa said, 'but they might have been half conditioned to accepting it.'

166

'I should be grateful they didn't try it on us,' Julie said. 'I suppose it wasn't worth it as we were only going to be there a month. I wonder how many of them haven't seen their families for years, maybe? What do they think has happened to them?'

'They try to target girls without close families,' Vanessa explained. 'With the rest I think they use the conditioning process to encourage them to break away from family and friends first. That way they're not so likely to be missed when they drop right out of sight.'

'Poor bitches,' said Julie with feeling.

'I'm sorry you haven't got any close family,' Vanessa said. 'That's what you need at a time like this.'

'I have so got a family,' Julie declared. 'The best you could ever want. All my chain sisters, the company . . . and you.' She kissed her. 'You're my big clever company sister who knows all the answers.'

'Don't start that again,' Vanessa warned her gently.

'Well, you are clever,' Julie said, coyly tracing a pattern round Vanessa's nipple with her finger. 'And very special.'

'They've been telling me that at Deedas, but it doesn't make it true.'

'It shows they recognise quality. That's why you're doing what you are. That's why you'll beat Rochester. I know it!'

Vanessa wished she were that certain.

Eleven

Angela was deploying a fresh swathe of green pins across the big map as new reports came in from the field. They augmented the gold that marked Rochester's houses and the blues that marked already identified slave houses and similar facilities.

'These show where we have monitor teams established, Miss,' she explained. 'The Alpha teams are shadowing the domestic locations as you instructed. All are in place. Their primary sensor units have been deployed and the operators have made their camps within transmitter range. All they can do now is wait.'

'Have they got the relief rosters worked out? They must stay alert.'

'They are mixed teams of staff and off-duty chain girls, Miss. You can rely on the girls to keep them both alert and entertained.'

Vanessa smiled. 'You're right, of course, Angela, we can. Anyway they deserve to be there. They so want to be part of this.'

'We all do, Miss.'

'And what about the Betas?'

'About two thirds in place as close to Rochester's suspected transit sites, storage depots and party houses as possible. The remainder should be established by tomorrow night. It has taken longer because they have to cover many more widespread sites.'

'That has to be where we're most likely to get the first signals. Anything detected yet?'

'Nothing reported yet, Miss.'

Vanessa chewed her lip and fretted. 'How long will it take to start using the new stock?'

'That depends on the pairs still in hand and the rate of turnover, Miss. We must simply be patient.'

'And how soon before Deedas make their move? I've made myself a pretty safe bet as potential slave fodder.'

'Don't do anything to rush the process, Miss.'

'I keep thinking about Kashika. It's only because of me that she's there. What's happening to her?'

'What happens to all slave girls, Miss: confinement, degradation, punishment and forced sex. But she knew that, and I'm sure she would not want you to make a mistake now to save her a little discomfort. She's strong like all her sisters. She'll do what has to be done.'

It was almost a relief to return to Deedas for her next session and slip back into her role as a proto-submissive. At least she was sharing some of the experiences Kashika was facing and not sitting in a comfortable office. As she stood naked before Lister and Banks in the lab reception room it seemed they were studying her with more than their usual degree of thoughtfulness, which gave her a glimmer of hope. Were things moving forward? There were also some interesting new devices on the table in front of them . . .

'In your response to our questionnaire, Subject 77, you revealed that you had two or three lesbian experiences in the past,' Banks said. 'Is that correct?'

'Well . . . yeah, I did a few times, Doctor,' Vanessa admitted, struggling to appear slightly defensive while trying not to think of the array of sweet pussies and their owners she had delighted in knowing so intimately during the past few months.

'We're not being judgemental, 77,' Lister reassured her. 'You understand this is all simply in the cause of scientific enquiry?'

'Yes, Doctor.'

'Did you enjoy the experience, 77?' Banks asked bluntly.

'It was different, Doctor,' Vanessa admitted. 'The first time I did it as a sort of dare. More like fun, you know, a bit of a game. Not the same as doing it with a man. It felt weird putting my tongue up her slot while she did mine, but after a while I got used to it.'

'Was it emotionally and physically satisfying, 77?' Lister asked. 'Did you achieve orgasms?'

'Not the first time, but I did later, Doctor. It was good. It got to be a regular thing with one girl . . . but she moved away.'

'How would you feel about having sexual intercourse, under laboratory conditions of course, with another of our test subjects, 77?' Banks asked. 'Subject 63 is a young healthy female like yourself who is also helping us with our research. She was further along in our research programme than you, but as you have made such excellent progress you have caught up with her, so to speak. Like you she has had some slight lesbian experience. She's already consented to participate in the test. We'll take the usual readings as you couple, and then we shall investigate how your initial encounter affects your attitude to her in a series of interactions between you. Under the pressure of external stimulation we want to see what choices you will make and your willingness to sacrifice her comfort to preserve your own. Then she will be given the opportunity to respond to your actions in turn.'

Vanessa didn't try to unravel the implications of that convoluted explanation. She would do whatever they wanted. What most interested her was the news that she was catching other test subjects up. That was progress.

She took a deep breath. 'Well . . . I'll give it a go, Doctor.'

'Good. You will wear the data collar as before and

170

also these new devices. Come here and bend over the table . . .'

Obediently Vanessa rested her hands on the table and bent forward. They were getting her to move to them to save them rising and in effect making her bow before them.

Lister fitted the data collar as before. Then she said: 'For reasons you will understand later, 77, it is very important during the test that you see and speak only when we permit you. However as you may be experiencing high emotions we cannot expect you to close your eyes or refrain from speaking when we direct you, so we have made it simpler . . .'

Banks held up a pliant band of clear plastic shaped like a pair of wraparound sunglasses with a fastening strap at the back on which was mounted a small silver box. He slipped it over Vanessa's head and tightened the retaining strap.

'Electro-sensitive liquid crystal lenses that darken when an electric current is passed through them,' he explained, holding up a small remote control box and pressing a button.

It was as though the lights had been turned out. The glasses had gone completely black. As Vanessa reached for them they cleared again, leaving her blinking.

'And to keep you from speaking at an inappropriate moment you will wear this,' Lister said.

She held up what looked like part of a ponygirl bridle but with the band that went around the back of the neck and the two narrower straps passing from the cheek rings over the bridge of the nose and under the chin made of clear plastic. There was another silver box on the back of the neckband and where there should have been cheek rings there were solid metal discs a little smaller than face powder compacts. In place of a bit there were two bowed plastic-coated wire cables that connected to the cheek discs.

Lister fitted the device over Vanessa's head and buckled it tight. 'Open your mouth and put your tongue out,' she commanded. Vanessa did so and Lister slipped the slender bowed cables over and under Vanessa's tongue. She could feel them in her mouth but they did not interfere with her tongue or lips moving, only prevented her from closing her jaws completely.

Banks pressed another button on his control box. Pulled in by motors in the cheek plates the cables tightened, forcing Vanessa's jaws wider as they cut into the corners of her mouth and pinched her tongue between them. She made an indistinct gurgle but the power of coherent speech had been denied her.

Then the wires binding her tongue loosened once more.

'Does it work properly, 77?' Lister asked.

'Yes, Doctor.'

She had been talked into wearing a high-tech slave gag and blindfold set, all in the name of science.

Vanessa only saw the outside of the door of the SEXUAL INTERACTIVITY CHAMBER. Then her blindfold darkened and the wire gag immobilised her tongue once again.

'It's important you do not see the other subject before the test is ready to begin, 77,' Lister explained. 'Subject 63 will be fitted with the same devices as you are. We want to record your initial reactions to seeing each other simultaneously.'

'Throughout the test we will only refer to you by your numbers,' Banks said. 'There are times when you will both be free to speak but you must not use your own names in any circumstances. This way . . .'

They took her by the arms and led her into the new room. Warmth and the ubiquitous background music enveloped her and there was rubber matting under her feet. She was backed around and then made to take a step up. She felt a smooth surface under her feet that seemed to curve up on either side of her.

'Raise your arms wide,' Lister commanded. Vanessa obeyed and she felt thick padded cuffs fastened about her wrists. The lines the cuffs were attached to were quite slack and twisting her hands round she found her fingers brushing across wire cables. A broad belt was then buckled tightly about her waist, held in place by unseen tethers on either side. Her feet were dragged further apart and cuffs were buckled round her ankles. Then electric motors hummed. The slack was taken in on the cables connected to her wrists cuffs. Her arms were dragged upwards and she was lifted off her feet. Motors hummed again and the tension increased on her waist and legs until she hung like a starfish in mid air, shivering with anticipation.

And there they left her for several minutes, mute and blind. Shufflings, motor hums and terse instructions given to a 'Subject 63' suggested her companion had been brought in and was being put into the same sort of restraints as she was. Then the outer door was shut.

Banks' voice came over a speaker. 'Attention, subjects 77 and 63. The first phase of the test will begin now . . .'

Vanessa's blindfold became transparent. She was in a room dark except for ceiling-mounted lighting tracks that supported several small spotlights that illuminated Vanessa's own spreadeagled body and that of the woman who was facing her no more than a couple of metres distant.

Subject 63 was a pale-skinned urchin-cut blonde perhaps a year or two older than Vanessa. Her dark deep-set eyes stared out in wonder and apprehension at Vanessa through the clear strip of her own electro-blindfold. The straps of a tongue gag ran over her nose and under her chin while her lips were drawn back by the taut wires of the bit, so the pink tip of her imprisoned tongue showed between her white teeth. She had a nice body and well rounded medium-sized breasts with very large brown areolae with erect nipple crowns in their centres. A small dark trimmed 'V' of pubic hair pointed down to a deep cleft from out of which protruded the crinkled tongue of her inner lips. Her body was decorated with red sticky labels in the same places as Vanessa, but displaying the number 63. A black data collar encircled her neck.

Like Vanessa, 63 was suspended spreadeagled inside a sturdy ring-shaped frame. Vanessa saw now that their cuffs were secured to wire cables that ran through power-driven windlasses bolted to the insides of the frames. The rings were mounted on black rectangular base blocks fitted with wheels that engaged with a few metres of twin rails on which they both ran.

Their unseen observers gave Vanessa and 63 a minute to get used to the sight of each other. 63's eyes roamed over Vanessa's body with hesitant, almost shameful fascination. As she did so her areolae seemed to grow a little larger and the tongue of her sex began to glisten. The possibility that 63 might be a plant to test her faded from Vanessa's thoughts as she saw her squirm in her bonds. Was she wondering what she had got herself into? Too late to back out now . . .

Motors in the base units hummed and the two frames with their helpless captives slowly moved closer together.

Vanessa saw 63's breasts trembling and her eyes widening. She could sense the heat of her body and a nice perfume.

'You will kiss,' Lister's voice commanded.

Their gags loosened, freeing their tongues.

Their nipples brushed. Vanessa felt the rougher texture of 63's wide expanse of areolae. Their breasts flattened into soft pliant fleshy cushions, rising up between them. Their bellies touched, then their pubic mounds. 63 was looking like a rabbit caught in the headlights.

Vanessa took the initiative. 'Just enjoy it,' she said

quietly as she ducked her head forward and kissed 63 on the lips.

For a moment 63 seemed frozen. Then she kissed back with sudden passion. Their tongues met. Vanessa touched the gag wires in 63's mouth. She tasted nice.

'You will make love,' Banks' voice boomed out. 'You will not be released until you have both climaxed.'

With a soft hum of electric motors both the ring frames began to move in a slow almost lazy rolling motion. They must have been running on rollers inside their bases. Both moved in synchrony but in opposite directions. Suspended within the frames Vanessa and 63's bodies were twisted across each other, pivoting about the centre of rotation, which was a point a little above their navels. Their lips were sheared apart and their breasts bumped, rippled and ground over each other, hard nipples dragging through soft pillows of hot flesh.

Vanessa's respect for the ingenuity of the Deedas designers went up another notch. They could use a set of these down in B3.

Each ring turned through ninety degrees. Vanessa's face was swung in an arc out across empty air until it passed over 63's hip and spread thigh until it halted opposite her smooth pale pouting cleft and its dark shaven 'V' crown. She was now hung sideways within the ring as was 63 who had been turned in the opposite direction and whose face now brushed her pubes.

The heady scent of 63's excitement filled Vanessa's nostrils. She dipped her head forward between 63's thighs and kissed and lapped the pretty sex mouth. She felt the other girl shiver. Then 63's lips kissed Vanessa's lovemouth and her darting tongue flicked over her hard clitoris.

The motors hummed and the rotation of the frames went into reverse. Vanessa groaned as her tongue was torn away from its sensuous delving. With their sweat-

175

slippery bellies sliding across each other they were carried back upright, bringing their faces back together and then halting.

63's cheeks were flushed and her eyes were sparkling. 'You taste lovely,' she said huskily.

They kissed, sharing the taste of each other's sex.

Then the frames started up again, carrying each of them in the opposite direction to their first quarter turn. Vanessa's face passed over 63's other flank until it was positioned opposite her vulva once more and she eagerly resumed her tonguing and lapping.

And that was how they coupled, being turned first one way and then the other as though on some sexual lathe, growing excited by the rubbing, bobbling motion of sweaty breasts being ground across each other and then the wet scented promise of their gaping sexes. They were total prisoners of the machines to which they were bound, timing their actions to their motions, being spied upon by an unknown number of cameras and human eyes and yet not caring.

They strained at their bonds as they came in each other's faces: not to escape, but to press closer and try to wrap their arms about each other and bury their faces a little deeper into their pulsing, dribbling sexes.

They were only given a few minutes to rest, with the taste of each other's juices filling their mouths. Then their blindfolds darkened and their tongue gags tightened. With a hum of motors their sweaty bodies were pulled apart as the frames rotated upright once more and were separated, rolling backwards on their tracks.

As she hung spreadeagled in her cuffs Vanessa heard complicated motor sounds and whirs of gears from 63's frame accompanied by muffled squeaks of alarm. Then Vanessa's frame started up. Something clicked and whirred and she felt a bullet-nosed object pressing into her anus. Her anal ring was forced open and a ribbed shaft flowed up into her. Another whir and click and some plug-like object was rammed up into her vagina and latched into place, squeezing inside her against the pressure of the thing up her rear.

Vanessa wriggled as far as her bonds allowed and felt a sluggish dragging resistance from the things plugged into her, as though they were connected to some soft of pivoting support. What the hell were they planning next?

'Attention subjects 77 and 63,' Banks said over the speakers. 'Phase two begins now . . .'

Vanessa's blindfold became transparent and her gag wires loosened. In front of her Subject 63 was half bent over with her pale backside jutting out towards Vanessa. The peach of her sex peeped from between her nervously clenching thighs. Her face showed over her shoulder wide-eyed and fearful. Her frame had been turned round and her cuff cables slackened off enough for her to stand on the base of her frame. An arm now extended up from the frame base between her legs and angled towards her lower stomach. Vanessa could not see what was on the end of it but it must have been something firm enough to keep 63 hunched over. With her arms, legs and waist still loosely bound this meant she had been forced into this humiliating posture appearing to offer her bottom to Vanessa.

And now Vanessa looked down at herself. A black dildo studded with electrode contacts jutted out from her pussy. It was connected to the plug up her rear and both were mounted on a pivoting telescopic arm that rose up from the base unit between her feet.

'Subject 77, you will use your phallus to penetrate Subject 63 by whichever orifice you chose,' Banks said over the speakers. 'This penetration will be accompanied by a series of shocks to her body delivered though the phallus.' 63's eyes grew wider in alarm. 'They will be mild at first but will grow stronger every minute. They will only cease when you have achieved an orgasm. Remember we are monitoring your bodily functions and you cannot fake this.'

The cuff cables slackened off, allowing Vanessa's feet to touch the ground. The arm supporting her groinal attachments compressed and moved with her. It allowed her a little freedom to position herself but she was still bound to the frame, which began to move slowly forward. Vanessa saw 63 shaking her head and chewing on the cable that bound her tongue. She looked genuinely alarmed.

Vanessa's thoughts raced. Was she really being tested to see how dedicated she was to Deedas and its strange experiments? Was this genuine or had they found out about her already? No, she had to assume it was what it seemed. But she did not want to hurt 63 to further her plans. If she had been a Shiller girl she would not have hesitated, but 63 was clearly a beginner and maybe no true pain slut at all. What would Josie do?

'Doctor,' she said anxiously, 'she looks unhappy . . . I don't want to hurt her.'

'You have both agreed to be test subjects to further scientific understanding, 77,' Banks said. '63 has passed every test you have and is more willing than she appears. Fortunately you do not have to feel any guilt over the matter as you have no choice . . .'

Vanessa gasped as the plug in her rear delivered an electric shock that seemed to zip right up her spine and burst in her brain.

'Now continue with the test, 77,' Banks said.

Vanessa blinked back her tears. She could fight this but Josie would not be so strong. 'Sorry,' she said to 63. 'I have to do this or they'll fry my arsehole. Just try to enjoy it. I'll be as quick as I can.'

63 nodded, looking even more alarmed as the bobbing phallus jutting out of Vanessa's groin got ever closer to her bottom. She was really quite pretty, Vanessa thought. If only she could enjoy having her.

'Tell her what you're going to do to her,' Banks commanded. 'Make her please you. The more aroused you are the sooner the test will be over and the less pain she will suffer.'

Had their scientific masters planned it this way all along? Still it made sense. It also made both her and 63 compliant in this little bit of sadism. Very clever.

Vanessa looked 63 in the eye and saw her give a tiny nod. 'I'm going to stuff this rubber dick up your pussy and you're going to like it, bitch. Legs apart! Wider! Let me see that snatch hot and ready.'

63 spread her legs and pushed her bottom out a little more, exposing the cleft pouch of her sex. Vanessa angled her hips and slipped the head of the phallus up inside her.

Their bodies were ground together. 63's bottom rubbed up against Vanessa's hips and thighs while her breasts flattened against 63's smooth back. 63 gave a little gasp and jerked as the dildo shocked her. Vanessa had to be brutal to get this over with quickly.

'Come on, bitch, work with me!' she commanded, thrusting with her hips and driving the dildo between 63's pussy lips to the hilt. 'Bump and grind! I want to feel this going all the way up you!'

63 whimpered with the thud of the phallus filling her passage and then flinched as its electrodes shocked her again. Sobbing she began to rotate her hips and work them to and fro. Vanessa leaned over the bow of her back, feeling the film of sweat on 63's buttocks, wishing she could hug her properly. She saw the padded bar on the end of the arm rising up from the base of 63's frame. It was dug into the pit of her stomach pushing her hips backwards and bracing her against Vanessa's thrusts. But there was also a second lighter sprung arm that rose up from the head of the first. Its curved crossbar was pressed into the undersides of 63's breasts, cupping them together. And the inside of the curve was lined with stubby spikes.

Every time Vanessa thrust into 63 she ground her onto the spiked bar, lifting her firm rounded breasts, mounding and pushing them together to form an amazing cleavage, rolling up her big nipples. 63 was snivelling in pain and her eyes were sparking with tears. She was suffering a double torment from stuffed and shocked vagina to pricked breasts. Vanessa was part of her suffering. It was both cruel and desperately exciting and she felt the liquid tension building in her loins.

Thrusting faster and harder she bent and kissed 63's cheek and whispered in her ear: 'When it's your turn you screw me as hard as you like and enjoy yourself. I'll be fine.'

Then she came.

The frames pulled their limp sticky bodies apart, dragging Vanessa's dildo out of 63's vagina, which clung and dripped helplessly, as did Vanessa's. Then the gags and blindfolds were activated.

Vanessa felt herself turned around. The plugs withdrew from her passages and were replaced by the pressure of a padded bar against the front of her hips. As she bent over and pushed her bottom out the second curving arm rose up and jabbed into the undersides of her breasts, making her gasp.

The blindfold cleared. She twisted her head round to see 63 now had an electric dildo plugged into her as she had. 63's face was wide with wonder as she looked down at herself and then at Vanessa. Her gag was relaxed, freeing her tongue, and she licked her lips.

The frame started its slow advance.

'Tell her what you're going to do to her!' Banks' voice demanded.

Did they expect her to want to take revenge for the pain she had inflicted? Was that what this was about?

'I'm going to screw her like she screwed me,' 63 said. 'But I'm going to put it up her bottom!'

Good girl, Vanessa thought.

The phallus hurt being rammed into her anus and it shocked her rectum from the inside, making it clench and spasm. With every thrust 63 made, the spiked bar jabbed the undersides of her breasts as it cruelly mounded and mashed them together. Tears streamed down Vanessa's cheeks and she snivelled and sobbed, biting on the wires that imprisoned her tongue.

She orgasmed a few seconds sooner than 63.

63 lay panting across Vanessa's back, her hips still pressed hard into her bottom so that her juices crossed the rubber shaft embedded deep in Vanessa's rectum and ran down into her cleft. Banks spoke again, but now his tone was congratulatory.

'That was very satisfactory, Subjects 77 and 63. You both behaved well within our projected parameters. We have gathered a lot of very useful information. Well done.'

And suddenly, seen through their blissful post-orgasmic haze, it did feel well done. All the pain and calculated cruelty was forgotten. The laboratory was such an exciting place to be. Vanessa twisted round and saw the shy smile on 63's face and knew they had both taken part in something wonderful and important.

After they were released from their frames they were separately allowed to use the lab's small shower and washroom to clean up. The glow of satisfaction still lingered and Vanessa had to remind herself that it had all been a sham.

Back in the lab reception Lister and Banks questioned them about their responses to the experiment. Still naked, Subject 63 and Vanessa stood before them on the other side of the yellow line with their hands meekly clasped behind their backs. 63 gave Vanessa a few shy sidelong glances but evidently she accepted it as part of the routine. How long had it taken Deedas to manipulate the attitude of a woman who was presumably at the most only mildly into BDSM into this state, Vanessa wondered? Perhaps being part of this pseudo-scientific process filled a gap in her life. It was an erotic adventure that pushed the boundaries of what was acceptable and yet it was also controlled. Maybe that was part of its appeal.

'So how would you sum up your feelings, 77?' Lister asked at length.

'Well, it was pretty pervy, Doctor,' Vanessa said, choosing her words with care. 'I mean those machines were pretty freaky things. Left my tits pretty sore. But once I knew 63 was OK with it I enjoyed it in the end. At least I came a few times.'

'The readings from your data collars confirm that,' Banks said. 'Both of you experience intense orgasms and prolonged states of positive emotion. This response to a situation involving strong elements of restraint and sexual threat is most interesting.' He looked at them thoughtfully. 'Would both of you like to take part in a special experiment this weekend?'

Back in the office that evening Vanessa explained the offer to Angela and Sandra.

'It's a full-day test this Saturday running from ten until six. I'm not sure what it means exactly but it's progress. Anyway I'll give it a go.' She grinned. 'For doing so I also get a double bonus entry into the holiday competition. A few more sessions of pervy machine sex bondage and I'm a shoe-in to win.'

Sandra looked concerned. 'They've never asked you to stay that long before. Is it safe?'

Vanessa shrugged. 'What's safe? This won't work if I stay safe, you know that. But I don't think they take people straight from Deedas. If what Cindy told us is right they've still got more work to do on them so they break up with family and friends first. Anyway I can't back down now. And I'm all kitted out.' She looked at Angela. 'You know what to do if I don't come back.'

'Yes, Miss. On that matter I'm pleased to report that every Beta team is in place. We're ready, Miss.'

'Now it's up to Rochester,' Vanessa said.

Twelve

Vanessa stood on the end of a line of five other naked Deedas test subjects, their arms folded neatly behind their backs, as they stood in a slightly shivery Saturday morning parade before Lister and Banks. Vanessa thought they looked a little like a group of trainee Shiller chain girls. Subject 63 and another dark-haired girl were more than averagely attractive but all at the very least had nice faces and reasonable figures. Deedas obviously took care selecting their potential recruits. Despite the circumstances she felt at home amongst them.

From the curious glances they exchanged Vanessa judged this was the first time they had been assembled in a group this large before. Perhaps like her they had only been involved in paired experiments so far. And yet they had given up half their weekend to be herded together with other naked strangers for some perverse piece of pseudo-sex research. Hadn't they anything more interesting or exciting to do? In truth, she had to concede, probably not . . .

Vanessa did not even know their Deedas numbers, apart from Subject 63 who had flashed her a quick smile as she came in, because they had not been applied yet. They had not even been permitted to talk to each other.

As each had entered Lister had commanded: 'Strip off, clothes on the pegs and stand by the wall. Please do not talk to any of the other subjects. It is important that the experiment starts from a neutral and unbiased state.'

Only when they had all arrived were they permitted to assemble in front of the yellow line facing Lister and

Banks as they sat behind their desk. Vanessa's eyes flickered over the new array of items laid out on it with interest.

'This will be the longest experiment any of you will have been involved in so far,' Banks told them. 'It will challenge both your physical and mental endurance and adaptability in unusual circumstances. Its purpose is to examine female reactions when deprived of the normal human means of interaction, such as speech and physical manipulation of your surroundings. We will see how quickly you adapt to being reduced to a more animalistic level of existence and, through a series of exercises, how you respond to each other as a group and to those in charge of your surroundings and well-being. You may find parts of it playful and amusing and others challenging but it is important that you treat the test as a whole seriously. When it is over we shall interview you to get your reactions, so make a careful note of them at each stage both good or bad.'

Smart, Vanessa thought. It made them feel involved and important while not promising they were going to enjoy themselves. She flicked a glance along the line. The other girls' faces were intent. They believed it.

Banks continued. 'I will not tell you any more now because we want you to respond naturally as far as your abilities and circumstances allow. These props should help you do this . . .'

He turned to the desk and took from a pile of similar objects a broad thick brown leather buckle-on dog collar of the sort any good pet shop could provide.

'As we anticipate a lot of extended and uncontrolled physical interaction your normal data collars will not be robust enough. So we have built the sensors and transmitter units into these regular animal collars . . .' He opened it wide to reveal tiny silver contacts lining the inside. 'For the same reason you will not wear your usual number stickers. Instead as you will see each

collar has a number on it for identification purposes.'
He pointed to the bold silver SUBJECT 35 repeated along
the length of the collar.

*So we'll be wearing real dog collars with no names on
them, only numbers*, Vanessa thought wryly. She glanced
along the line of girls again. *Has anybody else twigged
what that would make us?* She saw erect nipples and
expressions of wonder and fascination but nobody was
saying: Won't that be like wearing slave collars? That
was because they had been brought to this stage by
degrees. Their ID numbers had been innocent plastic
stick-ons and the collars had been data gathering devices.
Only when they were put together did they become
something else, but by then the subjects had got used to
them and didn't notice. Again it was all very clever.

'To limit your ability to interact with each other and
your surroundings you will also be fitted with these,'
Banks said. He held up a pair of thumbless black
mittens with rubber palms and fabric backs, and a thick
black ankle sock of the same combination of material.
'As you will find, the socks will reduce your mobility
and alter your posture. To limit your vocal range you
will wear these medical tongue sleeves . . .' He showed
them a strap loop connected to a complex piece of pink
moulded plastic. 'Come forward when we call your
number . . . Subject 35 . . .'

One by one they stepped up to the deck and had their
new collars, mittens and tongue gags fitted. As they did
so Vanessa was able to match a body with a number for
the four other girls she had not met before.

Subject 35 was a compact busty brunette with curly
hair, standout nipples and a fine thick pubic bush. 42
was a pale-skinned redhead with a ponytail, freckles on
her chest, very red nipples and a close-trimmed ginger
bush. 49 looked as though she might have some Latin
blood, with an olive skin, thick dark hair, perky brown
nipples rising from well-rounded breasts and close dark

186

pubic curls. 54 was a slim pale girl with brown hair tied in bunches, small conical breasts capped by pink nipples and neat hairless pubes. In all they made an appealing collection of girlflesh.

Vanessa thought the real dog collars were a little more comfortable than their old data collars, but it might have been the feel of leather. The mittens encased their whole hands, reducing them effectively to the manipulative capabilities of paws. The tongue sleeves were short ovoid tubes of semi-pliant plastic with curving side arms. The tubes slipped over their tongues, leaving the tips peeping through, and the side arms curved out of the corners of their mouths and returned over their cheeks where they fastened to the straps that went round the back of their necks. They did not totally immobilise the tongue but they made it virtually impossible to shape coherent words. And with the mittens on it was impossible to work the fastenings that held them in place.

The girls were trying to speak and giggling at the slurred animal sounds they made. *We've been muted and nobody is making any fuss because it's all in the name of science and we're all doing it together so it's a bit of a laugh*, Vanessa thought.

'Form a line, sit down, roll onto your backs, raise your legs straight into the air and clasp the backs of your knees,' Banks commanded.

They did so, raising a row of shapely legs into the air, clasping their knees tight with their mitten-sheathed hands and innocently displaying the pouting clefts of their pubes and anal puckers between their thighs. Lister and Banks went along the line fitting the thick socks onto their feet. Again the fastenings were too delicate to be opened with their now 'pawed' hands.

When they were done Banks said: 'Try to stand . . .'

A series of surprised yelps and whimpers issued forth as the girls tried to put their feet flat to the ground.

'There are short pins buried in the bottom layer of the soles,' Banks informed them. 'Putting weight on them makes them protrude through the sponge insoles. Go onto your hands and knees like animals and press only your toes to the ground. They have no pins in . . . that's right, practise moving about like that . . .'

It was possible to shuffle about on their hands and knees quite well as long as they did not attempt to rise. The pads on their hands helped. The lab floor filled with rolling bottoms, peeking fleshy oysters and freely hanging, jiggling and swaying breasts as they scrabbled about.

We've been turned into real bitches, Vanessa thought as she watched them with a helpless shiver of pleasure. *I'm entitled to get a kick out of this but you lot shouldn't.* She looked at their shiny excited innocent faces. *You think this is all a laugh. What have they done to you? Can't you tell it's a trap?*

There was one final crowning touch yet to come.

Tom and another white-coated young man with sandy hair, whom Vanessa had not seen before, entered the room. They were each carrying a bundle of dog leads. From their belts hung slender spanking paddles.

'For the duration of this test Tom and Mark will be your keepers and trainers,' Banks said. 'You will be totally dependent on them for your sustenance, punishment and reward, so you had better obey their instructions. You will be closely observed at all times, of course, but we shall try to keep it unobtrusive. Now line up again . . .' Obediently they did so, forming a pretty row of bare bottoms and regimented breasts. 'The test will begin when your leads are fitted . . .'

Tom and Mark took three girls each and began clipping the leads to their collar rings.

As the leash clip snapped about her collar ring Vanessa felt the warm tingle in her loins of a true submissive. She was where she belonged and she relished the dark thrill of it. Then she glimpsed the shadows of doubt cross the other girls' faces as they dimly realised what was being done to them. Was it a game or an experiment or something absurd and dangerous? Then she thought she felt the ubiquitous background music shift slightly.

The mood lightened. Everything was fine. The girls grinned, buoyed up by a sudden sense of anticipation and excitement. Any doubt was smothered and the urge to resist or question melted away. They were an animal pack subservient to their masters.

Tom and Mark tugged on their leads and the girls shuffled off along the corridor after them like dogs being taken for a walk. They had accepted another degree of humiliation disguised as science. Step by step they were being broken in to servitude and submission and they did not even realise it.

At the end of the corridor they came to a door marked EXERCISE AND ASSESSMENT YARD.

Beyond was an open chamber about the size of a tennis court, lit by ranks of fluorescent lights, that must have been the old factory space of the building. Above was the bare frame of the roof. The studwork partitions of the labs and offices formed an uneven wall down one side.

The middle of the open floor was laid out with a patchwork of old carpeting across which were traffic cones set out in rows and circles. Beside them were baskets of balls of different sizes, stacks of hoops and rails and other less identifiable items. In one corner was what appeared to be a raised sandpit. Along the walls were a row of wire mesh cages and several odd devices Vanessa could not make out. High up amongst the beams hung cameras and speakers, through which came the steady background wash of Deedas background music.

Tom and Mark did not give them time to think. Unclipping their leashes Tom said: 'Into line, you pretty bitches . . . quickly, quickly . . .'

His tone was playful and the girls accepted it as such. They formed a line between two cones. Vanessa felt the heat of their bodies on her flanks.

Mark went along the line at the rear. 'Come on, you can do better than that,' he said, flicking their rumps with his paddle. They were only light swipes and though they made the girls yelp and flinch in surprise they were not really threatening. The kiss of rubber across her own cheeks made Vanessa shudder with familiar delight. But for the others this might be their first taste of corporal punishment. She guessed there would be a lot more soon enough. Meanwhile she shuffled into a tighter line with the others like an obedient pack girl.

Tom pulled out a handful of small candies from his pocket. 'There's a treat for each of you bitches if you bring me back a ball. But you've got to do it properly. You drop it into my hand and then you sit up and beg properly with your tongues hanging out.' Mark scooped up half a dozen coloured balls from a basket. 'Ready, steady . . . fetch!'

Mark flung the balls into the far side of the yard and the girls shuffled off after them, going up onto their palms and toes and lifting their bottoms into the air to move faster, showing off their bum cracks and pussy clefts as they went. Vanessa scrambled away with them, her breasts jiggling and bouncing under her. It was just an innocent game you saw played in the park between dog and owner. It got them warmed up and was only deeply degrading if you thought about it. But then the whole thing was only some freaky Deedas science experiment and it was all right to feel humiliated so they could enjoy it and might even win a Caribbean holiday . . .

Of course being unable to use their hands they had to pick up the balls with their teeth, just like dogs. They bounded back to Tom with their prizes. One by one they dropped the balls into his hand and then sat back on their haunches with their curbed tongues hanging out.

190

Without being told they lifted their crooked arms up under their breasts with their paws hanging limp. Vanessa felt her stomach flip-flopping and pussy wetting as she rolled her eyes upward plaintively to her master. Her previous cynicism seemed rather mean now that she was getting used to the game. How wonderful it was simply to surrender and let herself be used like this.

Tom patted their heads and popped a candy into their mouths that they chewed on and swallowed awkwardly. Mark threw the balls again and again they bounded away after them, bottoms bobbing and weaving about, already lost in the perverse thrill of it all.

After the third round of this game Tom called them into line. They looked up at him, faces flushed and shiny, chests heaving, nipples hard and eyes bright.

'Right, you've shown you can fetch, but can you walk to heel?' he asked.

They nodded their heads and made eager throaty whines of affirmation.

Mark and Tom took it in turns to walk them round a course marked out with cones. They had to pad along perfectly to heel. When their master stopped they had to, sitting back on their haunches in an alert crouch, gazing up at him expectantly, waiting for his next move. If he made a turn she had to follow exactly. When they had completed a round successfully he patted them on their heads and said: 'Good girl,' and gave them another candy.

Vanessa felt the deep joy of simple obedience filling her as she scrambled along at Mark's heels, trying to keep in step, gazing up at him for any sign as to which way he was going to turn next. When he finally patted her head and smiled down at her in approval she shivered in delight.

'Good girl, well done.'

That's what she wanted to be more than anything: a good pet who pleased her master.

The men set out an obstacle course of cones and gates made out of stands set out over rubber mats with crossbars set high or low that they either had to jump or crawl under. The girls helped build the course, at the direction of their masters, taking hold of the mats with their teeth and dragging them across the floor. Vanessa had hold of the same mat as 63 who grinned at her as they tugged together, making small snarly dog noises of effort.

When it was ready they were sent round the course one at a time racing against the clock. The signal to start was a buzzer just like the one in the endurance chamber that signalled the floor was about to become electrified. They all sprang forward with little gasps of alarm at the sound of that and scampered at high speed, weaving round the cone lanes.

It was possible to take small jumps by diving over paws first and rolling on landing, as long as they did not mind a little pain on takeoff as their pin socks stabbed their feet. But the brief pain was worth it because they so wanted to please their masters and be the fastest. The crossbars they had to crawl under were no relief either because door mats with coarse scouring plastic bristles had been laid out under the bars. These scraped at their breasts and bellies. Nipples suffered especially, made worse by now being in a perpetual state of erection.

Vanessa's enlarged breasts were scraped almost raw but she did not mind. The suffering was all part of the game. This was the right place for it.

When they had all run the course candies were handed out again and heads were patted. They knelt before their masters, flushed and sweaty with red-streaked breasts and stomachs but feeling exhilarated by their achievement.

'You look like a thirsty pack of pretty bitches,' Tom said. 'Do you want a drink of nice cool water?'

They nodded and lolled their tongues.

192

'Well, you'll have to work to get it. This way . . .'

He led them over to one of the devices set beside the wall. It comprised two posts mounted on a flat platform with a rubber mat between them. On top of one post was a large inverted water cooler bottle. Angled upward out of the post below it and pointing across the mat was a phallus set at dog-girl head height. At the same height on the other post was a second phallus, also angled inward but perfectly horizontal.

'This works like an old-fashioned hand pump,' Tom explained. 'You, 42, plug your pussy onto that dildo and pump it while you suck the other one under the cooler bottle.'

With a blush 42 obeyed, crouching on her toes and palms on the mat between the two posts. She backed carefully onto the phallus, parting her pale cleft and ginger pubic curls. Her eyes rolled up as it slid inside her. Then she closed her mouth about the head of the other phallus. Flexing her knees she tried to pump up and down, but the phallus hardly moved and Vanessa saw her grimace.

'Try harder, 42,' Tom said, giving her rump a flick with his paddle.

With a grunt she tried again. There was obviously resistance built into the pump lever. Slowly it sank down and then up again, the shaft gouging and stretching her red-lipped slot. Bubbles rose in the cooler bottle and she gulped down a mouthful of water gratefully.

One at a time they all strained thighs and churned pussies to slake their thirst, adding a slippery sheen to the phallic pump handle with their accumulated juices. Vanessa thought that a drink from a water cooler had never been more arousing.

When they were done they were lined up again for the next test.

'All bitches need to be able to dig,' Tom said. He pointed to the sandpit in the corner. 'In there we've buried five rubber bones and you've got to dig them out and bring them back to me. The girl who doesn't gets a whacking. Ready . . . steady . . . go!'

They scrambled across the floor to the sandpit in a wild jostle of bare bottoms. It was about two metres square with raised plank sides and filled nearly to the brim with beach sand. The girls shouldered each other aside as they dived into it, scrabbling with their paws like dogs and sending sand flying out from between their back legs.

One by one they unearthed the coloured rubber bones, picked them up with their teeth and shuffled back to Tom with heads high looking triumphant. Vanessa finally found her bone and snatched it up, only to realise she and Subject 63 were the last in the pit. 63's hair was covered in sand and her face was a picture of desperation and distress. With her bone clamped between her teeth Vanessa started across the pit after the others but instead barged into 63, sending them both sprawling. As she fell she dropped her bone almost into 63's lap. 63 froze for a moment, her eyes locking with Vanessa's, and then she snatched it up and scuttled off.

With head hung low as though in fear Vanessa padded back to receive her punishment.

Tom took her by the hair and swung his leg over her back so he stood astride her as she knelt under him. He pulled her head up so the others could all see her face.

'This is what happens to girls who don't try hard enough,' he warned them.

Mark had taken up position behind Vanessa. Using his paddle he gave her a dozen crisp strokes across the backside. The crack of rubber on flesh rang out in the chamber. The tongue curb did a little to mute Vanessa's yelps of pain as her eyes filled with tears. Yet despite this she could not help pushing her haunches back against the blows, opening her legs a little wider so some fell on the plump swell of her pussy.

The other girls watched in fascinated horror, unable to tear their eyes away.

When Mark was done he said: 'Come here and see the blush on her.'

Nervously the girls shuffled over and peered at Vanessa's glowing bottom.

'Kiss her bum,' Mark said. 'Both cheeks. Taste how hot and sore she is.'

One by one they kissed her bottom. 63 delivered a lingering and distinctly deeper kiss.

'That's what you'll get if you don't do as you're told,' Tom warned, letting go of Vanessa's hair and stepping off her. 'Now I expect you're feeling the need to pee or poo after all that exercise. We'll show you how bitches do it.'

They shuffled after him as he led the way to an odd construction in a corner of the yard.

A shallow wooden ramp led up to a platform that had been built around the lower edge of the rim of a toilet bowl. An extension had been attached to the regular flush handle on the cistern.

'This is where you do your business,' Tom said. 'You kneel over it nice and wide. When you're done you stay there and pull the handle. It squirts water jets up from the rim and washes your pussy slots and bumholes clean, then it flushes and blows hot air to dry your pubes off. No need for paper. Who needs to go first?'

The girls shrunk back in embarrassment. They were coming to terms with their nudity and restraints but this was a whole new level of shame. To relieve themselves on a virtual podium in a barn of a building before a pair of men was too much.

'Come on, show us how you make pee fountains,' Tom said.

Mark slapped his paddle against his calf. 'You know what happens to bad girls . . .'

Vanessa shuffled up the ramp, turned round, knelt astride the bowl and peed gratefully. When she was done she pushed the handle down with her paw. The cleaning jet bubbled and foamed in her pussy. As the water flushed the bowl a blast of warm air dried her pubes off. It was actually quite pleasant.

When she clambered down 63 took her place, clenching her teeth bravely as she showed their masters how well the pee jetted from her cleft. Blushing and hanging their heads, the rest followed their leads. They were deeply embarrassed but did not resist, simply swallowed their pride and submitted to the inevitable. Though they did not realise it, this was the sort of exposure slave girls had to get used to.

Later that day when Vanessa used the toilet again she realised there was a speaker right above it. She was sure it had something to do with the little thrill she felt over and above what was natural each time she squatted down so publicly.

They were fed at a communal trough. Literally a metal trough that pigs might feed at. From a bucket Tom and Mark tipped a mass of dumpling-sized balls of food into it. They looked and smelled like a normal meat and three-vegetable meal chopped fine and pressed into bite-sized portions.

'Heads down, bottoms up and eat,' their masters commanded.

By now the morning's exertions had left them too hungry to waste time feeling humiliated at being made to eat like animals and they obeyed. It took some practice to nibble up the food balls cleanly and their tongue curbs made chewing and swallowing awkward but they persevered. While they were ringed about the trough Tom and Mark walked round them admiring the view and making intimate comments about the fullness of bottoms, the prominence and hairiness of pubic mounds and the tightness of anal mouths.

Vanessa saw blushes rise on several cheeks but they kept eating. They were beginning to learn they had no use for shame.

After lunch they played a new game.

'This is called pin the tail on the dog-girl,' Tom said with a grin. 'I'll show you how it's played in a moment, but first you'll need some of this up you.' He held up a tube of lubricating jelly. 'Heads to the ground and bottoms up . . .'

They bent over and presented their rears. He went along the line and they let him slide a finger loaded with the jelly up inside their tightest of passages. The familiar squishy sensation seeping inside her felt reassuring to Vanessa. A Shiller girl always had a clean and greased bottom.

Anuses glistening they rolled back onto their hands and knees.

'You'll each have one of these stuffed up your pussies,' Tom continued, holding up a pliant clear vinyl plastic tube closed at the top end. What looked like a mass of hair was packed tightly inside it with its root protruding from the open end of the tube. On this was fitted a rubber anal plug with a tapering point that flared to a wide base. Tom pulled it out of the sheath and it expanded into a curving dog-like tail bobbing about on its spring core.

'The idea is that you have to plug a tail up the bum of one of your pack sisters without getting one stuffed up yours,' Tom said, pushing the tail back into the sheath. 'The last girl with a tail-free bum wins. No holds barred. As an incentive all the rest will get six strokes of the paddle . . . across their tits, which will sting! And a dozen for the girl who still has a tail up her pussy when it ends. Right, on your backs and legs wide . . .'

As they lay back and exposed themselves Tom and Mark went along the line plugging in the tail sheaths, leaving the plug ends jutting stiffly out of their clefts. The girls squirmed and gasped a few times as their front passages were filled with the peculiar devices. The packed sheath felt strange inside Vanessa, but then she was used to odd things being lodged intimately inside her and assumed the other girls had become accustomed to something similar after the experiments they must have undergone to come this far. Such acceptance was essential in a slavegirl, of course.

When they were all fitted they rolled back onto their knees. The long plugs stuck out between their legs like slender penises. They eyed each other calculatingly, wondering who would be easiest to penetrate with a tail. Slim Subject 54, the lightest of the group, looked at the rest nervously and began to shuffle away. Suddenly the air was full of tension.

'Get ready . . . go!' Tom said.

35 and 42 both made a lunge at 54 who went up on her toes and scampered off with her tight pale bottom twinkling. Meanwhile 49 and 63 were rolling on the ground with breasts mashed together and thighs locked, each trying to get behind the other.

Vanessa ran off after 35 and 42. They had cornered 54 behind the sandpit and both had grabbed her. As she struggled they each tried to pull her round to present her rear to them, gasping and grunting with effort while 54 whimpered and squirmed between them. Unable to get a hand grip they were trying to lock their arms about her while batting at each other with their padded paws. Their earlier playfulness had vanished, so easily had they accepted the rules of their masters' game.

Finally 42 managed to push aside 35 who fell over backwards into the sandpit. Forcing 54 down on her face she mounted her from the rear, using her knees to spread her legs. 54 squeaked as 42's thrusts of the pointed plug found her anal mouth and rammed the device up into her rectum. Triumphantly 42 pulled back. The tail slithered out of her sheath and sprang up proudly from the cleft of 54's trembling bottom.

But 42 had forgotten about 35. Recovering from her tumble she scrambled back and grabbed 42 from behind, locking her arms about her and thrusting wildly with her hips at 42's pale freckled bottom. 42 bucked and grunted angrily as they rolled over and over, but she could not get free. Suddenly her eyes went wide as 35 found her target and the plug sank home.

But 35 did not pull the tail free of its sheath. Caught up in the delight of riding 42's body she continued to thrust with her hips, working the sprung tail in and out of her vaginal sheath and 42's anus in a sudden frenzy of arousal. 42 collapsed under her.

Vanessa crept up on the copulating pair, grasped 35's bobbing hips and rammed her tail plug into her bottom hole. But like 35 she could not simply pull out. This was too much fun. She added her thrusts to those of 35, ramming both of them into 42 who was gasping and moaning under them.

Paw-sheathed hands suddenly slipped round Vanessa's waist and jerked her off 35. It was 54 snatching her chance. As Vanessa's bottom lifted, the tip of a tail plug stabbed her anus, forcing her ring open. Before she could throw 54 off the tail was planted inside her and sprang free, bobbing merrily.

The four of them tumbled apart, sprawling panting and sweaty on the carpet, a little surprised by the intensity of their struggles. Tails wagged over all their bottoms and empty plastic sheathes hung out of their glistening sex mouths.

Vanessa look round to see how 63 and 49 were doing and saw 49 face down on the ground with a tail jutting out from her bum while Tom had hold of 63 by the hair as she knelt at his feet. 'The winner!' he declared.

* * *

With 63 kneeling on one side to watch, the rest of them sat back on their heels in a line with their arms folded behind their backs and their chests thrust out to receive their punishment. They still had their tails plugged in which curved up from between their buttocks. The mouths of their empty tail sheaths protruded from their vulvas, except for unlucky 49 who still had her plug showing.

She flinched and whimpered as she received her losing dozen across her smooth olive cones, which bounced, wobbled and shivered elastically as Mark swiped his paddle across them from above, left and right and with an upswing from below. Yet despite this she did not turn aside and her brown nipples were standing out stiffly by the time the last blow had fallen.

Tom took care of the rest of them, delivering the six each with practised efficiency. Vanessa knew he could have used much greater force but the crisp smacks still left their breasts red-blotched and smarting and eyes hot with tears. 42's pale flesh showed their new crimson glow to the best advantage. Like 49 their nipples seemed aroused by the pain and stood out proudly if painfully.

When he was done, Tom looked along the line of red and trembling breasts, a few wet with tears, in satisfaction. 'Very pretty,' he declared. He walked around them looking at their rears. 'You look like a proper pack of bitches with your tails in. I think you should keep them for the rest of the day. Mustn't leave you as odd girl out, 63.' He snapped his fingers. 'Head down and bum high. 49, you can have her now. Stick that tail up her.'

As 63 pressed her face to the floor and parted her thighs, 49 shuffled quickly up behind her and rammed her tail plug home. 63 gasped as her rear was filled. 49 pulled back and 63's tail seemed to emerge magically out of her pussy mouth and spring erect in the cleft summit of 63's posterior, wagging slightly as it did so.

Tom and Mark then went round pulling the empty and now glistening sheaths from them.

'You've got fifteen minutes to drink and use the loo,' he told them.

As they visited the drinking fountain and toilet, Tom and Mark set out a track marked by cones around the perimeter of the chamber, running along the strip of smooth concrete between the edge of the carpeting and the inside of the walls. Then they brought out some new equipment and laid it by the side of the track.

The girls were called back and commanded to lie on their backs with their legs in the air. What looked like sets of skateboard wheels attached to cut-down padded footboards fitted with heavy straps were buckled about their shins.

'Try them out,' said Tom.

Rolling back onto their hands and knees again they found the skates had been modified by the addition of ratchets on the wheels. These prevented them turning backwards and so gave traction with each push forward. With a little practice they got into a swaying rhythm with their hips as they swung one leg and then the other forward and kicked backward. With their padded paws to help keep balance they could build up quite a speed along the concrete track.

The girls' faces became flushed with delight as they sped round the track, thighs straining, bottoms rolling, tails wagging and breasts swaying in time. The rush of air over their naked flesh felt exhilarating and natural. This seemed like unadulterated fun. Then they were called back into line and saw the rest of the equipment and realised it would not be as simple as that.

These were more modified skateboards, one for each of them. They had rims screwed to their edges turning them into mobile trays, and rings bolted to their front ends to which were tied short lengths of rope which in turn plugged into red foam-rubber balls. By the track

201

were plastic water bottles, a pile of iron disc scale pan weights and a long trestle-like construction hung with straps and sets of cuffs bolted to its base frame.

The girls lined up across the track with knees spread wide and Tom and Mark positioned a skateboard behind each of them. They took up the balls, wadded them tight and stuffed them deep into their pussies. The girls shivered as stiff male fingers entered them. Vanessa felt the ball expand again inside her.

'Do a test lap and don't let the balls pop out,' Tom commanded.

Cautiously they circled the course with the boards rattling along at their heels, getting used to the tug of the tethers on their vaginas. Then Tom lined them up again.

'This is going to test your endurance, bitches, so listen carefully. You are to keep going until you drop or a ball pops out of your cunts. The first one to drop out gets sixty strokes of the paddle, the second fifty and so on. The last one skating gets away with just ten. Punishments at the end of the race. Every ten laps you get a mouthful of water and we add a weight to your boards. The last one to finish each heat gets an extra weight. Now get ready, set, go . . .'

They set off around the track with a mass burring of small wheels. Their faces were set. What had been fun was now a test of stamina and determination.

The first few laps were not too bad but by the fifth the strain began to tell on the inner thighs, but the threat of sixty strokes of the paddle kept them going. Vanessa tucked in behind the pale buttocks and ginger-fringed cleft of 42, who seemed to be a strong skater. She saw her vulva bulging from the pressure of the ball inside her and the strange sight of the rope emerging from between her weeping red sex lips.

The last lap of the ten became a serious race with the boards fishtailing along behind them as their hips waggled and strained. Sweat began to bead on their foreheads and down their spines. Vanessa was second after 42 with 63 and 35 close behind her. 54 and 49 battled it out to avoid last place. In the end 54 won by a head.

They were watered and the first weights were added to their skateboard carts with an extra weight for 49. Then they set off again.

49 lagged from the start and 54 was able to stay ahead of her all the way. Vanessa and the others concentrated on keeping ahead of them. 49 came last by a larger margin and received another extra weight. By now her face was flushed and she looked frightened.

On lap five of the third heat, accompanied by an audible sob of despair, the red ball popped out of 49's cleft. The towrope snaked away and the weighted board rattled off the track into the sidewall.

Tom and Mark stopped the race. They took a trembling 49 off the track to the trestle and bent her over its main beam so that she rested on her toes with her bottom raised high and facing the track. A strap went over her back to hold her down and her ankles and wrists were cuffed to the base frame. On her bottom cheeks they wrote in bold marker pen the number 60.

The rest of the girls were set off on another heat. Every time they passed 49 on display they were reminded what would happen to the next one to drop out.

But they were all feeling the strain now. The concrete of the track was stained with splashes of sweat and trails of girlish juices dripping from their helplessly stimulated sexes, worked into a state of excitement by the balls inside them and the tug and yaw of the ropes emerging from between their ever-redder labia. It made keeping the balls inside them even harder.

On lap four the tow ball slipped out of 54's smooth pussy lips. She was dragged off trembling and misty-eyed to be bound over the trestle bar beside 49. Mark drew a 50 on her neat rounded buttocks.

63 and 35 began to contest the last place in the diminishing pack. They were racing shoulder-to-shoulder, breasts swinging like bell clappers under them, when their knees clashed. Both swerved away. 35 hit a cone and the edge of the carpeting and tumbled over off her skates. 63 stayed upright but jerked on her towrope so hard the board unshipped a weight and jerked the ball out of her pussy.

Tom and Mark strapped them both over the trestle and drew a 40 on 35's bottom and a 30 on 63's.

Now it was just Vanessa and 42. By now both were lathered in sweat and aching with exhaustion. Only a sense of pride was keeping them going. They wobbled along level for three laps, the sweat dripping off their nipples. Vanessa's eyes stung, her gluteus muscles and thighs felt as though they were on fire and her weeping pussy ached from clenching onto the ball. The only difference between first and second was ten paddle smacks. That was nothing to her. Why didn't she just give up and let go of the ball?

Then with a gasp 42 shed her sodden tow ball onto the track and came to a halt, thighs splaying outwards, sinking her head down onto the concrete. Vanessa had won.

Tom and Mark bound them over the trestle and marked their bottoms 20 and 10. They swished their paddles through the air as they admired the row of red-rimmed sweaty pudenda and shapely female posteriors ready to receive their punishments, their shivering tails flying like flags of surrender.

Then Tom said: 'They've been good bitches all day and tried hard. Maybe they shouldn't get the full paddling.'

'How much would you cut it down to?'

'A tenth, maybe.'

At the end of the row 49 and 54 lifted their heads in sudden hope.

'That's going pretty easy,' Mark said.

'I think they deserve it.'

The other girls were stirring in hope.

'If they get their bums spared they've got to make up for the rest somehow. They mustn't think the rules don't apply. They've got to pay their due.'

'But how? They haven't anything to offer us instead.'

49 was making urgent gurgling noises, wriggling and tugging at her bonds and setting her tail bobbing. Tom and Mark went over to her.

'You want to say something, 49?'

She nodded desperately.

'If we take your tongue gag out don't waste your time asking to be let off.'

She shook her head. They undid the strap and pulled the sleeve off her tongue.'

'Please . . . screw me,' she said huskily.

'What did you say?' Tom asked. 'Speak up!'

'Screw me, please!' she repeated, so the whole line heard.

'So you're offering us sex to save you fifty-four lashes,' Mark said, squatting down by her head, taking hold of her hair and lifting so that she looked him in the face.

'Yes.'

'You'll take the six lashes and then you want one of us to screw you?'

'Yes.'

'And this is your own idea. We haven't made you do this?'

'No.'

Tom stroked the dark tangle of hair that fringed 49's sex and then tickled her slot. 'Do you beg for it?'

49 shivered and gulped. 'Yes . . . sir. I beg you to smack me six times and then screw me.'

'Well, you can't say fairer than that,' Tom said. He stood up and laid the paddle blade against 49's bottom.

205

'I want to hear you thank me for each swipe and then beg to have my cock inside you.'

'Yes, sir . . . thank you, sir.'

So every swish and crack of rubber on flesh was followed by a yelp of pain and then a choked: 'Thank you, sir!' After the sixth 49 said desperately: 'Please don't hit me any more, sir. Screw me instead, sir. Please put your cock up me . . .'

Tom had pulled his lab coat wide to expose a cock already straining free of its flies. Taking hold of her hips he slipped it between the lips of 49's wet and inflamed sex and thrust hard. The whole beam shook as he had her.

He had hardly pulled out of her sopping slot when 54 was wriggling and whining anxiously as well. Mark pulled out her tongue curb.

'Please sir, will you screw me too, sir? Just smack me five times and then fuck me good and hard.'

And he did.

The others strapped over the trestle could feel them coupling, smell her arousal and his spilt sperm. From then on it was inevitable that they all begged most sincerely for the same alternative to punishment.

Tom and Mark were young and virile and seemed to recover from each ejaculation within minutes. They worked their way down the line alternately availing themselves of the pussies that were pushed so eagerly at them. Perhaps they had been saving themselves for this moment for days.

It finished with Vanessa receiving her token single hard paddle smack and then taking Mark's shaft inside her. It was a balm compared to a rubber ball and a rope. A day of arousal without relief boiled up inside her and exploded.

Tom and Mark stepped back, zipping up, leaving them hanging limp over the trestles with red bottoms and dripping sexes. They had learned to trade their

206

bodies for sex to avoid a little extra pain and they actually felt good about it.

Banks' voice came over the speakers: 'The test is concluded. Repeat, the test is concluded. Bring the subjects back to Lab 3 reception for debriefing . . .'

The voice from outside came almost as a shock, bringing them back to Earth with a jolt. For eight hours the yard had been their special closed perverse world. Vanessa blinked, feeling a sudden sadness overwhelm her. It had been such fun. She'd been a good bitch and had pleased her masters. Then she shook her head. What was she thinking?

The girls were freed from the trestle and had their leads clipped back on. Vanessa saw confusion and even sorrow in their faces. As they were led back through the door to the lab some were looking behind them wistfully.

As they were lined up in the lab again along the yellow line, sitting back on their heels with their knees spread, pawed hands resting on their thighs and tails curling up from the humid depths of their buttocks, juices seeped almost unnoticed from their clefts and their eyes were still misty from their recent exertions. Their tongue curbs were removed.

Banks sat before them, notepad in hand. 'Tell me what you feel about your experience,' he asked.

At first they found it hard to express what they felt and the words came slowly. But a consensus soon emerged. They were amazed at what they had undergone and at their own daring. Their replies were infused by a sense of pride that they had been tough enough to enjoy experiences that might have broken lesser girls.

'I never believed before I could do anything like any of that,' 63 admitted. 'But it ended up being, well, fun. Especially the end . . .'

'Begging to be screwed was about the sickest sexiest thing I've ever done,' 35 said.

'It was so dirty but in a good way, you know,' said 42.

'Some of it hurt a lot and I was a bit frightened but at the same time my pussy was leaking,' 54 admitted.

'I was getting a buzz just squatting with my legs wide peeing where everybody could see me,' 49 confessed. 'What does that tell you about me?'

Oh yes, Vanessa thought, *they're hooked now. I know because I feel the same.* She added her own observation that was also a simple truth. 'I think having my bum smacked by a strong man when I know there's nothing I can do to stop him is about the biggest high there is.'

And the others agreed.

When they had all had their say, Banks concluded: 'Well, let me assure you we have gathered a lot of very important data from your efforts. You are very productive subjects.'

'In fact we were wondering if any of you were free for the whole of next weekend, Friday evening until Sunday?' Lister added casually. 'There's a country house in Surrey called Brysden Manor where we run more advanced sexual role-play laboratory events. Would you be interested in attending?'

They all were. None of them had any plans that could not be broken. It seemed nothing would keep them from participating in more of Deedas' experiments, however perverse.

Nothing would keep Vanessa away either.

Thirteen

'Brysden Manor, this supposed country house used by Deedas Research, does not exist, Miss,' Angela declared, turning aside from her computer screen that was displaying a list of postal addresses in Surrey. 'It may be another of Rochester's establishments in the same area going under a false name to ensure its potential recruits cannot identify it later.'

They were in the office late that evening after Vanessa's long day at Deedas. Vanessa was lying on the couch trying to ease the ache in her hips and thighs. Sandra was giving her a massage.

'That makes sense,' she said. 'We're supposed to meet at Deedas as usual and be taken there by private car, so there's no need for us to know that. A few detours along country roads and a fake sign put up at the gate and they're covered. Well, I'll find out more on Friday.'

'Shall we arrange for you to be followed, Miss?'

Vanessa thought for a moment. 'Yes, that makes sense. Trying to tie down the location of this place is the obvious next step. But it must be discreet.'

'We have plenty of volunteers with private cars, Miss. They can be coordinated via mobile phones. But you must still be careful, Miss.'

'Please,' Sandra said, and she lovingly kneaded Vanessa's buttocks.

Vanessa saw the concern in their eyes. 'As careful as I can be. But I don't think Rochester is ready to close in on this batch of girls quite yet. If they disappeared this weekend people would ask questions. They're getting hooked on the slavish life but they're not gaffed and landed. This is another phase in their conditioning, which is going well at the moment. Ending up over the trestles like that with the girls begging to be screwed was great . . .' She broke off, seeing the look on Angela's face. 'I know, I'm sounding like an eager recruit but they're good, I'll give them that.'

'I don't doubt it, Miss. But I'm worried this conditioning is affecting you more deeply than you realise.'

'Then you'd better hope something happens at this Brysden Manor place, or whatever it's really called.' She looked at the calendar marking off the number of days since Cherry and Dahlia chains were exchanged and thought again of what Kashika might be going through. 'It's got to happen soon . . .'

Angela's phone rang. She took the call, smiled, made a note on her pad and thanked the caller. 'That was from one of the Beta teams, Miss.'

Vanessa's heart thudded. 'Have they got a contact?'

'Yes, Miss.' She went to the big map, took out a red pin and pushed it into the map at a point near Maidstone.

Sandra bent and kissed Vanessa's bottom. 'That's the first . . . but there'll be more soon.'

It was working.

At six that Friday Vanessa walked into the lobby of Deedas Research. Slung over her shoulder was the overnight bag she had been asked to bring.

Miss Graves greeted her with her usual bright smile. 'Good afternoon, Josie.' She made a tick on a clipboard list she had by her computer. 'You're the last. The other girls are already here.'

'I'm not late, am I?'

'No, you're right on time as usual. I just think the rest are really eager to get going. They're all in Lab 3 for a briefing from Doctor Banks before you set off. Please go through . . .'

Vanessa went along the corridor and pushed the door open.

There were the other girls in their street clothes with bags over their shoulders. Tom and Mark stood either side of them. Vanessa opened her mouth to say hello but the words died on her lips.

They were five girls who only resembled subjects 35, 42, 49, 54 and 63. In a corner was a sixth girl, naked except for a red collar. She had light brown skin and dark fluffy hair and full breasts.

Even as Vanessa took this in Lister was by her side smiling through a transparent facemask, holding out a silver cylinder that she pushed into her face. There was a hiss and blast of gas and a chemical tang that filled her lungs. Vanessa took in one shuddering breath and tried to turn away, but the floor of the lab came up to meet her and the rest was darkness . . .

She could not move, but deep down she felt she was in motion. That disparity didn't help the sickly churning of her stomach. Her mouth tasted foul, her head was pounding and her bottom and nose felt sore. She tried to swallow but there was something preventing her lips functioning. Moving air caressed her body intimately. She was naked. She tried to open her eyes but it was still dark. She tried to move her arms and legs but they were held rigid, legs apart and arm pulled straight out from her shoulders. There were bands about them and across her body holding her in place. She was not lying flat but not upright either. And there was a slight steady droning vibration coming from below her. She moaned miserably.

'She's coming round now, boss,' said a man's voice.

'I want to see her eyes!' a harsh dictatorial voice snapped.

The pads that had been covering her eyes were pulled aside. Vanessa squinted into bright blurry lights. Gradually things swam into focus.

She was in a small boxlike room with studwork and quilted padding covering the ceiling and walls to either side and partitioned by a folding screen in front of her. Every so often the room swayed slightly. She was heavily strapped down onto some sort of tilted frame. A man in a blue boiler suit and balaclava mask with cut-outs for eyes, nose and mouth was standing over her. On a stand in front of her was a large plasma screen. Filling it was the graphic image of a single red eye with a glowing pupil.

Vanessa shivered. She'd seen that eye before. It was the image Rochester used when he wanted to hide his identity over a video link.

His voice came again from the screen's speakers. The pupil of the eye pulsed in time with the words. 'You certainly went to a lot of trouble, Buckingham, I'll give you that. It's a fine disguise. I nearly didn't believe it was you at first. But I prefer girls with paler skins. Mind you I'm not prejudiced, oh no. I've got some African girls that are worth their weight in gold. It's just that I think whip marks show up better on white skin.'

Vanessa growled at him round her gag.

'Want to say something? If I have him ungag you will you be polite and call me "Sir" like I told you last time?'

She shook her head.

Rochester chuckled. 'I didn't think you would. But I'll let you insult me if you want for now. I'll have you calling me "Master" soon enough. Take her gag out.'

The boiler-suited man pulled the plug of rubber from Vanessa's mouth, gave her a squirt of water from a plastic bottle and then left the compartment, closing the divider behind him. The eye vanished from the screen to be replaced by the head and shoulders of a thickset man in his late fifties with grizzled hair and a heavy jaw. He grinned hungrily at Vanessa's naked body, making her shiver.

'We keep meeting like this, don't we, Buckingham?' he said. 'But you aren't getting away this time. No friends on the other side of a trick mirror to help you today. Now you're all mine.'

'What happened to the real Deedas girls?' Vanessa asked.

'Ah, the reporter wants to get the facts straight, does she?'

'Yes.'

He chuckled. 'Very professional. Well, you see I've been watching your attempt at infiltrating Deedas for several days. I've seen all the test records. You screwing that blonde girl on the ring frames, by the way, was very enjoyable. But I decided you were probably getting impatient so I brought your little charade to an end. The other trainees got a call from Deedas saying the weekend had to be postponed. All except for you, of course. We found a close enough double from our stock. Once you were knocked out she dressed in your clothes and carried your bag out with the rest. If Shiller was having you tracked or followed they're welcome to waste their time watching a house in the country where nothing happens for two days. By the time they realise you're not amongst the party it'll be too late.'

'And I suppose I'm on one of your transport trucks. The ones you ship your girls around the country in?'

'So you've been doing your research like a good slut reporter? Yes. After they sent off your double we loaded you into a crate and took you out the back to where this was waiting. Plenty of HGVs coming and going all the time round there so nobody would look twice. Now it's driving around the motorways until I know you're safe to bring in and we can meet in the, ha, flesh at last.'

'Safe? You think I can hurt you like this?'

Rochester scowled. 'Don't take me for a fool, Buckingham, and I won't treat you like one. You wouldn't have tried to infiltrate Deedas without being prepared. So I had this truck set up to welcome you. Apart from being soundproofed it's fitted with a portable x-ray machine and a tech crew. They used it on you while you were unconscious. They've pulled the implants from your nostrils, but they were just plastic. Then they looked deeper . . .'

Vanessa stiffened.

'Oh yes, they found that capsule in your stomach. They weren't sure what to make of it at first so they fed you a laxative and flushed it out. A time-release micro radio transponder they tell me. The parts come together after a few hours after swallowing under the action of digestive juices but it's almost undetectable until then. Very clever. Of course it's been smashed.'

Vanessa clenched her jaws but said nothing. Rochester smiled.

'I do like to see a pretty girl looking distressed. Of course you're only here because you're a victim of your own successes. After you uncovered my agent at Glen Lothy it made me rethink my strategy. I stopped trying to ruin Shiller's business and saw how I could use it to my own advantage.' He chuckled again. 'You see, you can teach an old dog new tricks. Of course I wanted to pay you back for the trouble you caused, especially for betraying me the first time, but profit before pleasure.

'Once I had a chain in hand I considered asking for you in exchange, but I thought Shiller might not agree. She has this disgusting sentimental streak where slave-girls are concerned and might chuck it all in. Of course I knew you'd try something ingenious to get them back, despite my warnings about what would happen to them.'

'I didn't try to track them,' Vanessa said quickly. 'This was just me. You can't punish them for this.'

'Your concern for your fellow sluts is just what I'd expect of a Shiller company girl,' Rochester said contemptuously. 'But true enough you didn't try to track them so I'll keep to my side of the deal. It's going very nicely so far. These latest chains are top quality.'

Vanessa bit her lip. Rochester saw and laughed.

'After deciding not to ask for your tits on a silver platter I'd wondered about asking for Cherry Chain with your Indian girlfriend in. I knew that would be bound to make you try to make some move against me no matter what Shiller said. But I thought: no, don't rush things. Let the arrangement run for a while. Then Cherry Chain is delivered to me complete with your dusky blonde Indian lover.'

'There was a lottery,' Vanessa said quickly. 'It was the fairest way to choose.'

'So I hear from my informant . . .'

His image was replaced by one of Kashika. She was strapped to a door-sized metal grille with her arms and legs spread to the sides of the frame. A heavy black bridle gag strap covered her mouth, with thinner straps passing over her nose and under her chin. Her eyes were closed and her head hung forward against the broad neck strap that bound her to the frame. More straps crossed her chest, belly, thighs and knees. Lash marks covered her lovely body, concentrating about her breasts, pubes and inner thighs. She looked as though she was asleep or semi-conscious.

Vanessa felt a sick thrill of fear and strained at her own straps. 'Don't hurt her!'

Rochester laughed. 'Revenge is a dish best served cold, they say. I've been patient and now I have both of you. Which is just what you wanted, isn't it, Buckingham!'

'What?' Vanessa exclaimed.

'You wanted me to get my hands on Kashika and make her talk. Of course I'd recognise her when I reviewed the new intake. After a little persuasion she admitted you'd been away working on a special project. So I was ready when you tried to infiltrate Deedas. Might have missed you otherwise, but then it would have been unbelievable if you'd tried to do it with your own face so you had to be disguised.'

'I was doing it to get into your pleasure house system to smash it and free all your slavegirls!'

'There's no way you could find them all,' Rochester said. 'And now I can simply ask Shiller's for replacements. No, you wanted to be caught because you wanted to meet me in person.'

'Why would I want to meet a bastard like you face to face?'

'To incriminate me in some way and prove a personal link between my slave business and me, of course! After all, that's what I've been trying to do to Shiller for years. That's the only way to finish me and you know it! But you've failed.'

Vanessa sagged, turning her head aside and screwing up her eyes. 'All right . . . so you found out.'

'Stop playacting, Buckingham! You'd know I'd have you stripped and searched with a fine toothcomb. You know I'd never let you close to me unless I was certain you were clean. So you'd have one bug for me to find and be so pleased with myself I'd miss the second. I don't underestimate the technical resources at Shiller's disposal. Where is it?'

'You've found it, the capsule!' Vanessa protested.

'Don't lie to me any more, slut. Where is it?'

'There isn't anything else!'

'Too bad. Now I'm going to have to persuade you. Actually I was rather hoping you'd be stubborn. It gives me a chance to try out a device one of my special customers commissioned on your girlfriend.'

'No!'

'Just watch . . .'

The sound from wherever Kashika was being held cut in.

A black-clad and masked figure came into the frame. He was carrying something. The camera moved in close to capture the details.

It was a jar of set honey. He scooped some out and smeared it carefully over Kashika's breasts. She stirred and opened her eyes. She saw what was he was doing and began to struggle, shaking her head and making mewing, pleading noises in the back of her throat. The man ignored her protests. When her breasts were covered he knelt down to work on her pubes.

He took out a springy plastic ring the size of a teacup rim. It had short moulded spikes radiating about its outer edge. Prying open Kashika's inner labia he slipped the ring between them and let it unfold. The spikes dug into the soft lips of pink wet flesh and pushed them back, opening her vulva painfully wide and exposing the nub of her clitoris, the valley of her urethra and the mouth of her vaginal passage.

The man scooped up more honey and forced soft golden dollops of it deep up into her vagina with stiff fingers. It was almost the colour of her pubic hair. Kashika's passage clenched as it tried to resist him, but to no avail. When she was full he licked his fingers. The honey, warmed by her body heat, slowly began to ooze from her lovemouth.

Then, bizarrely, the man took out what appeared to be a tiny wire ladder some twenty centimetres long. The shafts at the top of the ladder curved outward to form springy hooks. He squeezed these together, slipped the end into the gaping mouth of Kashika's sex and let them spring wide. Kashika's whimper of pain was audible as the hooks bit into the flesh of her out-turned labia.

The man stepped back and the camera pulled away, revealing that the frame Kashika was bound to was supported by wire ropes clipped to eyebolts at its corners. A motor hummed. The frame was hoisted into the air and then rotated until Kashika hung face down with her honey-smeared breasts dangling freely. The little ladder hooked to her labia also swung down vertically from within the fleshy ramparts held wide by the star ring. She was shaking her head and moaning, looking ahead of her at something out of camera shot that cast light across her face. The winch unit began to move forward along a ceiling track and Vanessa saw what it was.

A glass-sided tank as large as the frame Kashika was strapped to was set on a sturdy table. The tank was half filled with sandy soil and illuminated by small strip lights set around its sides. It had a curious transparent roof that fitted the inside of the tank walls, supported by vertical corner channels. It appeared to be moulded plastic with a deeply indented pattern in it. The pattern was that of a woman posed as Kashika was, but there were holes where her breasts and pubes would be.

The frame halted over the tank and then began to lower. The tank lights showed Kashika's tear-filled eyes. She was dropped into the mould that fitted closely about her body. Her face showed through the plastic shell. There were two small holes over her nostrils. Her breasts slipped through circular paired holes and the rims pressed hard up against her chest. The tiny ladder hanging from her pubes dropped though its triangular curving hole, which also closed up tight about the swell of her wide-stretched sex mouth.

The moulding and frame, with Kashika sandwiched between them, now began to descend into the tank as one, sliding down against the resistance of springs in the corner channels. It came to a halt when the tiny pubic ladder touched the sand and dug in, leaving her honeyed nipples brushing the undulating surface.

Now in close-up Vanessa saw there were holes in the sand and the sides of the tank were honeycombed with tiny tunnels. She thought she saw small forms scurrying though them. Slowly warm trickles of honey were rolling off Kashika's trembling breasts onto the sand. A long heavy golden tongue was pouring out of her vagina.

'No! Take her out of there. You've searched me. I haven't got any other bugs.'

218

'You're lying, Buckingham, and your lover's going to pay for it . . .'

On the screen the black-clad man tapped the sides of the tank. Large black ants began to emerge onto the surface. Looking down through her plastic facemask Kashika's eyes bulged in horror and she began squirming and writhing against her straps. The scurrying insects, antennae twitching, moved towards the honey drips soaking into the sand.

'These are not common British garden ants but some foreign type . . . I forget the name,' Rochester said. 'It doesn't matter. You can see they're big and they like honey. They'll take that first but they like flesh as well. Amazingly sharp pincers, so I'm told.'

Kashika was crying now, her tears pooling in the plastic facemask. The desperate straining of her body was making the melting honey pour out of her even faster. The ants were forming a ring about her shivering breasts. Her sticky dusky nipples had picked up grains of sand. Curious ants sampled them as though suckling from her.

'Please take her out of there,' Vanessa begged. 'Please, sir . . . Master. Do you hear, I'm calling you Master? There's nothing else. Please!'

'I don't believe you.'

The ants were now climbing up the honey-sheened palpitating inverted brown domes of flesh that hung over them. Their legs were sticking but they continued on.

'How soon before they start nibbling her tits, eh, Buckingham?' Kashika began to flinch and jerk. 'Oh, look, I think they've already started.'

'Let her go, please . . .'

The ants were swarming about the pool of honey under Kashika's gaping sex. A few were climbing the ladder to investigate the golden orifice above them. Snaking lines of them led back to their nest holes.

219

'My toenails!' Vanessa shrieked. 'False toenails with circuits printed in them. Stacked together they make a resonant tracer. Clean off the varnish and you'll see. Please, Master!'

'I'll let her go when I know you're telling the truth.'

The ants had reached Kashika's sex, climbing through Kashika's honey-matted pubic hair. A few were investigating the mouth of her golden river. The camera zoomed in. They clambered over the pink ridges of her labia. One began nibbling at the mound of her clitoris.

The boiler-suited man came back though the partition. He bent over Vanessa's feet and sprayed a solvent over her toes.

Kashika's breasts were covered in ants now. She had her eyes closed and was whimpering continuously. Drool was running round the edges of her gag strap. Loosened by fear, her bladder suddenly cut loose. A hot fitful jet sprayed down over her tiny tormentors and splashed into the sand, forming a brief pool and drowning a handful of them. Others struggled out of the puddle that soaked rapidly away. The rest continued to gather honey.

The boiler-suited man had peeled off a toenail and was holding it up to the light. Etched into the clear plastic were tiny silver dots.

'Looks like she's telling the truth, boss,' he said.

Kashika's breasts and pubes were now black with swarming ants and she was yelping and screeching through her gag and shaking violently.

'Please get her out of there!' Vanessa shrieked.

Then the frame began to rise, shedding ants as it did so. As it reached the top of the tank it lifted clear of the moulded cover, exposing the underside of Kashika's trembling body. The black-clad man used a pump spray to wash the honey and remaining ants from her breasts and pubes. Underneath the skin looked reddened and blotchy with a few painful-looking pinpricks, but nothing worse. Kashika sagged and hung limply from her straps.

The boiler-suited man removed the rest of Vanessa's false nails and retired back through the partition. On the screen the image of Rochester replaced that of Kashika.

Feeling sick and numbed, Vanessa hung her head. 'That's all ... Master ...' she croaked miserably. 'There's nothing else hidden anywhere ... just me ...'

'I believe you, slut,' Rochester said, his face splitting in a broad grin of triumph. 'Now you'll both be put in cages small enough to fit in the boot of a car and then brought to me. Maybe Shiller will be watching my houses by now, but cars come and go all the time and there's no way of telling if one or none contain you. They might risk a raid but my private dungeons are very well hidden and without evidence what can they do? You'll be my special guests for as long as I want to keep you ...'

The boiler-suited man reappeared holding a silver cylinder. He pushed the nozzle up to Vanessa's face and pressed a trigger ...

Fourteen

The first thing Vanessa saw when she woke again was Kashika.

She was sitting slumped back against the angle of a brick wall just a metre away from her. She had a steel collar padlocked about her neck. From the back of the collar a heavy chain curved up to a slotted plate set high in the wall. Her hands were resting limply by her sides. They were encased in rubber paws. The whip marks and ant bites showed on her body but she was still achingly beautiful. Vanessa smelt the lingering aroma of honey.

With a sob of joy Vanessa feebly reached out to touch Kashika and found she was also wearing paw gloves. The straps of the wristbands looked as though they had been glued into place. As she moved she felt the weight of a collar about her own neck. Like Kashika's its tethering chain ran up to a slot in a wall plate above her.

Vanessa slumped back against the cold brickwork again, feeling sick and dizzy. She did not have the strength to move . . . but then there was nothing to move for now. It was done.

She realised she was sitting on a strip of rubber matting running along the wall that she shared with Kashika. It was about the only soft thing in the room, which was a windowless brick cell about three metres by four, with a concrete floor and ceiling. It had a single green iron riveted door with no handle on the inside. The light came from sealed garden-style lamps protected by wire mesh covers. In the corner adjacent to theirs was the pan of a small squat toilet with a showerhead over it. Set low down on the wall between herself and Kashika was a wide shallow grating. The rest of the walls and ceiling was hung with various rings, chains and pulley blocks. The room was furnished, if that was the word, with a low torture table, a restraint trestle, a device of wooden posts and a whipping block. On the far wall by the door was a rack of whips, canes, prods, lashes and assorted harness. High up in the corners of the room were small security cameras.

'Do you think he's trying to make us feel at home?'

Vanessa twisted her head round. Kashika had her eyes open and was smiling feebly.

Ignoring her sickness and pounding head Vanessa heaved herself over and hugged and kissed her. There was just enough slack in the chains for them to reach each other. 'I'm so sorry,' she sobbed. 'I saw what he did to you with the ants . . . are you all right?'

'I'll get over it,' Kashika said, hugging and kissing Vanessa back. 'I'll have nightmares but I'll get over it.' Then she started crying. 'I'm sorry . . . he used me, didn't he? To make you tell him the truth.'

'I couldn't let that go on,' Vanessa said. 'I should never have got you involved in this. It's all gone wrong and it's all my fault.'

For a long time they sat huddled together in silence. Then Kashika said: 'So . . . what happens now?'

Vanessa looked up at the cold glass eyes of the cameras. 'He does whatever he wants to with us.'

When they felt steady enough to stand they used the toilet and drank from the shower spray.

'I wonder where we are?' Kashika asked. 'They knocked me out right after the ant farm.'

'One of Rochester's private houses, I suppose.' She looked sorrowfully at Kashika. 'Was where you were bad, before the ants I mean?'

Kashika shrugged. 'Some of it. Our keepers were pretty strict, though we were fed well enough and they kept us looking clean and smart. All in red, even the stupid high heels. I suppose they made us easier to catch when clients were chasing us but I nearly twisted my ankle twice. Some of the other girls broke the heels right off.'

'And . . . did they give them new pairs?'

'Oh yes, shiny bright new pairs.' She looked down at her bare feet. 'I suppose they took mine off before they brought me here. Funny, they've cleaned off my nail varnish too.'

'He wasn't taking any chances,' said Vanessa dismally.

Without warning a hidden motor whirred into life and their collar chains began to reel in, rattling through the wall plates. They scrambled to their feet as they were pulled upright and then back against the wall. They tried to grasp their collars with their paws to stop them cutting their necks as they were pulled onto their toes. Then the motors stopped.

The green door opened, revealing a glimpse of a wall beyond with a set of pegs hung with clothes, and Rochester stepped into their dungeon.

Vanessa knew who it was even though he wore a purple silk mask over his head with slots for his eyes and mouth. He was dressed in a matching purple dressing gown and slippers, revealing bare calves. They would never be able to swear to his identity and they would not be blindfolded because, as Cindy had said, he liked to see their eyes when they were in pain.

'Let Kashika go, Rochester, she's nothing to you,' Vanessa said.

He took an electric cattle prod from the rack by the door, strode up to Vanessa and jabbed it into her stomach. As she clutched her arms across her middle howling in pain he jabbed at her breasts left and right, indenting them deeply.

'You will call me Master, nothing else,' he said simply, jabbing at her contorted body as it twisted about on her chain, stabbing the electrodes into the trembling flesh of her buttocks as they were turned towards him. 'You will demand nothing and obey my every command without question. I may free your friend when it pleases me but you were an uninvited guest and I shall keep you here until you cease to amuse me.' He pulled the prod away. 'Is that understood?'

'Yes . . . Master,' Vanessa sobbed, trembling uncontrollably, held upright only by her collar chain.

From his gown pocket he took out a small remote control box and pressed a button. Vanessa's chain slackened off and she sank to her knees.

He held the box up for both of them to see.

'Don't get any idea about grabbing this. Even if your pretty paws could work it, the release for your chains is outside the door and they won't reach that far.' He parted his robe to reveal an erect penis standing out stiffly from a thick tangle of greying hair. Thrusting his cattle prod sideways he jabbed the tip into the cleft of Kashika's vulva, making her yelp. Instinctively she made to push it away, but then closed her eyes and dropped her arms to her sides.

'This slut learns faster than you,' he said to Vanessa, twisting the probe to embed it deeper. 'Now you suck me off or your slut lover gets fifty thousand volts up her pussy hole . . .'

With tears still dripping down her cheeks Vanessa bent forward and took his shaft into her mouth and began to lick and suck lovingly. Meekly she raised her gaze to her master's masked face and saw the light of triumph in his eyes. And for the first time she saw the ruthless power of a natural dominant in those eyes and felt herself shrinking under them.

Her fear, her exhaustion, her submissive nature and Deedas conditioning seemed to combine as she sucked the cock of her enemy. He was her master and she was nothing. This was where she belonged . . .

He spouted hotly in her mouth and she swallowed every drop, licking him clean with desperate care.

He laughed. 'That's more like it, slut. You've got talent.' He pulled the prod from Kashika's pussy and Vanessa sagged with relief. 'Now, how do you like candles . . .'

Vanessa knelt on the low torture table, resting on her knees and elbows. Heavy metal clamps bolted to the planking closed over her forearms and widespread ankles, forcing her to kneel with her head low and breasts almost brushing the rough woodwork and her bottom thrust up high. The chain still connected her collar to the slotted wall plate, but it had been let out and passed over a hook in the ceiling so it hung straight down over her.

Rochester walked round Vanessa's helpless body, stroking the deep curve of her back and swell of her haunches. In one hand he carried a large red candle.

'This will sting a little,' he said maliciously.

The drops of wax splashed crimson onto Vanessa's back, tracing a line along her spine and over her buttocks. Gradually the candle got lower and the drops got hotter. She snivelled and whimpered, shaking her head. Rochester was holding the candle over her bottom cleavage, letting the drops fall onto the swell of her mound. Thank God she had no hair there any more for them to stick to.

'Now let's try it up your arse . . .'

He pried Vanessa's cheeks apart and slid the end of the candle into Vanessa's anus. Half the length vanished inside her until she could feel the warmth of the flame on her skin. The rest stuck up at an angle into the air. Wax splashed on to the wood between her knees.

'Shall I leave that up there until it burns down to your bumhole, slut?' he asked.

'No, please, Master,' she begged.

'Would you rather have your lezzy lover screw you instead?'

'Yes, please, Master.'

'With this?'

He took something from the rack and showed it to her. It was a huge black strap-on the size of a cucumber with knobs and ridges and a spray of spikes about its base. Still close-chained to the wall, Kashika gave a gasp of dismay.

'I call it the black mamba,' he said.

Vanessa's eyes bulged at the sight of it. 'No, please, Master, it's too big. Please don't make her use that on me.'

'Well, we'll let the candle burn down some more, shall we?' He moved round behind her, admiring the burning candle jutting out from her anus. 'It's lighting up your arse really well. Lot's of golden highlights. Can you feel the heat?'

Vanessa nodded miserably. 'Yes, Master.'

'Maybe I'll push it in a little deeper . . . there.'

Vanessa gave a shriek as she felt the cylinder of wax filling her rectum and the flame was suddenly hot against her pubic lips.

'Changed your mind about the screwing?' Rochester asked.

'Yes, Master!'

'Do you beg to have Kashika screw you with the black mamba?'

'Please screw me with the black mamba, Kashika.'

'Hard enough to make you cry,' prompted Rochester.

'Do it hard to make me cry . . .'

Rochester strapped the huge dildo onto Kashika and then loosened her chain far enough for her to reach Vanessa. He pulled the candle out of her rear.

'Now screw your girlfriend properly, Kashika,' he commanded. 'I want to see her cry . . .'

Kashika took hold of Vanessa's hips and pushed the head of the phallic monster to her cleft. She felt her lips parting and stretching as the thing was forced inside her. The head was inside her tunnel mouth and the shaft was following. Her stomach bulged and she sobbed with the shock of it. She screwed up her eyes as they filled with the tears Rochester had demanded. It was too big for her.

'No!' she shrieked. Kashika hesitated. There came a smack of Rochester's hand on her rump and she jerked forward. The head rammed into the end of Vanessa's passage. She was fully plugged.

Miserably Kashika began to pump her. Vanessa's lovemouth was squelching with every stroke and her juices were dripping onto the boards to mingle with the wax splashes. With every thrust the spikes at the base jabbed her stretched labia.

She moaned and dribbled. Her head dropped but Rochester grasped her hair and lifted it up again. He wanted to see every second of her pain until an orgasm was forced out of her, and Kashika's anguish at being made to inflict the suffering upon her. They were his helpless girlflesh sex puppets performing for his pleasure.

And so it began.

There was no natural day or night in the cell. In between Rochester's visits food on plastic plates with plastic cutlery was slid through the low grille in the wall between them on a tray. They put the dirty plates back through the same slot. Did Rochester prepare the food or did somebody do it for him? Who else lived in the house with him? Did they know they were being kept in this secret dungeon? Vanessa had no idea.

When the lights went off they slept. When they came on they knew Rochester might call at any time. Vanessa guessed he used them three or four times a day, but she was not sure. He was always dressed the same way. He kept his identity as a respectable businessman on the other side of the door. Inside the cell he was their absolute master, and they gave him whatever pain or pleasure he demanded.

Kashika was kneeling at Rochester's feet with his cock in her mouth licking and sucking for all she was worth, all the while rolling her eyes so she could look up at him with desperate pleading. He had a fistful of her hair in one hand and a cane in the other. Her mouth was held open by a heavy elastic band passing round the back of her neck with a pair of splayed wire hooks on the ends that dug into her cheeks and curled round and up under her teeth. Please enjoy me, her gaze said mutely.

Vanessa watched from the wall, unable to tear her gaze away from her lover's suffering. Her collar chain pulled her up onto her tiptoes and cut into her chin.

Kashika's arms were bent up and strapped behind her back, wrist to forearm. More straps crossed her chest over and under her breasts, binding her upper arms to her sides. She was squatting over a dildo mounted on a weighted base, the head of which was lodged halfway up her rear. There were strap loops about her ankles and upper thighs, holding her legs tightly bent together and keeping her on her knees.

Still holding onto her hair Rochester pulled his cock out of Kashika's open mouth, trailing saliva, and shifted his position so he stood to one side of her. Placing the cane across the upper slopes of her breasts that already bore the marks of his first assault he raised it and brought it down with an audible sharp smack.

Kashika gave an open-mouthed howl of pain as her pliant breasts flattened and rebounded from the blow and fresh tears ran down her cheeks.

After a couple more swipes that left blazing streaks in their wakes, darkening her coffee skin, Rochester said:

'Let's try a few underneath. I want to see those tits jumping . . .'

He whipped the next stroke upwards, impacting on the undersides of her proud softly rounded cones. They leapt as though in a vain attempt to escape the cane, and she shrieked again. Slowly the fleshy tremors settled and her breasts hung trembling, gently.

'Now let's see you suck me properly . . .'

Sobbing and red-eyed, Kashika gulped at Rochester's shaft again with desperate passion. It trembled and stiffened in her mouth and his eyes hollowed. With a grunt he pulled his cock out and spurted his come over her face and sore breasts.

'Better, slut,' he grunted, looking at her soiled features. 'But now I think I want to play with bigger tits . . .'

Vanessa hung face down in mid-air. Her arms were strapped behind her and her legs were doubled over as Kashika's had been. Above her a spray of ropes with hooks on their ends radiated down from a big ring in the ceiling. These were hooked into her binding straps, supporting her body at about waist height. A couple of extra short bungee cords had been added to her harness, linking the straps about her thighs to those about her chest. The tension pulled her doubled-over legs wide, showing off her anal cleft and the brown oyster of her sex pouch.

Her breasts hung pendant beneath her like inverted bells, showing off their extra weight. This was accentuated by lead weights clipped to her nipples by way of short chains and sprung crocodile clips. They drew her nipples into wineglass-stem cones. The pain was already making her eyes water.

'Time for a spin,' said Rochester.

He took her by one extended knee and set her spinning. The ceiling ring twisted in a pivoting mount.

The motion swung her nipple weights outward, stretching her breasts even further. She snivelled in pain. Rochester beat her thighs and flying breasts as they passed him, swiping in the direction of her spin to keep her turning. Tears were running down her cheeks.

Sick and dizzy, Vanessa was brought to a sudden halt, shrieking as her nipple weights briefly kept on going only to jerk and bounce to a stop under her, sending fluid shivers through her dangling breasts. Grasping her spread thighs Rochester stepped between them and thrust his shaft into her pussy.

Vanessa squeezed about him pitifully, holding his slug of hard flesh inside her as it pumped away. She was so grateful not be spinning or feel the cane on her flesh that having his cock inside her was bliss by comparison. She hated herself but could not help it. Pleasing her master was all that mattered. Was this how Cindy was broken?

She saw Kashika chained to the wall looking at her in pitying fascination as Rochester's thrusts set her swaying jiggling beasts in motion and her nipple weights dancing. She watched the piston-motion of his shaft as he slid in and out of Vanessa's gaping swollen sex and the drips of her juices to the floor and finally the helpless look of ecstasy on her face as she came.

'I call this the "Pussy Grater",' said Rochester proudly.

It was a construction of heavy black-painted wood: an upright hollow square section base out of which rose an inner square post whose height was adjustable with pegs pushed into a row of holes down its sides. Mounted on top of this inner post was a short transverse wooden block like a section of roof ridge tile, but with the crest carved into a cruel saw-tooth profile. The posts were set in a square outer frame some two metres along each side. Within this frame Vanessa stood, straddling the serrated wooden block with her arms and legs cuffed and chained and pulled out to its inner corners.

A fifth chain hung from a ring bolted to the middle of the horizontal frame. This was hooked to a ring in the crown of a slave bridle, where the nose and side straps crossed, that was buckled tight, forcing her to hold her head up and keep her neck straight. Rochester raised the grater block, pressing it into her groin and parting her cleft until Vanessa stood on tiptoe. He tightened the chains to her ankle cuffs, pulling her legs down and wide, and did the same to the wrist cuffs, pulling her arms out straight until her body was a taut shivering starfish.

Vanessa's head was held practically immobile by the tension of the bridle chain and her mouth was held clamped about its rubber bit by nose and chin straps. All she could do was swivel her eyes left and right to follow Rochester as he checked she was secure.

Then he used a long lash on her, working his way round the frame, laying the lash tongues across her breasts, belly, back and buttocks in turn. The broad soft lash tongues did not cut her skin but the hissing thwacks they made rang out clearly and the blows sent shivers through her flesh and brought tears of pain to her eyes. Foamy trickles ran from the sides of her mouth where the bit cut into it and dripped onto her breasts.

And with every jerk, twist or flinch of her body she ground her pubes over the wooden grater. Her outer labia were parted on either side of the ridge so that the wooden teeth cut up into the mouth of her vagina and jabbed her clitoris. The tension of her bonds meant she could not lift herself off the terrible wedge that seemed to be intent on cutting her in two. She could only suffer. But suffering was what her master wanted. That was why the wood was dark and wet with her juices and why the knot in her loins was getting tighter and tighter until it burst . . .

Vanessa moaned and jerked and hung still save for the heaving of her chest. She would have collapsed had her bonds not held her upright.

'You're a real pain junkie, Buckingham,' Rochester said with admiring contempt. 'Maybe I'll put you in one of my houses when I'm finished with you. You'd earn me thousands . . .'

He left her on her painful seat while he loosened Kashika's chain and dragged her over to a sturdy wooden trestle, the top and splayed legs of which were fitted with rows of eyebolts trailing lengths of rope and slotted through with wooden pegs that served as belaying pins.

He spread and bound Kashika's shins and ankles to the legs on one side of the trestle, bent her forward to clasp a pair of pegs halfway down the other set of legs and roped her wrists in place. Now she was secured, bent over and braced by her bound arms with her legs invitingly open and her breasts slightly pendant. He took a second slave bridle from the rack and buckled it onto her head.

Rochester paused to admire her bound form for a moment, fingering her slot and cupping her forward-hanging breasts. He read the fear in her eyes and twisted her nipples as a warning of what was to come. From the rack he took down a large polished steel hook with a bulbous tip, trailing a length of rope from the ring on its shaft end. He showed the hook to Kashika so he could see the look of dismay on her face, then he dug the tip up into her anus and pushed.

Kashika whimpered as it slid up into her, the unyielding metal forcing her rectum to conform to its contours, until she was fully plugged. The shaft of the hook sat in the cleft of her buttocks with its ring end and rope lying across her back. Rochester took up the rope and threaded it through the ring set in the top of her bridle and began to pull it tight.

With a strangled squeak Kashika's head was pulled back, forcing her chin up and her neck to bend, the straps of her bridle cutting into her cheeks and the bit stretching the corners of her mouth. At the same time the pressure of the hook up her rear made her hips lift as they were pulled forward. As the two were brought closer together her pliant spine was forced to dip, thrusting her stomach down and lifting her breasts.

Vanessa moaned in fear at the sight. He'd break her back. But just when she thought Kashika could bend no more Rochester tied off the rope, leaving her upper body trembling like a bent bow under the tension.

Once again he walked round Kashika, examining the effects of his new addition to her bonds. His finger slid into the mouth of her anus, which was stretched into a distorted oval by the hook.

He selected a hard rubber paddle with a cruel pattern of spiked ridges on its face and began tanning the coffee-tinted buttocks to an angry blush with flat stinging smacks, admiring the shivers they sent rippling through her flesh. He alternated with swinging the paddle up between her legs to smack into the heavy pouting curve of her vulva. Kashika howled and wailed and sobbed and frothed about her gag bit, her eyes red with tears. But the paddle still came away wet with her exudation, splashing it across the insides of her thighs.

We can't help it, Vanessa thought miserably. *Our pain just makes him more our master.*

Rochester parted his robe and took Kashika from behind, his rampant cock sliding up between her sore lovelips and into her sopping vagina. As he rammed into her he leaned forward and swung his paddle up between her spread arms, catching the undersides of her jutting breasts with meaty smacks, driving their hard nipples into their depths and setting them jiggling and bouncing.

Kashika writhed and shuddered in forced ecstasy.

When he was gone they huddled miserably together on their mat, soothing their abused bodies as well as they could.

'I'm so sorry I got you into this,' Vanessa said, kissing Kashika's raw buttocks.

'It's what we've got to do,' Kashika said bravely. But she looked and sounded deathly tired.

Vanessa stroked and caressed her as she drifted into sleep. 'It'll be over soon . . .'

They were jerked from their exhausted slumber by the door banging open. Rochester strode in, his face purple with fury. Vanessa felt his rage sweeping before him and they cowered back against the wall.

'Seven of my slave houses raided within five minutes of each other!' he roared. 'Seven! And a hundred girls gone, important clients frightened off!' He took a step forward and cuffed Vanessa about the head. 'This is your doing, slut! Somehow you passed their locations to Shiller. How? Tell me!'

'Please, Master,' Vanessa whimpered fearfully, trying to cover herself. 'I don't understand.'

'Please let us go, Master,' Kashika begged. 'I hate it here. Please let us go!'

Rochester took Vanessa by the hair, dragged her to her feet and slapped her face. 'Tell me how you did it!'

'I don't know what you mean, Master!' she sobbed.

Kashika was clawing feebly at his legs with her pawed hands. 'Please don't hurt her any more. You've screwed her and beaten her and made her suck you off. Isn't that enough?'

Rochester backhanded Kashika and she fell to the floor. Holding Vanessa against the wall with one hand he reached down to her sex, pinched her clitoris and twisted. Vanessa shrieked.

'Tell me the truth!' he thundered.

'You want . . . the truth?' Vanessa sobbed and gasped, blinking at him through tear-filled eyes.

'Yes, the truth.'

She took a deep breath and looked him in the eye.

'The truth . . . is that you should have remembered to put your mask on before you came in . . .'

Rochester reached a hand up to his face, as though for the first time realising it was uncovered. He was wearing an ordinary tweed suit and not his master's robe.

'I've seen you lose it before when you're angry,' Vanessa said. 'That was stupid of you . . .'

A phone rang in Rochester's pocket. He snatched it out. 'Yes?' His face contorted in disbelief. 'Who's at the gate . . . she says what?' He looked around wildly. 'That's absurd! How can she see me?'

'You can come out now,' Vanessa called.

They wriggled out from under the stands of the rack and torture bench. Three Robotikine screwsnakes each with a tiny video camera mounted on its head.

Kashika sat up, smiling despite her swollen lip. 'Surprise.'

'It's over,' Vanessa said.

For a long moment it appeared as though Rochester had been turned to stone.

Then he seemed to sag, suddenly looking a lot older. Woodenly he said into the phone: 'Let them in . . . and send her down.'

Then he sat down heavily on the corner of the torture table and closed his eyes.

Vanessa took Kashika in her arms and they hugged, rocking gently together and kissing softly. The said nothing. At that moment they were beyond words.

Two minutes later Shiller walked into the cell with a pair of security guards following at her heels. Vanessa's heart gave a leap of joy at the sight of her. Shiller looked at Vanessa and Kashika and then at Rochester. 'Free them,' she said.

Rochester seemed unable to look at her. 'The red key . . . outside the door . . .'

Shiller found it and unlocked their collars herself. They bent and kissed her feet and she stroked their heads. 'Well done,' she said. 'I'm proud of you beyond measure.'

Vanessa felt hot tears of joy in her eyes. The terrible weight had lifted from her shoulders. It had worked. It really was over.

'Are my chain sisters safe, Director?' Kashika asked.

'They're safe. And the Dahlias. Thanks to you they're all safe now.' She looked at Rochester. 'You will cease your girlflesh trade immediately. You will provide a list of all your slave facilities, fixed and mobile, and girlflesh stock. You will withdraw from all aspects of the slave business and submit to regular monitoring to ensure you comply in future. If you do so I will not release the recording of you abusing Vanessa and Kashika while they begged you to stop, or your earlier torture of them. Is that understood?'

Rochester nodded. 'Yes,' he said simply.

That one single world marked the end of his slave empire.

With an effort he stood up, then paused and looked round at Vanessa. 'How did you do it?' he asked.

'Tell him, Vanessa,' Shiller said. 'He deserves that much. And this is your victory.'

Vanessa faced the person who had dominated her for days, who was now just a beaten middle-aged man.

'You were right that I wanted to get caught all along. But the toenails and the tracer capsules were both red herrings. I had another backup, one you could never find. But it would only work if I was in a fixed location . . . with plumbing. You arranged that. We've had teams camped outside all your houses for days. Posing as workmen they put sensors in the sewer drains. They're attuned to my unique biochemical fingerprint, carried in my pee. When they got a result they knew I was in here, even if they hadn't seen me brought in. And if I was here so would you be, having fun with me in one of your private dungeons. I knew they'd be well hidden, but I also knew they were fitted with toilets. So the snakes were sent through the drains following my trace until they came up in here, where they hid and watched. But even film of you screwing and beating us was no good if you kept your hood on. We had to see your face.

'That was the hard part. Making you so mad you'd forget to be careful, even just for two minutes. It had to be timed just right. The snakes told our people when you were upstairs, in your office I suppose. That was when the raids on your slave houses must happen. But how could we hit enough of them in one go to tip you over the edge? A girl you once abused in one of these dungeons told me about those distinctive high-heeled shoes you had your girls wear. That was my way in.

'I was searched by Shiller guards for fun once, but they hardly looked at my collar. Why, because it was a company collar. The company provided it, so it already belonged inside the building. I hoped the same would work for your shoes. We modified the last batch. Your people ordered them and they were a regular purchase so they weren't suspicious. Even if they had scanned them they wouldn't have found anything. It's only when you put them on the girls' feet that they work.

'There are micro-generators in their heels powered by something called the piezoelectric effect. If you compress certain crystals they generate a current. Some gas lighters use it. That charges a capacitor linked to a segmented transmitter like the one in the capsule I'd swallowed. Every so many steps it comes together and emits a brief tracer pulse. At all other times it's inert.

'As the new shoes were put into use our teams were able to track them down and see which of your sites had girls in. When they identified enough of them they made the simultaneous raids. That was the trigger I hoped would send you in here in a rage without taking time to put on your hood . . . and it did.'

Rochester was nodding slowly. 'All right, Buckingham, I admit it, you were too clever for me. Now get out of my house . . .'

But Shiller's manner seemed to have softened. To Vanessa's surprise she took Rochester by the shoulders and looked him in the face until he met her gaze. Almost regretfully she said: 'You should have loved your slaves like I do. See how loyally they serve when there is that bond. That is why I have won and you have lost. Now, for your own peace of mind, accept that it's over . . . brother.'

Fifteen

Wrapped in blankets, Vanessa and Kashika rested in the back of Shiller's limousine as it pulled out of the driveway of Rochester's house. They sat on either side of the Director who had her arms about them as though they were children. The tinted windows muted the sunlight, for which Vanessa was very grateful. After days in the cell it hurt her eyes.

For the first time they saw the exterior of Rochester's Hampshire mansion in the bowels of which they had been held captive. It was a comfortable and highly respectable-looking ivy-clad country house. No outsider could have imagined that the confrontation that had just taken place within would affect so many lives for the better.

As they sped smoothly back towards London, isolated by a screen from the chauffeur, Shiller answered some of the questions that had been passing through their minds since she had spoken that simple word to the man whom they had thought of until that moment as her arch enemy.

'Harvey is in fact my half-brother,' she said. 'We share the same father. However we were brought up in different countries and did not meet until we were in our twenties. Perhaps due to our common genetic inheritance we found we had the same sexual tastes. But Harvey could never cope with my being a woman and sharing his desires. He thought it was unnatural and that I was a freak. He hated me and, I'm sad to say, made me hate him in return. And so our rivalry, both personal and commercial, began. This was the first time we have met face to face in fifteen years. Siblings should never be brought to such a state of enmity. Cain and Abel were warning enough. Perhaps that is why I have always wanted my slavegirls to care for each other like a family should, because the only family I had was so divided.'

She looked at each of them solemnly. 'I would greatly appreciate it if you did not reveal this information to anybody else. It is a personal matter and no longer has any bearing on company business.'

'Of course, Director,' they said.

Shiller smiled. 'But now let us look forward to happier days. First we must get you both healed. Take a week's rest. After all, we want you to look your best for the other girls . . .'

A throng of bare, beribboned, bangled and perfumed girlflesh filled the training yard once more. But whereas the last time Vanessa had been there the mood had been one of proud defiance, this time it was jubilant.

She knelt on the podium to one side of the group of trainers. Beside her was Kashika, who was looking about with shy excitement. Once again they were properly clad in their own collars and sandals and nothing else. The remodelling of Vanessa's face had been reversed, the tinted contact films had gone from her eyes and the stain was beginning to fade from her skin. But as agreed with Kashika she had retained her fuller breasts and her pubes would remain smooth and bare. It was one unplanned positive legacy of her deception she was determined to enjoy.

Along the front of the ranks of slavegirls were the chains most closely involved in recent events: Canary, Cherry and Dahlia. To one side stood Angela and Sandra, looking on proudly. Kneeling leashed by her master's side and looking more content than before was

Cindy. Beside her was Zara, personally reporting on the occasion for *GN*.

The Cherry girls waved and Julie 5 gave a sly thumbs-up. When Kashika had told her Cherry sisters that their chain had been deliberately chosen as part of Vanessa's plan to destroy Rochester they had said simply: Of course you had to do it. Don't feel guilty. We'd already volunteered . . .

The memory of their words brought a lump to Vanessa's throat.

Shiller stepped forward to speak.

'This is a happy day,' she said. 'Today I can tell you that the last of Rochester's slavegirls have been returned to their homes. A few potential natural submissives have been sent to our Felgrish facility for further tests and assessment. We hope they may soon join this company as your new chain sisters.'

The girls cheered and clapped.

'But the conclusion of this long and bitter struggle would not have been possible without the ingenuity, effort and sacrifice of many people throughout the company. To those who designed intricate technical devices and those who went out in the field and monitored them patiently over many days, your sisters amongst them, we all say thank you.'

More applause.

'There are of course two amongst us who deserve special mention,' Shiller said. 'I refer to Kashika 5 Cherry and Vanessa 19 White.'

There were even louder cheers at the mention of their names. Vanessa felt a blush rising to her cheeks and her stomach flip-flopped.

'These two girls both endured personal danger and suffering to bring this conflict to an end, and showed great courage and fortitude. We are here to honour them in the traditional company manner. Bring them forward . . .'

A pair of male trainers each took Kashika and Vanessa by the arms. On each side of the podium were two heavy board panels ringed by straps and mounted on pivoting stands, which were tilted at an angle towards the arc of watching girls. Kashika and Vanessa were lifted off their feet and laid back against the frames. Broad straps went over their necks and waists. Their arms were drawn up, bent back and strapped down. Their legs were lifted and spread wide, their knees were crooked and similarly secured at the ankles and thighs so they were held flat against the panels. They hung on the boards displaying the pink gashes of their vulvas to the crowd.

Shiller stepped up to Kashika. She held a metallic device no larger than an office stapler in her hand, a set of silver pliers and a small gold ring. There was an intake of breath from the watching girls. The Director was going to do this personally . . .

'Kashika 5 Cherry, for outstanding bravery and dedicated service to the company I award you a second gold ring . . .'

The Director bent over Kashika's exposed pubic mound. There was a faint snick of a bodkin being driven through soft flesh and Kashika gave a little gasp. Then Shiller threaded the split ring through the new hole in Kashika's labia and closed it tight with the pliers.

She stepped back so everybody could see Kashika now had a matching pair of rings in her pink love lips. As the girls applauded, her Cherry sisters loudest of all, Vanessa felt a thrill of happiness and pride for her lover. Nobody deserved such an honour more than she.

Shiller now stepped up to Vanessa.

'Vanessa 19 White, for ingenuity, perseverance, courage and exemplary service to the company, I am proud to restore the two gold rings you have already earned and add a third . . .'

Vanessa gasped as the sprung needle drove through the petals of her labia and then the hood of her clitoris,

243

but it did not really feel like pain. The cold metal slipped through her flesh and then Shiller stepped back. The crowd whooped and applauded and Vanessa craned her neck to see the sparkle of gold rising from the crest of her mound. She looked sideways at Kashika and saw tears of joy in her eyes.

Then Shiller stepped forward again and carefully draped a folded white leather leash over the corner of Vanessa's frame.

There were breathless 'Ohh . . .'s and 'Ahh . . .'s from the watching girls. Vanessa did not know what it meant. Then she saw Sandra and Angela beaming at her and nodding happily, and then she understood.

That evening, on the end of her white leash, Vanessa shuffled along at Shiller's heels as the director led her through her penthouse apartment.

It was warm and white, very neat and elegantly but sparingly decorated. It matched its owner perfectly. In the bedroom, facing the large white bed with its polished steel frame, was a vertical polished steel rack mounted on a glossy black dais, looking almost like a piece of abstract art.

'What do you wish for?' Shiller asked Vanessa.

Vanessa said meekly: 'I want to be your perfect slave, Mistress, to serve you in any way you wish. I beg to suffer pain at your hands so I can prove my love and devotion.'

'Then mount the rack . . .'

Steel cuffs and powered winches held Vanessa rigidly spread-eagled within the rack frame. To add to her pain the Director slipped plastic rings over the roots of her breasts with stubby spikes cast into them that dug into her flesh. A smaller ring she slipped between the thick lips of her outer labia, pushing them wide as though they were crying aloud and exposing her already engorged clitoris. A last crescent of ring on a plug she pushed into Vanessa's anus so the arc of spiked plastic curved up within the deep cleft of her buttocks.

'Thank you, Mistress,' Vanessa said, just before Shiller put a rubber bit between her teeth for her to bite on.

Before taking up a lash to grant Vanessa's wish, Shiller stripped naked.

She had a lean slender body with few wrinkles and clear skin, small breasts that sagged little, and a mound of Venus capped by a close-cropped delta of tight curls. But even unclothed she still had the same sense of power and authority that had captivated Vanessa months before.

Shiller selected a lash with long broad thongs and began methodically to beat Vanessa. She walked slowly round her stretched and helpless body, applying the thongs with a firm hand. The hiss and crack mingled with Vanessa's grunts and whimpers of pain. She lashed her bottom from left and right, setting her full buttocks shivering and rippling, grinding the spiked crescent between them. She swung from side to side, below and above at Vanessa's breasts, made even more prominent by their spiked collars. They tossed and bounced like living things, driving the spikes even deeper into her soft curves. She swiped the lash up between Vanessa's widespread thighs, from both front and back, sending the thongs curling up into the gaping mouth of her stretched vulva and licking her naked clitoris. Vanessa's juices darkened the lash thongs and splattered across the floor.

As this steady rain of leather set her flesh on fire Vanessa whimpered and groaned and yelped and howled, writhing in her bonds. She bit on the rubber bar between her teeth and drool ran from the sides of her mouth. But every stroke of burning pain was followed by an intimate caress from her mistress, and so they were happy tears that ran down her cheeks.

245

Vanessa orgasmed while the lash licked across her weeping lovemouth and then hung limp in her bonds, her chest heaving.

'Good girl,' Shiller said, running her fingers through her own sex and bringing them away wet. 'Now you are ready to serve and I am ready to be pleasured . . .'

Vanessa lay face down on the Director's bed, her lash-marked body simmering happily. Her arms were cuffed behind her back and her spread feet were cuffed to the footrail of the bed. A telescopic rod extending forward from the bedrail held a dildo embedded deeply up her vagina, keeping her in place and giving her something to squeeze and suck on. A dark passion stain was already forming on the sheet under her groin.

Vanessa's head rested between Shiller's thighs as she reclined on her pillows and her tongue was busy inside her mistress's sticky sex, lovingly bringing her to a second orgasm. As she did so Vanessa's mind sang with joy. This was where she had wanted to be for so long, with the taste of her Mistress' delight in her mouth, knowing that at last she had proved worthy of her trust and respect. And below in B3 was Kashika, the love of her heart. Life could hardly get any better than this.

Shiller stroked Vanessa's hair as she lapped and sucked. 'Now my battle with Harvey is over I can look to the future again,' she mused. 'There are plans to be made. I must think one day about retiring . . .'

Alarmed, Vanessa raised her face, glossy with her juices, from Shiller's cleft. 'No, Mistress, please don't speak about that! I never want you to retire.'

Shiller smiled indulgently at her outburst. 'It will not be soon, but I must think of these things, Vanessa, and you know it. But the company will go on. And I must consider who shall direct it after I leave . . .' She pushed Vanessa's face back down into her pussy to resume her amorous duty. 'It must be somebody who understands the needs of the girls, who can both love and dominate them and command their respect. Whoever took on the job would have to be quite exceptional. In the past the prospect of finding somebody worthy to fill that position has troubled me . . .' She stroked Vanessa's hair. 'But I'm not worried any more . . .'

For a moment Vanessa froze as the enormity of her mistress' casual words sank in, setting her heart racing. Then once more like a good slave she began to suck and lap and nibble and slavishly give joy and so receive it redoubled in return.

There was no need to say anything more for it had all been said.

The girlflesh company would continue in its unique way.

Everything really was perfect now.

nexus

The leading publisher of fetish and adult fiction

TELL US WHAT YOU THINK!

Readers' ideas and opinions matter to us so please take a few
minutes to fill in the questionnaire below.

1. Sex: Are you male ☐   female ☐   a couple ☐?

2. Age: Under 21 ☐   21–30 ☐   31–40 ☐   41–50 ☐   51–60 ☐   over 60 ☐

3. Where do you buy your Nexus books from?
☐ A chain book shop. If so, which one(s)?

_____

☐ An independent book shop. If so, which one(s)?

_____

☐ A used book shop/charity shop
☐ Online book store. If so, which one(s)?

_____

4. How did you find out about Nexus books?
☐ Browsing in a book shop
☐ A review in a magazine
☐ Online
☐ Recommendation
☐ Other _____

5. In terms of settings, which do you prefer? (Tick as many as you like.)
☐ Down to earth and as realistic as possible
☐ Historical settings. If so, which period do you prefer?

_____

☐ Fantasy settings – barbarian worlds
☐ Completely escapist/surreal fantasy

- ☐ Institutional or secret academy
- ☐ Futuristic/sci fi
- ☐ Escapist but still believable
- ☐ Any settings you dislike?

_____

- ☐ Where would you like to see an adult novel set?

_____

6. In terms of storylines, would you prefer:

- ☐ Simple stories that concentrate on adult interests?
- ☐ More plot and character-driven stories with less explicit adult activity?
- ☐ We value your ideas, so give us your opinion of this book:

_____

_____

_____

7. In terms of your adult interests, what do you like to read about? (Tick as many as you like.)

- ☐ Traditional corporal punishment (CP)
- ☐ Modern corporal punishment
- ☐ Spanking
- ☐ Restraint/bondage
- ☐ Rope bondage
- ☐ Latex/rubber
- ☐ Leather
- ☐ Female domination and male submission
- ☐ Female domination and female submission
- ☐ Male domination and female submission
- ☐ Willing captivity
- ☐ Uniforms
- ☐ Lingerie/underwear/hosiery/footwear (boots and high heels)
- ☐ Sex rituals
- ☐ Vanilla sex
- ☐ Swinging
- ☐ Cross-dressing/TV

☐ Enforced feminisation
☐ Others – tell us what you don't see enough of in adult fiction:

_____

_____

_____

8. Would you prefer books with a more specialised approach to your interests, i.e. a novel specifically about uniforms? If so, which subject(s) would you like to read a Nexus novel about?

_____

_____

_____

9. Would you like to read true stories in Nexus books? For instance, the true story of a submissive woman, or a male slave? Tell us which true revelations you would most like to read about:

_____

_____

_____

10. What do you like best about Nexus books?

_____

_____

11. What do you like least about Nexus books?

_____

_____

12. Which are your favourite titles?

_____

_____

13. Who are your favourite authors?

_____

_____

14. **Which covers do you prefer? Those featuring:**
    (Tick as many as you like.)

☐ Fetish outfits
☐ More nudity
☐ Two models
☐ Unusual models or settings
☐ Classic erotic photography
☐ More contemporary images and poses
☐ A blank/non-erotic cover
☐ What would your ideal cover look like?

_____

15. **Describe your ideal Nexus novel in the space provided:**

_____
_____
_____
_____

16. **Which celebrity would feature in one of your Nexus-style fantasies? We'll post the best suggestions on our website – anonymously!**

_____

THANKS FOR YOUR TIME

Now simply write the title of this book in the space below and cut out the questionnaire pages. Post to: Nexus, Marketing Dept., Virgin Books, Random House, 20 Vauxhall Bridge Road, London SW1V 2SA

Book title: _____

NEXUS NEW BOOKS

Other titles by Adriana Arden in the Girlflesh Series:

THE GIRLFLESH INSTITUTE
Adriana Arden

Probing the lowest levels of the outwardly respectable London headquarters of Shiller plc, Vanessa Buckingham stumbles into a hidden world of Twenty-First Century slavery. Turned into a living puppet by Shiller's enigmatic director, Vanessa is forced to record every detail of the slavegirls' lives; from intimate psychological testing at the mysterious Fellgrish Institute, through strict training and ultimate submission to the clients who hire them. In the process Vanessa must confront both her own true nature and a terrible dilemma: can there be such a thing as a willing slave? Should she expose Shiller's activities as immoral – or let herself become another commodity in its girlflesh trade?

£6.99 ISBN 978 0 352 34101 3

THE GIRLFLESH CASTLE
Adriana Arden

Vanessa Buckingham has discovered strange contentment in the bizarre and secretive underworld of commercially organised slavery. Having accepted her own submissive nature, Vanessa is now happily working for the powerful Shiller Company as a 'slave reporter' for *Girlflesh News*. She has also found a lover in the form of the beautiful slavegirl Kashika. But there are forces at work that wish to destroy Shiller's carefully run 'ethical' slave business. Shiller's rival and arch enemy – the media mogul Sir Harvey Rochester – has not given up trying to take over the operation. Having failed to use Vanessa as his unwitting pawn to expose Shiller, Sir Harvey now turns to more extreme methods.

£7.99   ISBN 978 0 352 34504 2

New titles for 2009

ON THE BARE
Fiona Locke

Fiona Locke's *Over the Knee* has become a cult classic and is considered a definitive work of corporal punishment and fetish fiction. This anthology of short stories is even stronger, portraying the bratty, the spoilt and the wilful as they each get their stinging just deserts from masterly purveyors of discipline. Full of the authentic and exquisite details her fans adore, these stories are spanking masterpieces for true connoisseurs.

£7.99   ISBN 978 0 352 34515 8

THE GIFT OF GIRLS
Chloë Thurlow

Magdalena Wallace scores a great summer job as an intern at City accountants Roche-Marshall. But she omits to tell her boss, the mysterious Simon Roche, that she works nights as a waitress at Rebels Casino. When Magdalena learns a 'secret' system from a high-roller, she plays the tables only to lose all her university savings. Soon she is dipping into clients' money and it is not long before Simon Roche catches her in the act. As an alternative to notifying the police, he suggests she become his slave until the debt is paid. She agrees but never envisages just how far she will have to go to break even.

£7.99   ISBN 978 0 352 34520 2

WICKED OBSESSION
Ray Gordon

Eighteen-year-old Anne has always been jealous of her attractive and successful older sister, Haley. Feeling second best is something she has grown used to. But when a handsome young man rejects her advances and takes a shine to Haley instead, it is one humiliation too many. Seething with envy, Anne decides to take revenge the only way she knows how – by using her young body and sexual charms to destroy Haley's relationship. Before long behaving wickedly becomes an obsession and Anne relishes the rewards of her promiscuous behaviour. Prepared to go to any extreme to trump her sister, Anne makes plans to seduce Haley's future husband on the night before the wedding.

£7.99   ISBN 978 0 352 34508 0

NEXUS CONFESSIONS: VOLUME 6
Various

Swinging, dogging, group sex, cross-dressing, spanking, female domination, corporal punishment, and extreme fetishes . . . *Nexus Confessions* explores the length and breadth of erotic obsession, real experience and sexual fantasy. This is an encyclopaedic collection of the bizarre, the extreme, the utterly inappropriate, the daring and the shocking experiences of ordinary men and women driven by their extraordinary desires. Collected by the world's leading publisher of fetish fiction, these are true stories and shameful confessions, never before told or published.

£7.99   ISBN 978 0 352 34509 7

If you would like more information about Nexus titles, please visit our website at www.nexus-books.co.uk, or send a large stamped addressed envelope to:
  Nexus
  Virgin Books
  Random House
  20 Vauxhall Bridge Road
  London SW1V 2SA

NEXUS BOOKLIST

Information is correct at time of printing. To avoid disappointment, check availability before ordering. Go to www.nexus-books.co.uk.

All books are priced at £6.99 unless another price is given.

NEXUS

☐ ABANDONED ALICE	Adriana Arden	ISBN 978 0 352 33969 0	
☐ ALICE IN CHAINS	Adriana Arden	ISBN 978 0 352 33908 9	
☐ AMERICAN BLUE	Penny Birch	ISBN 978 0 352 34169 3	
☐ THE ART OF SURRENDER	Madeline Bastinado	ISBN 978 0 352 34013 9	
☐ BARE, WHITE AND ROSY	Penny Birch	ISBN 978 0 352 34505 9	£7.99
☐ BEASTLY BEHAVIOUR	Aishling Morgan	ISBN 978 0 352 34095 5	
☐ BEHIND THE CURTAIN	Primula Bond	ISBN 978 0 352 34111 2	
☐ BEING A GIRL	Chloë Thurlow	ISBN 978 0 352 34139 6	£7.99
☐ BIDDING TO SIN	Rosita Varón	ISBN 978 0 352 34063 4	
☐ BLUSHING AT BOTH ENDS	Philip Kemp	ISBN 978 0 352 34107 5	
☐ BRUSH STROKES	Penny Birch	ISBN 978 0 352 34072 6	
☐ BUTTER WOULDN'T MELT	Penny Birch	ISBN 978 0 352 34120 4	£7.99
☐ CALLED TO THE WILD	Angel Blake	ISBN 978 0 352 34067 2	
☐ CAPTIVES OF CHEYNER CLOSE	Adriana Arden	ISBN 978 0 352 34028 3	
☐ CARNAL POSSESSION	Yvonne Strickland	ISBN 978 0 352 34062 7	
☐ CITY MAID	Amelia Evangeline	ISBN 978 0 352 34096 2	
☐ COLLEGE GIRLS	Cat Scarlett	ISBN 978 0 352 33942 3	
☐ COMPANY OF SLAVES	Christina Shelly	ISBN 978 0 352 33887 7	
☐ CORRECTIVE THERAPY	Jacqueline Masterson	ISBN 978 0 352 33917 1	
☐ CORRUPTION	Virginia Crowley	ISBN 978 0 352 34073 3	
☐ CRUEL SHADOW	Aishling Morgan	ISBN 978 0 352 33886 0	
☐ DARK MISCHIEF	Lady Alice McCloud	ISBN 978 0 352 33998 0	
☐ DEPTHS OF DEPRAVATION	Ray Gordon	ISBN 978 0 352 33995 9	
☐ DOMINANT	Felix Baron	ISBN 978 0 352 34044 3	

☐ EXPOSÉ	Laura Bowen	ISBN 978 0 352 34035 1
☐ FORBIDDEN READING	Lisette Ashton	ISBN 978 0 352 34022 1
☐ FRESH FLESH	Wendy Swanscombe	ISBN 978 0 352 34041 2
☐ THE GIFT OF GIRLS	Chloë Thurlow	ISBN 978 0 352 34520 2
☐ THE GIRLFLESH CASTLE	Adriana Arden	ISBN 978 0 352 34504 2 £7.99
☐ THE GIRLFLESH INSTITUTE	Adriana Arden	ISBN 978 0 352 34101 3 £7.99
☐ INDECENT PURSUIT	Ray Gordon	ISBN 978 0 352 34196 9 £7.99
☐ THE INDISCRETIONS OF ISABELLE	Penny Birch (writing as Cruella)	ISBN 978 0 352 33882 2
☐ THE INDULGENCES OF ISABELLE	Penny Birch (writing as Cruella)	ISBN 978 0 352 34198 3
☐ IN DISGRACE	Penny Birch	ISBN 978 0 352 33922 5
☐ IN HER SERVICE	Lindsay Gordon	ISBN 978 0 352 33968 3
☐ INSTRUMENTS OF PLEASURE	Nicole Dere	ISBN 978 0 352 34098 6
☐ THE ISLAND OF DR SADE	Wendy Swanscombe	ISBN 978 0 352 34112 9
☐ LEAH'S PUNISHMENT	Aran Ashe	ISBN 978 0 352 34171 6
☐ LONGING FOR TOYS	Virginia Crowley	ISBN 978 0 352 34138 9
☐ LOVE JUICE	Donna Exeter	ISBN 978 0 352 33913 3
☐ LOVE SONG OF THE DOMINATRIX	Cat Scarlett	ISBN 978 0 352 34106 8
☐ LUST CALL	Ray Gordon	ISBN 978 0 352 34143 3 £7.99
☐ MANSLAVE	J.D. Jensen	ISBN 978 0 352 34040 5
☐ MOST BUXOM	Aishling Morgan	ISBN 978 0 352 34121 1
☐ NAUGHTY NAUGHTY	Penny Birch	ISBN 978 0 352 33976 4 £7.99
☐ NEIGHBOURHOOD WATCH	Lisette Ashton	ISBN 978 0 352 34190 7
☐ NIGHTS IN WHITE COTTON	Penny Birch	ISBN 978 0 352 34008 5 £7.99
☐ NO PAIN, NO GAIN	James Baron	ISBN 978 0 352 33966 9
☐ THE OLD PERVERSITY SHOP	Aishling Morgan	ISBN 978 0 352 34007 8
☐ THE PERSIAN GIRL	Felix Baron	ISBN 978 0 352 34501 1
☐ PETTING GIRLS	Penny Birch	ISBN 978 0 352 33957 7
☐ PORTRAIT OF A DISCIPLINARIAN	Aishling Morgan	ISBN 978 0 352 34179 2
☐ THE PUNISHMENT CAMP	Jacqueline Masterson	ISBN 978 0 352 33940 9
☐ THE ROAD TO DEPRAVITY	Ray Gordon	ISBN 978 0 352 34092 4 £7.99
☐ SCHOOLED FOR SERVICE	Lady Alice McCloud	ISBN 978 0 352 33918 8

☐ SCHOOL FOR STINGERS	Yolanda Celbridge	ISBN 978 0 352 33994 2
☐ SILKEN EMBRACE	Christina Shelly	ISBN 978 0 352 34081 8
☐ SILKEN SERVITUDE	Christina Shelly	ISBN 978 0 352 34004 7
☐ SINDI IN SILK	Yolanda Celbridge	ISBN 978 0 352 34102 0
☐ SLAVE OF THE SPARTANS	Yolanda Celbridge	ISBN 978 0 352 34078 8
☐ SLIPPERY WHEN WET	Penny Birch	ISBN 978 0 352 34091 7
☐ STRIP GIRL	Aishling Morgan	ISBN 978 0 352 34077 1
☐ STRIPPED BARE	Angel Blake	ISBN 978 0 352 33971 3
☐ SWEET AS SIN	Felix Baron	ISBN 978 0 352 34134 1
☐ A TALENT FOR SURRENDER	Madeline Bastinado	ISBN 978 0 352 34135 8
☐ THAI HONEY	Kit McCann	ISBN 978 0 352 34068 9
☐ TICKLE TORTURE	Penny Birch	ISBN 978 0 352 33904 1
☐ TOKYO BOUND	Sachi	ISBN 978 0 352 34019 1
☐ TRAIL OF SIN	Ray Gordon	ISBN 978 0 352 34182 2 £7.99
☐ UNEARTHLY DESIRES	Ray Gordon	ISBN 978 0 352 34036 8 £7.99
☐ UNIFORM DOLL	Penny Birch	ISBN 978 0 352 33698 9
☐ WEB OF DESIRE	Ray Gordon	ISBN 978 0 352 34167 9 £7.99
☐ WHALEBONE STRICT	Lady Alice McCloud	ISBN 978 0 352 34082 5
☐ WHAT HAPPENS TO BAD GIRLS	Penny Birch	ISBN 978 0 352 34031 3
☐ WHAT SUKI WANTS	Cat Scarlett	ISBN 978 0 352 34027 6
☐ WHEN SHE WAS BAD	Penny Birch	ISBN 978 0 352 33859 4
☐ WHIP HAND	G.C. Scott	ISBN 978 0 352 33694 1
☐ WHIPPING GIRL	Aishling Morgan	ISBN 978 0 352 33789 4
☐ WHIPPING TRIANGLE	G.C. Scott	ISBN 978 0 352 34086 3
☐ WICKED OBSESSION	Ray Gordon	ISBN 978 0 352 34508 X £7.99
☐ THE WICKED SEX	Lance Porter	ISBN 978 0 352 34161 7
☐ ZELLIE'S WEAKNESS	Jean Aveline	ISBN 978 0 352 34160 0

NEXUS CLASSIC

☐ ANGEL	Lindsay Gordon	ISBN 978 0 352 34009 2
☐ THE BOND	Lindsay Gordon	ISBN 978 0 352 33996 6
☐ THE DOMINO ENIGMA	Cyrian Amberlake	ISBN 978 0 352 34064 1
☐ THE DOMINO QUEEN	Cyrian Amberlake	ISBN 978 0 352 34074 0
☐ THE DOMINO TATTOO	Cyrian Amberlake	ISBN 978 0 352 34037 5
☐ FAIRGROUND ATTRACTION	Lisette Ashton	ISBN 978 0 352 33927 0

☐ RITES OF OBEDIENCE	Lindsay Gordon	ISBN 978 0 352 34005 4	
☐ THE SUBMISSION GALLERY	Lindsay Gordon	ISBN 978 0 352 34026 9	
☐ TIE AND TEASE	Penny Birch	ISBN 978 0 352 33987 4	£7.99
☐ TIGHT WHITE COTTON	Penny Birch	ISBN 978 0 352 33970 6	

NEXUS CONFESSIONS

☐ NEXUS CONFESSIONS: VOLUME ONE	Various	ISBN 978 0 352 34093 1	
☐ NEXUS CONFESSIONS: VOLUME TWO	Various	ISBN 978 0 352 34103 7	£7.99
☐ NEXUS CONFESSIONS: VOLUME THREE	Various	ISBN 978 0 352 34113 6	
☐ NEXUS CONFESSIONS: VOLUME FOUR	Various	ISBN 978 0 352 34136 5	£7.99
☐ NEXUS CONFESSIONS: VOLUME FIVE	Various	ISBN 978 0 352 34144 0	£7.99
☐ NEXUS CONFESSIONS: VOLUME SIX	Various	ISBN 978 0 352 34509 7	£7.99

NEXUS ENTHUSIAST

☐ BUSTY	Tom King	ISBN 978 0 352 34032 0	
☐ CUCKOLD	Amber Leigh	ISBN 978 0 352 34140 2	
☐ DERRIÈRE	Julius Culdrose	ISBN 978 0 352 34024 5	
☐ ENTHRALLED	Lance Porter	ISBN 978 0 352 34108 2	
☐ LEG LOVER	L.G. Denier	ISBN 978 0 352 34016 0	
☐ ON THE BARE	Fiona Locke	ISBN 978 0 352 34515 8	£7.99
☐ OVER THE KNEE	Fiona Locke	ISBN 978 0 352 34079 5	
☐ RUBBER GIRL	William Doughty	ISBN 978 0 352 34087 0	
☐ THE SECRET SELF	Christina Shelly	ISBN 978 0 352 34069 6	
☐ UNDER MY MASTER'S WINGS	Lauren Wissot	ISBN 978 0 352 34042 9	
☐ UNIFORM DOLLS	Aishling Morgan	ISBN 978 0 352 34159 4	
☐ THE UPSKIRT EXHIBITIONIST	Ray Gordon	ISBN 978 0 352 34122 8	£7.99
☐ WIFE SWAP	Amber Leigh	ISBN 978 0 352 34097 9	

NEXUS NON FICTION

| ☐ LESBIAN SEX SECRETS FOR MEN | Jamie Goddard and Kurt Brungard | ISBN 978 0 352 33724 5 | |

---- ✂ ------------------------

Please send me the books I have ticked above.

Name ....

Address ....

....

....

.... Post code ....

Send to: **Virgin Books Cash Sales, Direct Mail Dept., the Book Service Ltd, Colchester Road, Frating, Colchester, CO7 7DW**

US customers: for prices and details of how to order books for delivery by mail, call 888-330-8477.

Please enclose a cheque or postal order, made payable to **Virgin Books Ltd**, to the value of the books you have ordered plus postage and packing costs as follows:
   UK and BFPO – £1.00 for the first book, 50p for each subsequent book.
   Overseas (including Republic of Ireland) – £2.00 for the first book, £1.00 for each subsequent book.

If you would prefer to pay by VISA, ACCESS/MASTERCARD, AMEX, DINERS CLUB or SWITCH, please write your card number and expiry date here:

....

Please allow up to 28 days for delivery.

Signature ....

Our privacy policy

We will not disclose information you supply us to any other parties. We will not disclose any information which identifies you personally to any person without your express consent.

From time to time we may send out information about Nexus books and special offers. Please tick here if you do *not* wish to receive Nexus information.   □

------ ✂ ------------------------